Praise for *The First Principles of Dreaming:*

"Beth Goobie blends generous servings of sex, religion, the supernatural—even horror—into a deliciously creepy coming-of-age tale unlike any other you're likely to have read. The award-winning author of numerous young adult novels, Goobie knows the mind of teenagers—especially teenaged girls—like few others, and puts that knowledge to terrific use in this most adult of stories which ultimately transforms itself into a beautiful tale of healing and redemption."

—Dave Margoshes, author of
Wiseman's Wager and *A Book of Great Worth*

THE
FIRST
PRINCIPLES
of
DREAMING

Beth Goobie

Second Story Press

Library and Archives Canada Cataloguing in Publication

Goobie, Beth, 1959-, author
The first principles of dreaming / by Beth Goobie.

Issued in print and electronic formats.

ISBN 978-1-927583-27-2 (pbk.).—ISBN 978-1-927583-28-9 (epub)

I. Title.

PS8563.O8326F48 2014   C813'.54   C2014-903454-7

C2014-903455-5

An earlier version of the first half of chapter two
was published in *The Pottersfield Portfolio.*

Editors: Stephanie Fysh, Carolyn Jackson
Copyeditor: Kelly Jones
Cover: Natalie Olsen
Design: Melissa Kaita

Printed and bound in Canada

*Second Story Press gratefully acknowledges the support of the Ontario Arts Council,
the Ontario Media Development Corporation, and the Canada Council for the
Arts for our publishing program. We acknowledge the financial support of the
Government of Canada through the Canada Book Fund.*

MIX
Paper from
responsible sources
FSC® C004071

Published by
SECOND STORY PRESS
20 Maud Street, Suite 401
Toronto, ON M5V 2M5
www.secondstorypress.ca

for Sue and for Edna

ONE

My mother had a private kingdom of high, bright pain—it was her solace and comfort, her secret delight. Angels dwelled above her head; she had only to close her eyes and she would be with them, lifted upward into constant wingbeats, the currents of passing spirits. My mother endured the temporary war that was her earthly body; within this war existed the flicker of her true self, the divine spirit that spied on the rest of her life, tabulating moments of good and evil, acts of obedience and acts of the will. This true spirit lived always in waiting—the war might be temporary, but the waiting was eternal—for my mother knew she was one of the chosen few, the 144,000. Someday, the Rapture would take her on a rush of angel wings; the gates of light would open; she would enter and receive a small white stone with her secret name written upon it, and then she would understand everything—the reason why, the meaning.

My mother did not trust meaning that carried an earthly stench. A tall, plump woman with glasses and a beaked nose, Rachel Hamilton never acknowledged her physical appearance in any way. The year I turned fifteen, she was forty-three. For the last thirty years, she had twisted and pinned her hair into tight pin curls every night before going to bed; it had never occurred to her that this could change. My mother fenced herself in with words like *sacrifice* and *surrender*, read books by Billy Graham and William F. Buckley Jr., never allowed a negative word to be spoken against my father, a positive word to be spoken about herself. If I said, "Mother, you look nice," she would respond, "Oh no, I don't look nice. I'm very plain. But your *father*—he's so good-looking. You're lucky you got your looks from him."

Any insistence on my part would send her from the room in a rush of anger. My mother brooked no disagreement; as I grew older, the wooden spoon disappeared and she ruled me with her wound—that unspoken sacrifice she had made for her only child and continued to make daily through every action, so that my father and I ate her homemade bread and apple kuchen as if from an invisible altar, ate them like the flesh of her body while her spirit floated above our heads, trapped in the ether, waiting for the gates of Heaven to open so she could enter and learn her secret name.

Everything my mother did carried the echo of her pain. A member of the Waiting for the Rapture End Times Tabernacle's Women's Auxiliary Prayer Group, she met weekly with other female members to pray, gossip, and legislate what

Waiting for the Rapture children could eat, speak, wear, and watch on TV. Throughout childhood and adolescence, I was not allowed to wear pants, and my mother sewed all my clothing—the Women's Auxiliary Prayer Group exchanged sewing patterns until their children looked like a Christian fundamentalist Mickey Mouse Club minus the big ears. Since I was the only Waiting for the Rapture child in our neighborhood, I survived elementary school relatively unscathed, but junior high meant several girls from my Sunday school class walking the same halls in the same McCall's sewing patterns, each of us with our arms crossed over our chests in a vain attempt to hide the darts none of our mothers seemed able to sew in properly. In a Waiting for the Rapture family, sacrifice and silence were the highest fashions. If my mother pulled out a pattern and I mentioned that I had seen Elizabeth Morgan or Janey Carruthers wearing that particular dress, wings began to beat in my mother's head and her compressed mouth trembled, but she did not speak. Instead, her wound spoke for her, a wound of silenced lips and waiting eyes—ah, those years and years, those decades, *millennia* of waiting.

There was no arguing with such eloquence. And so I would watch, digging deeper into agony as she chose department store fabrics with plaids, paisleys, and stripes. The darts she sewed into any patterned cloth turned my bust into a hallucinogenic apparition, and no matter how carefully I rotated, standing on the kitchen stool, the hemline that she chalked onto each new skirt never failed to make me look as if I wobbled as I walked. While other girls wore hot pants and miniskirts, my hemlines never left the fifties, yet my suffering could not compare to the way my mother's wound burned in silence. It might have been her only beauty, but it was glorious; she transformed her shame into magnificence and laid down her life as an altar to it. My mother taught me this—it was her greatest gift to me—but even so, I was never able to explain her secret heart to anyone else—the way it ruled me. In the end, I was simply her only daughter, for whom she opened secret gates that remained closed to everyone else. I had seen into those places, and they had shaped me.

When I was eight, my mother began reading aloud to me after school. Daily I came home to find her seated on the couch and hunched over Billy Graham's *My Answer* or *Peace With God*; as I entered the living room, she would point silently to a nearby chair, flip to passages she had marked earlier that day, and start to read.

"Oh, Mary-Eve," she would say throatily after finishing a section. "Isn't that powerful?"

Awe vibrated her voice as her unfocused eyes fixed on some distant place, and my unblessed vision strained after hers, desperately trying to catch a glimpse of that high, bright world where angels with flaming swords stood all around, protecting souls from communism and the lesser forces of evil. Sometimes at these moments, the veil fell from my eyes and I suddenly saw the four horsemen of the Apocalypse galloping through our living room on waves of white light while the lake of fire burned below, awaiting the imprisonment of the Beast. Ponderously, full of portent, my mother would read on, words like *Antichrist* and *revelation*, *apocryphal* and *doctrine* spilling from her tongue—each a drumroll of syllables, majestic and divine; later, I conjured their sounds in my head as I lay awake in the dark, sending them out to do battle with the evil I was certain lurked everywhere, hiding in the four apocalyptic corners of my bedroom.

My mother knew the second that I lost interest. The last months of junior high, I came awake within myself and realized I did not want to become my mother—did not want to dress like her, talk like her, or live in her high, bright world. Her pain was still my pain; it was a small, precise tongue licking my secret wound—keeping it alive and within her reach, familiar to us both. In spite of this, however, changes had begun to ripple through me—quick, shimmering tremors that left me trembly as a horse's nose, wanting to whicker and run. My mother's pain reached out to me, the Apocalypse and the four horsemen guarded me close, but she knew the moment I slipped free, the moment she lost me and I lost her. It was a spring afternoon in 1972, the lilacs in full bloom, their mauve scent calling through an open window; as my mother read aloud, I began to drift. Some minutes later, I caught and returned my wandering thoughts to find myself confronted by silence and the full weight of my mother's hooded gaze.

Quietly, she set *World Aflame* aside. "Well," she said, glancing out the window. "I suppose that's the end of that." Without another word, she got to her feet and left the room.

"Mother," I called after her, but my betrayal had been evident to us both—I was no longer the chosen one who believed enough to forsake earthly pleasures and follow her through the fiery gates of faith to walk the mind of God. After she exited the room, I sat staring at a nearby coffee table piled with copies of *Christianity Today*, *Moody Monthly*, and *Reader's Digest*. Within me beat a wild huge-winged pain, for I knew she was right—something had come to an end; without being aware of it, I had broken faith and no longer believed.

That night at dinner, my mother's eyes were red. She did not look at me, did not speak to me for the next two weeks. If I entered a room in which she was present, she walked out, except during meals and church services, when she tolerated my presence. Finally, she began speaking to me again, but I remained fallen from grace; it was obvious she held no more expectations of me than she did for the children of mundane women.

• • •

After they had been friends for several months, Mary-Eve Hamilton learned that when Dee Eccles turned fourteen, her mother gave her the keys to the family Volkswagen Bug and said, "It's yours. Now stay out of trouble until you get your goddamn license." It was, Mary-Eve reflected, the sort of incident that typified the enormous difference between them—her own mother still had not applied for her learner's permit, preferring to sit, staring vaguely through the front passenger window, while her husband piloted their 1962 Valiant to and from the Waiting for the Rapture End Times Tabernacle. Dee's mother, on the other hand, drove a '70 Chevy, her father a '72 Ford, and her older brother had just placed a down payment on a Camaro the year Dee inherited the Bug and entered grade nine, Eleusis Collegiate, and the outer perimeters of Mary-Eve's life. The two girls shared no classes, as Mary-Eve was enrolled in the academic stream and Dee was not. Dee then went on to fail grade nine; for these reasons they became aware of each other only gradually, Mary-Eve watching from classroom windows as Dee erupted through school exits with the smoking crowd for midmorning break. Short-sleeved and shivering from the cold, individual smokers huddled together, silky white laughter sifting from their mouths. United by an invisible rapport, they swallowed anyone with a cigarette into their ranks, and above their heads, Mary-Eve thought she could see a unique brand of angel hovering—nicotine angels, each cradling the raw cigarette ember of one smoker's fiercely burning heart in its hands.

From grade nine onward, Dee Eccles was one of the tallest girls in the school, but it was the size of her laughter that marked her—the way it reverberated through a surrounding throng. Ignoring her own age group, she lit up with her older brother and his friends, breathing fire and riding their brain waves as if they were a temporary joyride created just for her; and from where Mary-Eve stood, trapped behind window glass, it seemed Dee knew everything there was to know about guys, everything there was to know about being a girl among guys. Year after year, Mary-Eve studied Dee Eccles like a textbook—memorized the angle at which she held her head when she spoke, the number of degrees the sky tilted as she laughed, the way she could drop every aspect of her surroundings along with her chin and stand scuffing one bored heel in the dirt. Without consciously admitting it to herself, Mary-Eve also kept track of Dee's extensive wardrobe of halter tops, tube tops, Levi's 501s, and jean jackets, from a distance sliding them casually off the other girl's body and studying her heartbeat, the olive sheen of her skin. Each time she watched Dee light up a cigarette and inhale, Mary-Eve came alive within herself—surfaced into warm spots and wet spots and sweet tingling currents, as if the ember at the tip of Dee Eccles's cigarette were Mary-Eve Hamilton's fierce burning heart and she needed that specific pair of sucking lips to feel it, to see exactly how cherry red she could become.

For four full years, Mary-Eve lived off the idea of Dee Eccles—dragging on that ember, sucking its smoky addiction deeper and deeper in. Walking along city streets, she would let herself slide into the low-slung rhythm of the other girl's hips; staring into her bedroom mirror, she peeled out of her mother's insane darts and watched the soft hope of Dee's breasts surface into her own. Mary-Eve wanted Dee's dark shagged hair and long angular face; she wanted her red-lipped, mobile mouth; and some nights as she kissed, licked, and sucked her pillow, those cherry-red lips did seem to melt into her own— for one crazy, ecstatic moment, Mary-Eve *became* Dee Eccles, and together they rubbed against the vague necessary boy in her bed.

Dee had carnal knowledge of guys—it was obvious from the way she moved among them, the way they watched and touched her. She sinned often, on a whim; her daily list of things to do could not have been further removed from Mary-Eve's. In fact, it probably would have been accurate to say that nothing whatsoever in Dee Eccles's life related directly to Mary-Eve's. Dee had an older brother; Mary-Eve was alone. Dee swirled with the school's rebel current; Mary-Eve attended Inter-Varsity Christian Fellowship. But while even Armageddon would not have had the power to drive Dee through the front doors of the Waiting for the Rapture End

Times Tabernacle, still Mary-Eve knew that delicate, unspoken currents connected the two of them. For sometimes, as she stood watching through a classroom window, her nerves began to resonate in an invisible siren's call. And each time, as if in answer, Dee's head lifted, her nostrils flaring so intensely that even at a distance Mary-Eve felt the other girl's sharp intake of breath and stepped quickly out of the line of sight.

By the beginning of grade thirteen, Mary-Eve had been observing Dee Eccles in school hallways, assemblies, and across the cafeteria for so long, the other girl seemed to exist on an alternate plane. If they passed each other in the rush between classes, Mary-Eve's brain went into overload—Dee was a metaphysical Ziggy Stardust; the light show she carried was all internal, and she was *loaded*. Mary-Eve wanted that light show; she wanted the ember of that fierce heart burning between her own sweet lips; so in mid-September 1977, she entered the IGA on Wimple Street and handed over a week's allowance for one pack of Player's cigarettes—Dee's brand of cool.

The cigarette box sat slim but defined between her fingers, a necessary weight. The plastic wrap came off with a satisfying crinkle; the cardboard lid scraped open onto an acrid, dusky scent; then, *unbelievably*, Mary-Eve was sliding out the pristine shape of her first cigarette, placing its delicate tip between her lips, and striking a match. Hidden in the shadow of the Dumpster behind the IGA, she watched the ember of her heart catch fire, smelled the smoke of its burning, and sucked in. The next few weeks were lonely, coughing work, accompanied by the rustling of falling leaves and the reek of the IGA Dumpster, but for some reason she felt the need to return day after day to the same place; it was a chosen place, a sanctuary—the trees there watched her with knowing, the breeze whispered a silent pact through her hair, and finally, *finally* came the moment she could breathe smoke like air, triumph drifting, an easy silken white from her lips, to dissipate into the long, blue afternoon.

Several days later, on a windy, golden October afternoon, Mary-Eve stood hesitating outside Eleusis Collegiate's east exit, scanning the smoking crowd that had congregated on the school lawn. The face she was seeking, however, wasn't among them, so without a second thought, she passed on by, headed for Wimple Street and her sanctuary behind the IGA. Then, halfway down the block, she caught sight of a powder-blue Bug idling at the corner, the driver's dark shagged head bent as if in prayer. Without warning, the head jerked upright and a small yellow object came flying out through an open window.

"Fuckin' lighter!" howled a voice.

Three heartbeats passed as Mary-Eve stood frozen; then she was veering off the sidewalk into the come and go of after-school traffic and flicking her Bic into the terrifying possibilities of an open car window. As if from a great distance, the dark shagged head turned toward her and a pair of large, deep-set blue eyes widened; for a long, stretched moment, two girls stared wordlessly over an orange Bic butane lighter. Finally, the one in the car leaned toward the lit flame. Dragging deeply, she scanned the face in her window, blew out an emphatic line of smoke, and asked, "Who dresses you?"

Mary-Eve blinked twice. Then, rapid-fire, she reeled

off, "The Waiting for the Rapture End Times Tabernacle's Women's Auxiliary Prayer Group."

"Shit," Dee said slowly. "Any chance they'll stop praying for you soon?"

"Let 'em pray," said Mary-Eve. "Just make 'em stop sewing."

Dee's head dropped back and she laughed soundlessly. This close, Mary-Eve could see a small blue butterfly tattoo that flew the tanned skin of the other girl's upper arm. "Your name's Mary-Eve, right?" asked Dee, taking another drag off her cigarette.

"Mary-Eve Hamilton," Mary-Eve said immediately, as if reporting for duty. "Mary for the mother of God, Eve for the mother of mankind."

Dee lifted an eyebrow. "You don't talk like you look," she said, revving the Bug's engine, then added casually, "You hang around school windows a lot."

Mary-Eve shifted foot to foot, fighting a flush. "Any way out of a trap," she said.

"You got it," agreed Dee. "This is my last year, and then I'm outta here. Okay, I owe you one—for the light. I'll drive you home."

Stunned temporarily stupid, Mary-Eve stammered, "What—in your car?"

"No, Jesus-girl," grinned Dee. "My fire engine. C'mon— get in."

Mary-Eve made it to the passenger door so swiftly, she practically leaped the Bug in a single bound, but all Dee said as she climbed in was "Jez. I'm calling you Jezebel, for the mother of fun. Jez for short."

"Short fun," said Mary-Eve. Shakily she lit up, dragged in, and blew out the long, smoky line of her soul. She couldn't believe it—she was actually sitting beside Dee Eccles *in her car*—the Blue Bug of Ultimate Cool. "Know what happened to the first Jezebel?" she asked, trying to fake casual.

Gazing over her shoulder, Dee pulled into traffic with a lurch. "Died of syphilis?" she quipped.

"Uh-uh," said Mary-Eve. "Syphilis would've been too good for Jezebel. She was the queen of iniquity, you know." Relishing the phrase—*the queen of iniquity*—Mary-Eve repeated it in her head. She had always liked the sound of *iniquity*—it did fascinating things to the tongue. "Eunuchs threw her out a window, and wild dogs licked up her blood."

"Eunuchs?" asked Dee, glancing at her with a frown.

"Y'know," Mary-Eve said vaguely, not wanting to get into specifics. "Men who haven't got them anymore. They used to do that to slaves."

Ignoring traffic, Dee gave her a long stare. "Gotcha," she said. "Guys without dicks. What a completely useless world that would be."

"Would you like the official King James version on Jezebel?" Mary-Eve asked quickly. Without waiting for a response, she dug into her brain for the first phrase, then was off and running. "'And he said, Throw her down,'" she recited with practiced ease. "'So they threw her down: and some of her blood was sprinkled on the wall, and on the horses: and he trode her under foot. And when he was come in, he did eat and drink, and said, Go, see now this cursed woman, and bury her: for she is a king's daughter. And they went to bury her: but they found no more of her than the skull, and the feet, and the palms of her hands. Wherefore they came again, and told him. And he said, This is the word of the Lord, which he spake by his servant Elijah the Tishbite, saying, In the portion of Jezreel shall dogs eat the flesh of Jezebel: And the carcase of Jezebel shall be as dung upon the face of the field in the portion of Jezreel; so that they shall not say, This is Jezebel.'"

Recitation completed, Mary-Eve sat staring intensely ahead. She had done well, she knew that—every word had been correct. In her Waiting for the Rapture End Times Tabernacle Sunday school class, her teacher and fellow students would have been murmuring in approval: *Praise the Lord. Praise the holy HOLY God. Shame on Jezebel—shame, shame. Shame on the wanton woman sinner.*

From beside her came the sound of fingers tapping the steering wheel. "Nice story," said Dee, her voice laconic. "That's the fucking Bible, isn't it?"

"Second Kings chapter nine," said Mary-Eve. "Verses thirty-three to thirty-seven."

"You've got the whole book memorized?" asked Dee.

"Just the interesting parts," said Mary-Eve.

"Shit," muttered Dee, shaking her head. "Ever read anything else?"

"I started *Carrie*," said Mary-Eve, "but the Bible's more interesting."

Dee's face twisted. "It *is*?" she demanded.

"God's a better writer than Stephen King," said Mary-Eve. "Weirder. Think about it—why would wild dogs eat everything except Jezebel's skull, her feet, *and the palms of her hands*?"

Dee frowned, dragging on her cigarette. "That *is* weird," she agreed.

"Even the wild dogs wouldn't shake her hand," said Mary-Eve. "Even when she was *dead*." Dragging on her own cigarette, she blew out her thoughts and watched them settle. "I mean, I know she was bad, but…"

An intense moodiness came and went in Dee's face. "Ever notice how all the interesting chicks end up on the rocks?" she asked. "All through history. Joan of Arc. Anne Boleyn. Marilyn."

"Marilyn who?" asked Mary-Eve.

Braking in the middle of traffic, Dee stared at her. "Marilyn," she intoned precisely, "*Monroe.*"

For a long moment, the two girls assessed one another— Dee's gaze openly scornful, Mary-Eve's lips parting slightly as a flush rose in her cheeks. Then a car horn honked behind them, Dee floored the gas pedal, and they jerked onward into her silent disapproval. "Well," she said, taking a deep breath. "That isn't happening to me, I can tell you that."

"What isn't?" asked Mary-Eve, still trapped in the heated dregs of her shame.

"The rocks!" yelped Dee, hitting her own forehead with the heel of her hand. Certain she had been terminated, declared social refuse, Mary-Eve cringed, but then, without warning, Dee's mood flipped and she asked, "What size jeans do you wear?"

Confused, but willing to adjust to any topic of conversation, Mary-Eve pulled at the waistband of her dress. "How would I know?" she asked. "I've never worn hips."

Dee hooted, then grinned, "We'll get you hips, Jez baby.

Not today—I've got to be somewhere in five—but later this week. I bet we're the same size. You can borrow some of my jeans."

Astounded, Mary-Eve tried to keep hope from flying off with her face. "No kidding?" she whispered.

"No kidding," Dee echoed softly. "No kidding, Watch-Me-Through-the-Window Jezzie-Jesus-girl."

She looked at Mary-Eve then, her lips slightly parted, a strand of dark hair blowing across her face, and Mary-Eve's skin touched itself in wildly sweet, terrified places.

"You want to come play Barbie dolls with me, Jez?" Dee asked.

Reaching through her open window, Jez flicked the accumulated ash off the end of her cigarette and took a deep, steadying breath. "Yeah, sure," she said calmly, "maybe later this week," and smiled at a gloriously wide and windy world.

TWO

When I was eight, my father was transferred to the city of Eleusis, population 65,000, one hour northwest of Toronto. The city's core was redbrick Victorian, but expanding rapidly into suburbs of split-levels and apartment blocks, and my father initially started looking at houses in the outskirts, which was where a family like ours belonged. Soon into the search, however, my mother's prayers guided our car toward the university area, then onto a street where a handwritten FOR SALE sign was posted in the window of 59 Quance Crescent—a three-story redbrick house that had been built at the end of the previous century and was almost as old as the woman selling it. Taking one look at my carefully rag-curled ringlets, polished patent-leather shoes, and the Sunday school paper I clutched in my right hand, she agreed to sell her house for the first offer my father made, at one-fifth its market value.

The house had hardwood floors, beige flame-shaped lightbulbs, and radiators with clawed feet. We arrived early one July morning to take up residence, an hour ahead of the moving van. My father led us up the white porch steps, where we stood outside the front door for a long flowering moment, surrounded by hanging pots of geraniums and petunias, the old woman's garden rooted in wind. Then my father unlocked the door, and we stepped over the threshold and separated into a vast emptiness. Leaving my parents, I walked alone into the gloom, where each room led into the next, a series of echoing caverns. For some reason, the old woman had left several antique mirrors hanging on the second-floor walls, and they kept catching me at odd angles, so that I found myself suddenly doubled and walking toward myself from across an empty room or twinned at the opposite end of a hall. Transfixed, I stared at reflections that seemed to be stepping through glass veils, coming and going through layered mystery, while from the ground floor came the sound of my father pushing up kitchen windows and opening the house to subtle breezes, a chorus of cicadas, the rustling innuendos of maple and oak.

To either side of our new home, Quance Crescent unrolled—a tidy sequence of several-story stone and brick houses inhabited by professors, architects, a former mayor, and the wisdom of maple trees; my father was the only salesman, my mother the only housewife-for-Jesus, and we constituted the only Waiting for the Rapture family on our block. Century-old gray stone churches inhabited nearby street corners—Anglican, Presbyterian, United, and Roman Catholic. Most of our neighbors attended these services, and over the years, my mother allowed me to accept invitations to accompany friends and their families so I could learn about "other faiths," though it was assumed that these congregations did not hold a true understanding, would not be included among the Waiting for the Rapture 144,000, and did not stand among the chosen as the Hamilton family did.

So I never revealed to my mother the way I felt these churches rise out of the earth, solid as heartbeat. I never spoke of the spirits I saw soaring through the great stone arches, how I would sit on dark pews staring upward, a roaring in my ears, until the shimmering, quivering air appeared about to split open onto some other place of color and light. Soundless singing filled my head—singing that I sensed like vibrations, calling voices that I knew could be heard with just a little more faith. These aged churches seemed to resonate with doorways that would become visible on the other side of knowing. Whatever the mystery was, it never revealed itself, though I watched beady-eyed as a robed man mounted an iron staircase to a pulpit where secrets were carved deep into the wood, a Bible splayed open like a huge dead bird, candles gusted and smoked, and stone walls opened into glorious stained-glass windows that intoned scarlet, royal blue, and forest green in all the silences of the heart. Seated in churches that had been built out of the very thoughts of God, I knew I had found the Rapture, but since it belonged to "other faiths," I never told my mother of its mysteries, of the way my thoughts ascended that vaulted air, tiny insect wings riding sacred waves of shadow and light.

At the Waiting for the Rapture End Times Tabernacle, the shape of God's thinking was different—held no inner spaces, no silences, no slowed-down places to watch your own wings. Instead, the air seemed to tense against itself, arguing and whimpering as if it carried secret voices that wailed like babies, crying to be let in. I never got the sense that anyone else heard these voices; the faces of this congregation shone like fierce closed flames—careful, prearranged shapes like the candle-flame lightbulbs in our house on Quance Crescent. Calling each other Brother and Sister, members cried out and hugged in the church lobby like prodigals returning from enemy territory; with each embrace, the secret baby voices grew more frenzied; Sunday after Sunday, the congregation's faith shone brighter, their faces sealed more tightly shut. This Waiting for the Rapture congregation was composed of crusaders, the Bible their sword and faith their shield; they sang choruses projected from overheads onto the white sanctuary wall, clapped and performed dance steps, and often crowded the aisles, raising their hands and speaking in tongues.

My mother received the gift of tongues the first Sunday we attended the Waiting for the Rapture End Times Tabernacle. Before this, she had always stood calmly in church—holding her hymnal like a duty and singing in a markedly resigned marching rhythm. That Sunday, however, something seized her as we entered the sanctuary; her nostrils flared and she seemed almost to be sniffing the air, touching it with her skin. When, partway into the service, the congregation began to moan and lift up their hands, she raised hers too, crying out in a voice no one could turn His back upon. As if in response, the very air split open above her head and a white glowing tunnel appeared. Inside its rapidly rotating form, a bird of fire in swift descent was observed by everyone present. Touching down on my mother's head, it hovered a moment—a flickering opalescent vision the size of a small dove. Then, spreading its wings, it laid a single pearl-white flame upon her crown. Briefly, its fiery beak opened, but if the iridescent bird cried out, its sound was so high and otherworldly that it could not be heard by human ears. Abruptly, the apparition launched itself upward, re-entered the tunnel, and disappeared from view. Once it was gone, the spinning tunnel also vanished, but the white flame continued to glow atop my mother's head, and her voice, like a parallel visitation, also took on the shape of fire—burning with the inexpressible, the unattainable, that lovely heat.

For some years after that day, Pentecost visited her anew every Sunday. With an ecstasy the rest of us could only imagine, my mother saw visions, called out to angels, foamed at the mouth, and fell down rigid. Each time she collapsed, the congregation retreated behind rows of fanning bulletins, a silent wall of flesh and faith that watched, narrow-eyed, as Pastor Playle approached her rigid, foam-flecked form, went down on his knees, and waited. In spite of my mother's strange suffering, or perhaps because of it, God answered her call—converting her grating gut-punch sounds into a drifting petallike loveliness, an unintelligible rush of liquid syllables only Pastor Playle seemed able to understand; unfailingly, the good pastor translated for the rest of us, his voice rising and falling with hers so they seemed joined in parallel ecstasy, riding vibrations above our heads.

Sometimes my mother spoke of the heavens—not a

single place, but many connected worlds, seemingly formed from crystal and jewels, the prismatic thoughts of God. Other times she warned of apocalypse and global catastrophe, the evil that lurked both as potential and realized action. But what most caught the congregation's attention were her more personal references. Often, pointing at individual members or visiting strangers, she was able to give uncannily accurate descriptions of crises they were experiencing, and she could successfully diagnose illness and predict pending death in the family, spousal infidelity, or financial calamity. Word spread quickly about this extraordinary prophet, and attendance at the Waiting for the Rapture End Times Tabernacle soared as people flocked to hear her testify. Soon Pastor Playle began meeting with my mother privately for midweek prayer and praise sessions, and within a year, she was anointed the Divine Sister—a position created to recognize her unique gift that also granted her the privilege of offering up praise at important church functions, even national Waiting for the Rapture conferences.

Through every stage in her rise to celebrity, Pastor Playle was at Rachel Hamilton's side, appearing with her on stage to introduce her to other congregations, then kneeling in humble devotion to translate her enraptured visions for the lesser, uncomprehending elect. But however the euphoria joined them, it left Pastor Playle and my mother differently—the good pastor striding vigorously to the podium as if reborn while the pearl-white flame faded from my mother's head and she collapsed into a trembling heap. After particularly intense sessions with the Spirit, deacons had to be summoned to carry her from the sanctuary, and it could be days before she recovered from the seizures and headaches that ecstasy left in its wake.

No tongue of fire ever touched my scalp, though I cut orange flames out of construction paper and held them above my head, imitating the sounds I heard coming from my mother's mouth. Sunday mornings I stood beside her, raised my hands and swayed, and sometimes a sweet white fire seemed to descend onto me and a new voice to sing from my mouth, but it always sang in English, always "Just as I Am" or "Swing Low, Sweet Chariot." For several years after my mother's first visitation, I was certain a nurse had accidentally switched me with another infant after my birth, and somewhere a poor, confused, *truly* Christian girl—one of the 144,000—was fervently speaking in tongues while her Anglican, Presbyterian, or United parents whipped her with chains and locked her in a dark basement until she learned to speak good, solid, plain old English.

My mother assured me that it didn't matter, God heard my words as clearly as hers, but there was a line of satisfaction around her mouth as I begged her to sound out Heaven's words slowly so I could learn them one by one. "It's a gift, Mary-Eve," she told me flatly. "You get given it or you don't. You can't *ask* to become one of the chosen few."

"But what if I'm not a chosen one?" I asked fearfully. "What if God chose you and He didn't choose me? What if only people who speak in tongues get into Heaven?"

"Nonsense!" snapped my mother, turning to leave the room. "You're my daughter and you'll go to Heaven. That's all there is to it."

Approximately one year after our move to Eleusis, I

retreated into a game I called The Chosen Ones. The game always started with the pulling down of my bedroom window blind, and then, midmorning or in the afternoon, I would be standing in a curved shadowy realm—a place I thought of as the catacombs into which the early Christians had fled to worship. Closing my eyes, I imagined them—the *truest* Chosen Ones—and gradually I would begin to hear the rustle of robes and soft chanting. Then, if I continued to concentrate, they appeared to me—a long line of robed figures materializing into clearly defined form. Concealed within the openings of their hoods, their faces remained a mystery, but, pulling my bathrobe over my head, I fantasized that I was one of them—one of *The* Chosen Ones gathered deep in the bowels of the earth where death stood all around, the walls were crowded with tombs, and the bones of the poor had been piled high in a vast pit. If the odd spirit came drifting past, it did not frighten me; I felt comfortable in this place between the living and the dead, whispering code words like *agape* and making the secret sign of the fish.

The Chosen Ones had the gift of tongues and conversed frequently with the Spirit—an entity that revealed itself through glowing flames scattered across their heads and arms—and they knew how to speak to the tall transparent shapes of the dead. Each robed figure carried a bone-handled knife in the left hand, which was raised in song or chant. Deep in the shadows of my mind, I watched candlelight glint off curved blades as knives arced through the air then sank into the folds of The Chosen Ones' robes like a kind of mysterious speech, a retelling of old stories—Cain and Abel, Abraham and Isaac, the ancient temple sacrifices. Familiar with these myths, I thought I understood the holy requirements of this secret priesthood; obviously, there were rituals to be obeyed, and The Chosen Ones were waiting for me to prove myself worthy. If I had no fatted calf, my toy box was packed with dolls, my mother kept a large can of tomato juice in the fridge, and the sharp knives were stored in a drawer beside the kitchen sink. Having collected the necessary ingredients for a good sacrifice, I pulled down my window blind, laid one of my dolls on my bedroom chair, and made the secret sign of the fish. The robes of The Chosen Ones made anticipatory rustles; I felt their watching eyes as I sliced open the doll's cloth belly, poured tomato juice onto the cotton stuffing, and offered up her soul to the Lord.

Nothing changed. As before, The Chosen Ones continued their unfathomable chants and dancing but did not speak to me, did not draw me in. Somehow I had displeased them; the sacrifice of the doll had not been enough, for it had not allowed me to break the code that would have granted me entry into their ranks. For days I was stymied; then intense cogitation brought my error to me—God, of course, required the sacrifice of something alive, *real* blood. One of the *truly* chosen ones would not sacrifice a mere doll, nor would she flinch from the holiness of the task set before her.

I did not flinch. Sneaking past my mother, who was sitting on the living room couch, engrossed in First Corinthians, I spent a good fifteen minutes stalking a neighborhood cat with a bread knife hidden behind my back before I was noticed. That was the end of The Chosen Ones. My window blind was snapped firmly up, the sharp knives locked away, my sacrificed doll thrown into the garbage. And The Chosen Ones blamed me. No matter that none of this had come of my volition—nothing I could do or say enticed them to return, and my room resonated with their absence as completely as Christ's Easter-morning tomb.

A kind of desperation seized me then, and I began walking down the Waiting for the Rapture End Times Tabernacle's central aisle once a month to be saved. I would have gone forward weekly, but Pastor Playle put out the call for salvation solely on the last Sunday of the month, not wanting to wear out his flock. After my second trip down the aisle, my mother carefully explained that I could only be saved once, I had offered my spirit to the Lord when I was four and nothing could undo this, and, most importantly, God did not want me repeatedly traipsing down the aisle and wasting His Very Godly Time. But deep inside I knew I was lacking—I might be officially saved, but it did not feel as if it had been a thorough job. Every month, Pastor Playle put out the call, and every month, I heard the secret baby voices wailing; nothing seemed able to shut them out—not the depth or breadth of the congregation's singing, not my mother's warning whisper "Mary-Eve, you're *already* saved," not her hand reaching to grab me as I slipped into the aisle, not the look of alarm on Pastor Playle's face as I came forward yet again to fall, sobbing, to my knees. I put on a good show; if I could not speak in tongues, still I *had* a tongue and I was my mother's daughter. One Sunday I cried, "God, oh Jesus, listen to me, I'm a sinner, I need to be saved, I want to be saved good like my mother, I want to be filled with glory-talk, save me, please give me white holy blood, crucify me and let it pour out of me like Jesus, except I'll be better, I'll have pure white blood, it'll run down my arms and legs and drip onto everyone wailing at my feet, they'll be covered in my pure white blood and that'll save them, I'll be pure and holy like my mother, maybe I'll get into Heaven's gates and be one of The Chosen Ones, the 144,000—"

At this point, Pastor Playle clapped his hand over my mouth, which put an end to my ecstatic outburst but annoyed me—no one ever clapped a hand over my mother's mouth, probably because they couldn't figure out what she was saying. So I put up a struggle so intense, it took two deacons to carry me into the lobby; there they pinned me, grunting and spitting, to the floor until my mother came out to tell me that I had shamed her, and my father would be dealing with me. This, predictably enough, meant a spanking, but first my father took the unusual detour of making me repeat three times that I was saved and a child of God before bending me over his knee.

In spite of their efforts, however, the following month, the frenzy seized me anew. As Pastor Playle put out the salvation call, I was once again overcome by the secret wailing-baby voices; raising my hands, I poured imaginary ashes over my head, tore open the front of my dress, and began to crawl down the central aisle, intent on kissing the pastor's shiny black shoes. But before I could get to them, my father darted out of our pew, grabbed me by the arms, and dragged me to the lobby, then out through the church's front doors to the car. I answered the call once more after that, danced down the aisle and fell rigid at Pastor Playle's feet, even foamed at the mouth, but all that emerged from my lips was the same boring English—everyone understood what I was saying, so no one was impressed. This time Pastor Playle dealt with me, alone in his office. "You come walking down that aisle again, I'll knock your teeth in," he hissed, and I never did.

Perhaps it was the mundaneness of the architecture that led to the congregation's excesses. The Waiting for the Rapture End Times Tabernacle was an unimpressive stucco building in a suburb of apartment blocks. The plain front doors could have led into a dentist's office, the lobby was lined with coatracks, and small utilitarian tables displayed the collection plates in full view. Several opaque puke-amber windows divided the lobby from the sanctuary, and the sanctuary itself had no windows, no stained glass that resonated the wondrous mind of God. Ceiling fans whirred constantly, the walls' only decoration was a single large cross, and the stage had no pulpit—simply a podium on wheels that could be shoved to one side when the choir came up to perform. Stage left, a trapdoor opened onto a baptismal tank that did not seal properly; sometimes it leaked, and there was always the odor of chlorine. What could such a setting do for God's thoughts, much less mine? At the Waiting for the Rapture End Times Tabernacle, there were no wings, no silent, widening ripples of the mind. Hands searched for these, they lifted ceaselessly upward; ceiling fans spun; baby voices wailed unheard; and the glory of the Lord spilled incomprehensible rivers of sound out of my martyr mother's holy throat.

• • •

The room Dee had above the garage sat apart from the rest of the world. Situated at the far end of her parents' backyard, and enclosed on three sides by aspen and birch, the garage's upper floor had a single south-facing window that opened onto an alley and a row of neighborly fences. The afternoon Jez first came into that place whirled russet-golden with leaves, a dense wine scent layering the air as several nearby apple trees dropped overripe fruit to the ground in quiet thuds. Two endless days had passed since she had offered Dee the flame from her Bic. When they had passed in the halls, the other girl hadn't glanced her way, and for the first time, as Jez had pressed against classroom windows, waiting for a glimpse of the smoking-crowd goddess, no sirens had pulsed her nerves and the air had swallowed her like dead breath. Then, without warning—no signs, no omens, not even the slightest change in the weather—she had come out of Eleusis Collegiate through her usual exit, en route to her IGA sanctuary on Wimple Street, and there had been the powder-blue Bug idling at the curb, with Dee sitting cross-legged on its roof.

"Jez," she had grinned. "Still wanna play Barbies?"

Sticky Fingers was playing on the tape deck. After Jez lit cigarettes for them both, they traveled with their windows down, bright leaves gusting the hood. Dee headed for one of the newer suburbs and parked in front of a colonial-style house, saying the garage was reserved for her father's Ford. Then, crossing a manicured front lawn, she opened a gate in a freshly painted white fence, and the two girls entered a long backyard that hadn't been mowed in weeks. Rose petals drifted through tall grass; a fairy-tale fountain gave out the sound of running water; an enormous maple scattered gold across an endless blue sky. With a sigh, Dee pulled her Pink Floyd T-shirt over her head, dropped it to the ground, and stretched. Eyes wide, Jez watched the other girl's back bra strap shift to reveal an unbroken tan. Along the left side of her spine, three blue butterflies rose in tattooed flight.

"Warm out, eh?" said Dee, breathing deeply, hands in her back pockets, breasts taut against the black lace of her bra. It was an open invitation for scrutiny, Jez realized, her throat tightening. Too open. Uneasily, her eyes skittered away.

"Come on," said Dee, striding toward the back of the yard.

"Where to?" asked Jez. Hesitantly, she followed, a kaleidoscopic headache in her green paisley midi dress and blue-and-white oxfords.

"Where I live," said Dee, pointing to a small run-down garage surrounded by a cluster of trees. Close up, the white clapboard building looked sturdy enough, though badly in need of paint. A steep wooden staircase ascended the west side, taking the two girls out of the scent of warm grass and grounded apples to a landing perched high among rustling trees. As Dee unlocked the narrow door, a birch leaf spiraled onto her naked shoulder; letting it rest, she crossed to the room's only window and propped it open with a wine bottle covered in candle wax. Then, turning to face the open door, she called "Don't be shy," and Jez stepped out of the high tug of wind, the shift and sigh of trees, into the mind of that place, the thoughts of Dee Eccles; the adult world lost all claim on them.

Coming through the door, she was hit with a solid wave of odor: stale cigarette smoke, musty throwaway furniture, the muted stench of oil and car exhaust from the garage below. On the wall opposite sagged a Union Jack, torn in the bottom right corner. Beneath it stood a brown plaid couch, obviously in survival mode. Magazine pictures of the Rolling Stones were taped to the walls, and Rod Stewart leered from a poster, satin shirt unbuttoned to his navel. Directly under that navel hunched an unsteady-looking burgundy love seat piled with laundry. Over by the window, a stereo and a small fridge competed for space, and a kicked-around coffee table sat in the middle of the room, covered with ashtrays, *Playgirl*, *People* magazine, and *TV Guide*. Behind Jez something crinkled, and she whirled, nerves rattled, to see a gust of wind bell out a poster of Farrah Fawcett that had been tacked to the inside of the door. Turning back to the room, she watched Dee cross to the love seat and stand in front of it, where she regarded Rod Stewart thoughtfully.

"Who," Dee asked, tapping her upper lip, "do you think would look better if Farrah and Rod traded hair?"

Charlie's Angels wasn't on the Women's Auxiliary Prayer Group's approved TV list, but Jez had caught sight of Farrah and her red swimsuit taped to the inside of many an Eleusis Collegiate male student's locker. Now, narrowing her eyes, she gave the poster a thorough going-over. "You know," she said, keeping her voice as cool and even as Dee's, "Jehu would've tossed this one out the window without a second thought."

"Jehu?" asked Dee, glancing at her with a frown.

"The guy that splattered Jezebel," Jez reminded her.

One beat passed, then comprehension entered Dee's face and she nodded. "Jehu would be really pissed with this window," she said, leaning through it to survey the alley. "Couldn't even break your leg from here. No wild dogs to lick up blood, either."

"Farrah's safe then," said Jez, scanning the wardrobe, dresser, and queen-size bed that engulfed the other end of the room. Dismay hit full force as she recognized the pouting features of Marilyn Monroe splayed across the cherry-red quilt. "You sleep under a dead person," she said slowly.

An amber leaf drifted through the open window and floated on the pause. "Nice of you to notice," said Dee.

No one usually noticed Jez's casual comments; she felt the danger. "The Women's Auxiliary Prayer Group does not allow Marilyn," she explained rapidly. "Or Farrah. Or any of those"—she pointed at the Stones—"guys. They wouldn't allow me to live up here alone, either. How did you talk your mother into it?"

"I doubt she's noticed," said Dee. Languidly, she dropped onto the couch, and another butterfly was revealed, fluttering out of the crease between her breasts. "Last Easter," she continued in deliberately bored tones, "Mom threw the bread knife at Dad, so he moved out here until two weeks ago, when they started fucking again. He insulated this place over the summer, just in case he had to live here all winter, so they couldn't really complain when I decided to move in." Angling her head to catch Jez's eye, she mouthed the word "fucking" several times. "My parents' *favorite* hobby," she added. "You like that hobby, Jez?"

Carefully, Jez shifted foot to foot. Though she had sized up every inch of the room, she still had to take more than one step into it; here she stood awkward in Dee's space, on Dee's terms, and they both knew it. Even the vocabulary belonged to Dee.

"Do you know what *fucking* means, Jezzie-Jesus-girl?" Dee asked, her voice prowling.

Jez took a quick breath. "D'you think I'm stupid?" she asked hoarsely. "It means getting carnal."

Softly, *softly*, Dee laughed. "You ever get carnal?" she sing-songed.

For one brief, piercing moment, Jez wanted to fly out of that place to her mother's high bright realm—the world of Billy Graham and *My Answer*. Even Armageddon had rules; this conversation was like climbing a hillside of loose shale. Still, she *had* come here looking for something. There was no point in hiding her light under a bushel.

"At an Easter church retreat," she said slowly. "And… summer camp."

"*Bible* camp?" asked Dee, one eyebrow lifting.

Jez shrugged. "Sorry you missed out," she said.

Dee grinned, and both girls won. "So, what's your favorite position?" she asked.

"Come on," Jez scoffed. This one was easy. "Missionary."

Now they were both grinning.

"How many different guys you been with?" asked Dee.

Jez shrugged again. "The adults went to bed," she said. "We snuck out. Sometimes there was a group."

They assessed each other, Dee half-naked and sprawled on the couch, Jez one step up from a Hutterite, waiting just inside the door. This was Dee's sanctuary, and Jez could feel it—the fiery heartbeats that guarded it close, a kingdom of burning hearts, burning bridges. Quickly she reviewed everything she had learned watching the girl across from her—the way, for instance, Dee used small gestures to set up rules in conversations then abruptly changed them with a tilt of her head. No one held her for long; she was a radio constantly switching stations, tuning people in and out. Jez had seen Dee make and destroy guys with small movements of her body, and nothing lost her more decisively than backing down…or accepting a conversation on her terms.

"I've spent four years watching you," she said finally.

"I know you have," drawled Dee.

"So I know you four years better than you know me," said Jez.

Dee's face came alive with interest. Opening a purse that lay beside her, she extracted her cigarettes, then swore softly. Without comment, Jez tossed her the orange Bic. Also without comment, Dee lit up and tossed it back.

"Okay," she said, inhaling. "You've watched me for four years. So what did you learn?"

Jez's skin sang with stark realization; she pushed it away.

"Careful," Dee said harshly. "I'm watching for the way you lie."

"I want to know what you know," Jez whispered, her voice hoarse with the effort of half-truths. "Whatever it is, I want to know it too."

Dee's eyes narrowed. "All right," she said after a moment. "But this time I'm watching *you*. Take off your clothes."

In the long pause that followed, Jez almost admitted defeat, turned, and fled. For the miserable, unmentionable, *agonizing* truth was that, under the safety of her voluminous paisley midi dress, obvious tan lines divided her body into good and evil: at the neck, just above the elbow, and two inches below the knee. Over the years, the Women's Auxiliary Prayer Group had seen no reason to vary anything except the sleeve length in their seasonal sewing projects; as a result, from neck to knee, Jez's skin retained the exact shade of pale she had been born with—a color she was certain she shared with bloated underwater corpses. None of the dreamy predictions that she had been engaging in for the last two days had prepared her for a scene like this; she had assumed that the clothing Dee planned to lend her would miraculously cover any defects, and there would be a washroom for changing purposes. In this small, shadowy room, there was nowhere to go except Dee's eyes, and they were predatory.

"I can't," she stammered.

"You can't?" echoed Dee, her head lifting, nostrils flared. "You *can't?*" she repeated ominously.

"All right," mumbled Jez, suddenly sweaty. "But I'm warning you, it gets ugly. I'm not allowed to suntan, and I have to wear these ugly midis all the time, even in the summer. Why would you want to see—"

"Jez," Dee said intensely, sitting up, her entire body focused into her thought. "*Everyone* wants to know what's underneath. You can't tell me that you've watched me for four whole years with my clothes *on*. Not if you really want to know what I know." Getting to her feet, she crossed the room, placed her cigarette between Jez's lips, and began to undo the buttons on the front of Jez's dress. "Jesus!" she muttered derisively. "Paisley is *sperm*, y'know. You're walking around in a sperm midi. Christ, you're a sperm whale."

Jez's mother had a penchant for keeping things closed; this particular midi had forty-three buttons, and Dee swore her way through each one. Casually, her hands glided over the give of Jez's breasts, the bodice parting gently under her touch, Jez's heart another layer sighing open underneath.

Together, the girls' breathing fell into the same quick tobacco-scented rhythm as Dee's hands pressed against Jez's belly and the dress slid from her hips.

"Could you shut the door?" Jez whispered. Instead, Dee crossed to the stereo and turned it on—Rod Stewart, perfect backup for a strip, Jez realized—so she shut the door herself, then allowed Dee to inch the cotton slip up her body, exposing the bargain panty hose, the extra-large underwear, and the stained, stretched bra. (Jez's mother saw no reason to own more than one.) Slowly, languorously, the slip lifted over her head, and fingers fumbled with the hooks of her bra. A small sound happened in Jez's throat. "Shh," soothed Dee, bending to work off the panties and nylons. Finally, they were gone, and Jez stood free of it all and terrified in her skin, the all-consuming fullness of it, as if she had been reborn or newborn, as if Dee had removed some invisible numbness, an unspoken citizen's agreement to a taming, and now her skin was rising from within itself to reclaim everything—body, mind, fire, air, the first principles of dreaming. With a whimper, Jez stepped toward the bed, intending to dive headlong into Marilyn Monroe's gleaming smile, but the thought came to her: *She's dead and I'm alive.* Taking one long breath of the living, she turned directly into Dee's gaze, the single breath that shuddered open-mouthed through them both.

Dee's eyes were vague. "Did anyone at Bible camp see you like this?" she asked.

"It was always dark," Jez mumbled.

"So I'm the only one?" asked Dee.

"Yes," said Jez.

"Then we're even," said Dee. "No one's ever watched me the way you have. Turn around."

Trying to shrink into invisibility, Jez made the required pirouette. "Okay, so I told you I was ugly," she babbled. "Anita Bryant looks better *without* a girdle."

"You could pose for the virgin centerfold," murmured Dee.

"I am *not* a virgin," protested Jez.

"Okay, okay," said Dee. Her gaze was still vague; she seemed to be pulling herself in from a great distance. "I think we *are* the same size. Close enough, anyway." Crossing to the dresser, she pulled out a pair of pink panties and a matching underwire bra, and tossed them onto the bed. "Try these."

Thankful for the camouflage, Jez scrambled into the skimpy panties and the bra, which compressed her breasts into a high-rise shape even her mother's darts hadn't been able to imagine. Then it was Stevie Nicks singing "Rhiannon" as Dee pulled her to the dresser, lit two white candles, and began tilting her face this way and that, applying lip gloss, eyeliner, mascara, and blush. Unfamiliar with makeup, Jez was surprised at its heaviness, the drag on her skin, but she quickly forgot it as Dee whispered, "Now tell me who's ugly," and turned her toward the mirror with its candlelit reflection of pink satin, the shadowy hollows of throats, the huge questions of eyes.

"Do you like it?" Dee asked softly.

Slightly stunned, Jez avoided the question. "Is this what you want me to wear to school?" she stammered. "I mean, do I get to wear anything over it?"

"Just a sec," said Dee. Crossing to the wardrobe, she

began tossing clothes onto the bed, and eventually Jez decided on jeans and a *Starsky and Hutch* T-shirt. "Jehu would love you, baby," teased Dee, giving her the once-over. "Meet me at a quarter after eight tomorrow morning at the 7-Eleven on Dundas. You can change into those in Sinbad's backseat."

"Sinbad?" asked Jez.

"My car," said Dee. "Sin *bad*. Sin, for short."

"Of course," said Jez.

They sat outside on the top step in jeans and bras, smoking a last cigarette. Jez had asked to wear the underwire bra home that night as a practice run, wanting its pink shimmering presence, its two secret hands stroking her this way and that under the paisley midi, forbidden and closer than the touch of a mother. For the last ten years, Rachel Hamilton's monster midis had been a stranglehold on her daughter's life, numbing it and stealing it away, but tonight Jez would sit at her mother's table, eat her roast beef and apple pie; they would take turns reading Bible verses and praying, and Jez's softest, most innermost prayer would be the shimmering satin bra—a reminder that buried alive, she still breathed. Playing with this thought, she watched the blue butterfly on Dee's upper arm darken to black in the fading light.

"Monarch," said Dee, catching her glance. "I've got them all over. Even two down here." She traced a finger along her inner thigh. "I'll show you sometime."

"How many are there?" asked Jez, amazed.

Dee shrugged. "Not as many as I want. Did you know monarchs migrate like birds? They fly south to California and Mexico. Cerro Pelon—that's the name of a mountain in Mexico where a hundred million monarchs spend the winter.

Huge flocks of them roost together, all winter long. Imagine if they all took off at once. Sky of wings, man."

"Hard to imagine a butterfly flying all the way to Mexico," said Jez.

"How far can you send your mind?" asked Dee, her eyes intense in the late afternoon shadow. "Butterflies are the way you think, man. Flit-flit-flitting, inch by inch. A tiny cosmic detail, but they can go anywhere. Just think—they're in Cerro Pelon, and we're stuck here." Briskly, she slapped Jez's leg. "When are you supposed to be home?"

Jez had been keeping an eye on her watch. "I have half an hour," she replied. "I told my mother I'd be working on a history paper at the library."

Stubbing out her cigarette, Dee got to her feet. "Shit," she muttered. "Where'd I leave Pinko?"

"In the backyard," said Jez.

"You put on that sperm mural while I get Sin," said Dee, heading down the stairs. "I'll pick you up in the alley in five."

Still seated on the top step, Jez watched her jump the bottom three and take off running across the yard—a girl composed of a flock of monarchs, each butterfly traveling its own tangent. Until the day, Jez mused, they all came awake together and rose in a great blue tattooed spiral, transforming Dee into a skin of wings.

THREE

My mother rarely slept at length. Retiring at eleven, she typically dozed off for several hours, then rose and prowled the house. My father, on the other hand, was a sound sleeper and so remained largely undisturbed by her wanderings, but it was not unusual for me to wake at three or four to the sound of footsteps in the hall or the running of water in the kitchen sink. To a child's ear, these were guardian sounds—my mother an angel patrolling the divine pathways of our home, guided by an inner but audible map of voices that led her, free from human error, through the denser material realm. That these voices were archangelic and of the highest celestial order was never then in question, for it was mere days after her baptism by the Tongue of Fire that they initiated contact, thereafter summoning her nightly out of mundane sleep to visions of the sublime.

From the beginning, my bedroom was of interest to them, and I often woke to see my door opening so silently, it felt like a crack in my brain oozing wide. Then the stooped shape of my mother appeared, standing in that opening, darker than the darkness of the hall. If I stirred, the door closed as soundlessly as it had opened, and I heard the quiet pad of angel's feet leaving me. If, however, I managed to remain motionless, my mother entered and crept about the room, running her fingers over my stuffed panda, my library books, the mirror on my dresser.

Opening my dresser drawers, she sifted through my clothes, all the while whispering in soft hissing sounds. Restlessly, her fingers traced the carpet's border design and ran along the floorboards; sometimes she knelt at the center of my room and drew a circle about herself or patterned the air above her head. Less frequently, she approached my window, drew apart the curtains, and sent out her voice in a low hum; but always she completed her activities by opening my closet door and emitting a low digging sound—a grave-digger's call that dug the dead deeper, piled earth higher over what had been buried, and kept it down.

On occasions of significance—birthdays, holidays, notable changes in the weather—she circled my bed, stroking the edge of the mattress and braiding the bedspread fringe, and sometimes she shaped her hands into a soft-flowing mold and ran them over my body, whispering, always whispering, inward to herself. At these times, I felt something lift from me and depart—some inner shimmery membrane of breath and nerves that passed from the darkness of my flesh into the darkness of hers; as it entered her body, she took a quick shuddery breath and turned from me, deeper into night, into another level of the mind, and left the room.

I rarely thought of these moments during the day, for they seemed to belong to the dark—that fabric of consciousness that fades into the dawn. Signs and warnings, the faint drumming of angel wings, a whisper of prophecy in the blood—my mother and I never spoke of these matters, simply knew they had a place in the order of things, necessary and familiar as the sound of one's own breathing. Instead, I learned to tune to the nocturnal shuffle of her feet passing my door, to watch in my sleep as she crept along house corridors, touching framed prints of *The Last Supper* and the *Crucifixion*, so often awake within my dreams that if I physically climbed out of bed, crept to the door, and opened it, I could not be certain if I was still dreaming or actually saw what transpired next.

Houselights were not turned on at night, and in the dark, sounds magnified. A heavy wind might fill the lungs of the backyard trees, the rustle of my mother's bathrobe carve out a long, cavernous tunnel. Creeping in her wake, I would stand in a doorway and watch her progress around a room, tracing her fingers over the walls as if looking for cracks or holes. Sometimes she came to a halt, humming all the while deep within herself, and circled her fingertips endlessly about a single spot; when she moved on, her fingers remained on the wall's surface without breaking contact. To my child's unimpeded mind, she seemed to be sending into and receiving from some kind of divine circuitry. When, several times, I managed to sneak up behind her and touch a point in the wall she had just stroked, a shock shot through me, accompanied by a swiftly cut-off current of voices or a series of brilliant images that flashed by too quickly to comprehend.

Some nights my mother appeared to actually summon angels. Certain voice tones and colors seemed necessary to invoke their presence; she often used flowers or colored candles, cupping her hands around the blossom or flame and humming until a second glow appeared between her palms. As this new glow grew, the space between her hands widened until, taking sudden form, a luminescent figure stepped forth, but whatever happened next was lost to me—the circuitry of my mind not strong enough to handle such intensity—and all that I perceived were vague shape-changing forms that swirled about my mother in restless communion.

If, indeed, I occasionally witnessed Rachel Hamilton communing with illuminated beings from another dimension, most nights she walked alone, tracing her fingers along the walls and whispering, it seemed to me, only to herself. Though she gave no sign of noticing my presence, I was careful to keep my distance, aware without having to be told that the path we were on had been granted only to her and that I was trespassing on forbidden ground, violating sacred law. There came a time, however, when in spite of my caution I was abruptly trapped at one end of a hallway as my mother made an unexpected turn and came back toward me. That night, she was carrying a pale green candle that lit the underside of her face and cast the upper half into leaping shadow. Heart thudding, I pressed to the wall, but my eerily lit mother brushed past without acknowledgment, leaving me in her wake as merely another bit of the unworthy, a speck of the dingy material world.

From that moment on, I knew my mother could not see me. The landscapes we inhabited were too different—what she saw was not what I saw; what surrounded her disdained and shut me out. By haunting her footsteps, I was able to catch occasional glimpses into her realm, but she wandered a part of the mind I could not enter; I stood on the edge of a world she had passed through to, a world I had been refused. While as a child I resented this, for years it seemed the natural order of things, dictated by my mother's chosen status, her direct line, as it were, to the divine. But as I came into adolescence, I realized that the situation was more complex—as complex, in fact, as the careful web my mother wove about my bedroom, closing gaps and cracks, any openings onto other planes. Was she indeed attempting to protect me by preventing evil influences from reaching through to me from other levels of reality, or was she preventing me from reaching toward them? Was it actually true that she had the sacred sight and I had none? If so, why did she have to expend so much effort, night after night, spinning her spiritual web—a web I finally understood to be accomplishing more than simply closing me in? Rather, it was draining me of something vital, blinding me to what I needed to see of my own means, to *know*.

I did not tell my mother about Dee Eccles for months, but she sensed it, and started coming into my room more often, hiss-whispering to herself as she sent her fingers spider-walking the walls. During that early period, while I moved away from her toward Dee, toward myself in the context of Dee, my mother's searches intensified. As I lay nightly in bed, she reached to touch my bedroom wall and I felt that touch on my skin; she stroked my dresser mirror and invisible fingertips were suddenly traveling my face. Once, her touch reached out to connect with me during the day. It was weeks into my friendship with Dee; I was on lunch break and had crowded into the backseat of her Bug with several others; abruptly, a door opened inside my head and the dark whispering outline of my mother appeared. No one else noticed, not even Dee. High on a shared joint, she and the others continued to crack up over yet another snide comment, leaving me trapped and alone within my mother's questing current, shuddering like a startled horse as her fingertips brushed lightly over some section of my brain.

• • •

The following morning Sinbad idled at the 7-Eleven, "Smoke on the Water" blasting from the tape deck as Dee sat slumped in the front seat, her eyes fixed in a dull stare. Overnight, the weather had turned cold, a sharp frost withering colors and curling the edges of leaves. Huddled against the store's side wall, Jez was a blaze of lime in a jacket her mother had bought on sale at Zellers. Inside her left pocket rested the pink satin bra, carefully folded. She had come to return it, and had spent the last fifteen minutes perfecting the polite, impervious smile she intended to wear as she handed the bra pleasantly but firmly through the car window.

"Yesterday was a mistake," she planned to say, her voice dispassionate and impersonal. "*My* mistake. I'm sorry I wasted your valuable time." Then, turning from the car window, she would walk the last few blocks to school alone.

As she stood considering her next move, cars veered into parking spaces and a stream of adults hurried in and out of the store's main door, cradling steaming cups of coffee. In contrast, Dee looked completely unplugged. Jez had never seen her this wasted, almost lifeless—as if an inner switch had been flicked and her circuitry shut down. Her skin was pale, her eyes two hollowed-out charcoal caves, and she wasn't even smoking. Whatever lived in Dee—all those transitory quick-winged wishes that flew her skin—seemed to have migrated south overnight, leaving her facing a winter without dreams.

Jez knew about being exiled from dreams. If no butterflies flew her skin, still she had been a slave in Egypt and had wept by the waters of Babylon; she had knelt at the cross, wrapped the mutilated body in the tomb, and gone underground to await the Second Coming. Years had passed as she had waited alone in the catacombs of her gut, waited so long she sometimes forgot what it was she was waiting for. But last night she had been reminded. Last night, she had finally recognized all those years of loneliness as a sanctuary carefully carved out around her—a period of preparation necessarily keeping her separate and alone. It was a dream that had brought this revelation to her—a dream sent by The Chosen Ones. In this dream, she had seen the hooded faithful, knives raised as they whirled around an underground cavern. At their center had stood a large stone altar with two girls laid across it, their throats about to be slit like pigs. When Jez had woken from this dream, the memory of it had been so strong that she could still feel the altar beneath her back and see the firelight arcing off the raised blades.

The dream's message had been clear: in spite of her failings, in spite of everything she did not yet comprehend, The Chosen Ones had claimed Mary-Eve Hamilton for a purpose, and she belonged to them. If the purpose had not yet been revealed, still that was no reason not to trust it. If it seemed bewildering and unfathomable, The Chosen Ones had carried the secret mind of God throughout the history of mankind; they moved in mysterious ways and were not to be questioned. Dee Eccles was an outsider, one of the unchosen. If Jez continued her association with the wild butterfly girl, The Chosen Ones would spit them both from their holy mouths as unclean vermin.

Did anyone at Bible camp see you like this? she remembered longingly. *Then we're even. No one's ever watched me the way you have.*

The parking lot's black asphalt stretched out before her—dark, dense grief; then, without warning, a lucid ache opened within Jez, rippling up from the inner place that holds all that is unknown. In that instant, everything about her seemed to lose its form, as if stores, cars, houses and schools, family and friendships, all of human history, including Jez herself, were simply molecules playing a game at the surface of some deep ongoing knowing. A liquid exquisite, she felt it for several seconds—a knowing that had never, and would never, reveal itself fully to the human mind. Then this knowing faded, returning her to the mundane—Dee sitting slumped and dull-eyed in the Bug, cars pulling in and out of the parking lot, the curse of the normal once again pressing its thumb down upon the world...everything empty of call, the heart cored, the pulse of the possible lost.

All that remained was faith. The Chosen Ones had always possessed the gift of great faith—they were, after all, the spoken forms of the Logos resonating within the world of flesh. Perhaps, Jez thought suddenly, the realization hitting her in a delirious, delicious flash, she had misunderstood the dream; perhaps The Chosen Ones had been *protecting* the girls on the altar. *That's it!* she thought jubilantly. *It was a dream of approval, not condemnation.*

And if not, if she was wrong and The Chosen Ones came after her and Dee for this unintentional transgression, then she would voluntarily lay herself down on the altar, bare her throat, and say, "Take me. I've got enough for the both of us."

Tentatively, Jez approached the powder-blue Bug and knocked on the passenger window. As if touched by a bare wire, Dee jerked upright, then jabbed a finger at the backseat, where the *Starsky and Hutch* T-shirt and a pair of jeans had been tossed, and returned to her slump. Opening the passenger door, Jez ducked into the backseat and began unbuttoning the front of her green and red plaid midi.

"Shit," croaked Dee, her voice hoarse with the day's first words. "Someone'll see you. Hold on." Without further warning, she burned rubber out of the parking lot, Jez hanging tightly to the front seat as Sinbad veered into a nearby alley. "Okay, fine now," said Dee, killing the ignition and settling back into her dull-eyed stare. "No one'll see you here."

Jez decided to make a quick job of it. Erupting out of her mother's darts, she pulled on the triumph of the pink satin bra, Starsky, and skintight jeans, then sucked in and dragged the zipper closed. Eyes shut, she took a careful breath. After almost a decade as a Women's Auxiliary Prayer Group sewing experiment, Jez's fast-growing impression of jeans was that they were a well-disguised tourniquet applied no-holds-barred to the crotch; for the life of her, she couldn't see how they would tempt anyone into a life of sexual debauchery. How was one supposed to wear them and function?

Gingerly, she levered one leg, then the other, over the top of the front passenger seat. "Look, Mom," she said, jerking her blue and white oxfords up and down. "No socks."

Dee shot a quick glance at Jez's naked ankles and swore softly. "Cold skin, cold turkey," she shrugged.

Radiating exultation, Jez edged out of the back of the car and carefully lowered herself onto the front passenger seat. If her new jeans were a well-disguised chastity belt, still, after seventeen endless years, she was sitting on an undeniable *ass*; she had tits Mick Jagger would put his lips onto and *suck*. The unexpected excitement pouring through Jez was so volatile, she wanted to howl, but beside her Dee continued to slump oblivious, a yawn eating half her face. Small bugs were definitely crawling out of every pore.

"So, um, what's up?" ventured Jez. "Your mother feed you the Abomination for breakfast?"

"Huh?" croaked Dee. The gaze she turned toward Jez was the palest purple—two complete blanks.

"You know," explained Jez, "666 on your toast, the Beast hiding at the bottom of your oatmeal. Your stomach a burning lake of fire."

"You got the last part right," groaned Dee. Straightening, she reached across Jez and opened the glove compartment. "I'd better do your face," she added, taking out a makeup kit. "Otherwise no one'll believe you're my friend."

Taking Jez's chin into her hand, she stared as if searching for a hidden code, then sketched a series of quick, sure lines. "Okay," she said, leaning back against her car door and giving Jez the once-over. "You're for real now."

Tilting the makeup case's small mirror this way and that, Jez caught angled reflections of a bold, pouting face she had seen previously only in the sweaty touch-alive fantasies of her own mind. How had Dee found this and coaxed it onto the surface? she wondered. How had she looked at Mary-Eve Hamilton in her green and red plaid midi and known it was there?

"C'mon, we've gotta make tracks," Dee said abruptly, shifting in behind the wheel. "I forgot my compass set at home, and I can't do isosceles shit without it."

Punching in the Deep Purple eight-track, she turned up the volume and drove straight past Eleusis Collegiate. They entered the suburbs, Jez perched carefully on the edge of the passenger seat, still trying to ignore the crotch of her jeans. Idly, she picked up the *Sticky Fingers* eight-track by her feet, realized what she was looking at, and started to put it down. Then she brought it back up and stared with unabated curiosity. Though she wasn't a virgin—had, in fact, repeatedly managed to lose her mythical virginal status—every one of her acts of carnal abandonment had taken place in complete darkness. To date, she hadn't managed a single direct look at the damn thing.

"Next time they play Eleusis," yelled Dee, tapping the eight-track's cover, "they're mine." Lifting the tape from Jez's hands, she placed it between her thighs and rocked. Wild giggles took Jez, and she stared fiercely through the passenger window as the Bug turned into the alley behind the Eccles' home and pulled up next to the garage. The engine died, terminating Deep Purple and leaving the girls alone with the slanted rush of wind. Several drops of rain splattered the windshield. Tossing the eight-track onto the floor, Dee swiveled left and pushed open her door with both feet.

"Day off," she announced, and got out without looking back.

"Day off from what?" asked Jez, emerging uncertainly from the passenger door.

Dee was already halfway up the stairs. "Didn't you know?" she called over her shoulder. "It's a national holiday. Deeday. Y'know—Monday, Tuesday, Wednesday, Deeday. Whenever it's Deeday, we get the day off."

Jez hesitated. Truth be told, she would have preferred more options, but all she was being offered was a view of Dee's back as the other girl disappeared through the garage's second-floor doorway, the green and red midi slung over her shoulder. A brief burst of rain hit Jez in the face, startling her into momentum, but after darting up the first several stairs, she slowed—as she was all too quickly beginning to discover, movement in tight jeans was an art form, learning it a baptism of fire, and these particular stairs looked to be an especially long burn. A fleeting vision of her homeroom class whisked through her mind, everyone in postures of boredom, safe and secure at their desks. Deep-throating nicotine with Dee after school had let out for the day was one thing, she thought grimly—breaking a straight-A average quite another. With a loud moan, the wind tore into the trees around the garage, releasing a long spirit-line of leaves. Watching it from the landing, Jez waited, but no last-minute angels revealed themselves, no sirens keened in her blood. Even her dream of The Chosen Ones had vanished, leaving her empty, without sanctuary. She was no one. She could become anyone. In front of her a doorway stood open; she walked through it into Dee's place.

"Close the door," said Dee.

Inside the room, Jez found everything draped in black— the window, the bed, the couch. On the coffee table a single black candle gusted wildly, and Stevie Nicks's "Rhiannon" once again haunted the stereo. But it was the two long-haired guys smoking on the couch that claimed Jez's attention. Though they were no longer Eleusis Collegiate students, she recognized them immediately—Dee's older brother and a former bass player from the school band. Like everything else in the room, both were dressed completely in black. Uneasily, Jez's eyes flicked toward Dee's T-shirt—also black, and dominated by a large white skull—then down to her own black *Starsky and Hutch*.

"What is this?" she asked. "Stephen King's home-decorating kit?"

The air was gag-heavy with smoke. Butting out his cigarette, the bass player got up and closed the door, then leaned against the black sheet tacked across its inner face.

"Cute," Dee's brother said softly, his eyes giving Jez the slow slide.

"Jailbait," agreed the bass player, his hands coming around Jez from behind and pulling her in hard against his crotch.

"Dee!" hissed Jez, stiffening, and the other girl's gaze

slid across hers, wide-eyed, an animal being dragged toward fear. Slowly, the bass player's hands started to move and Jez's stomach inverted, turning on its axis. Lifting her left foot, she kicked backward, and felt the thud of a sturdy blue and white oxford entering flesh. With a howl, Bassie let go and Jez pivoted, reaching for the doorknob. But before she could grasp it, Dee's brother grabbed her around the waist and swung her onto the bed, his full weight coming down onto her like a gut punch.

"So you're Dee's new friend," he murmured, his face one inch from hers—Dee's face but more angular, the blue eyes deeper set.

"Take it easy, Andy," said Dee, edging onto the side of the bed. "She's religious."

"Jesus-bait," grunted Andy, thrusting with his groin, and a jagged fear swept Jez, filling the air with tiny, scratchy sounds. "Want to fuck, Virj?" he breathed, his mouth pressing hers so hard, she could feel his teeth through his lips. Abruptly, he pulled back, and Jez became aware of Dee leaning over them, nudging her brother's face with her own.

"C'mon, Andy," she said. "We know you're not a dog, so stop acting like one."

"Who're you saving her for?" growled Andy, glancing up at her.

"Shh," said Dee, slapping his face playfully.

Andy tensed, his expression shifting to neutral, everything going into the eyes. "Make new friends but keep the old, eh, Dee?" he murmured. Without warning, he launched himself, taking Dee facedown onto the bed beside Jez and pinning her as a grinning Bassie pulled down her jeans. For a single taut breath, the two guys stared, transfixed, at Dee's naked, heaving ass. Then, leaning forward, Andy bit her hard on one buttock.

Whooping loudly, both guys climbed off the bed as Dee struggled, choking on her own breath, to pull up her jeans. "Come and get it, Dee. Come and get it," they chanted. "Rape me, rape me."

Wordless, Dee threw herself at them. Andy and Bassie ducked, guffawing, but instead of attacking, Dee lunged past them and grabbed an object lying on the coffee table. Suddenly her brother and his buddy started fighting each other for the door. Frantically, they yanked it open and shoved themselves through the gap, then slammed it shut just as a jackknife thudded into the wood behind them. Muffled footsteps rumbled down the outside stairs, and the walls reverberated from several emphatic kicks. Still lying stunned and wide-eyed on the bed, Jez realized that under the quivering black sheet tacked to the inside of the door, Dee's jackknife had nailed Farrah Fawcett right in the kisser.

Moaning softly, Dee stumbled against the coffee table and the candle toppled. In the sudden complete darkness, there was only the sound of Fleetwood Mac and two girls' harsh breathing.

"I have a lighter," Jez said into the void. "For the candle. It's in the pocket of my dress."

"I got a new one," Dee replied. With a quiet click she came into view, her face flickering as she knelt at the coffee table and relit the candle. The thought came to Jez then of a cat she had seen once—the lower half of its body run over and squished flat, the upper part dragging itself off the street, looking for a place to die.

"Deeday always like this?" Jez asked carefully, wiping the taste of Andy from her lips.

"Deeday," Dee said bitterly. "*Andy*day. Every day is fucking Andyday. Sometimes I want to kill him so much, I dream of peeling his skin off with my fingernails." Hugging herself tightly, she took a long shuddery breath, then added, "Only kids are lucky. D'you have a brother?"

"No," said Jez. "I'm an only-only. Think you'll need a rabies shot?"

With a snort, Dee wiped her eyes, smudging her makeup. "Isn't that for wild animals?" she asked.

"He's an animal," said Jez.

Dee rocked slightly, staring at the candle with dazed eyes. When she spoke again, her voice was barely audible. "Check to see if the skin's broken, okay?" she whispered.

Jez swallowed, her throat clenching like a fist. "Yeah, sure," she said.

Unzipping her jeans, Dee bent over the couch. Slowly, disbelievingly, Jez leaned toward the other girl's naked ass and ran her fingertips over the reddish-purple bite mark on the right buttock. A single blue monarch flew the other. Two breaths left Jez; she wanted to trace her mouth—soft, open-lipped—across them both.

"Skin didn't break," she said. "It's smooth."

"Thanks," said Dee, and pulled up her jeans. Turning, she knelt with her eyes lowered and concentrated on lighting a cigarette. "So," she said, inhaling, the rasp of smoke deep in her lungs. "You've met my brother and you're not running off screaming into the black night?"

Jez shrugged. The thought hadn't occurred to her, at least

not since Andy had taken off. *No*, she realized then—the longer she remained in this place, the further its candlelit shadowiness seemed to move *into* her, creating a kind of oneness. In a way she could not have explained, its very darkness felt familiar, almost like home. Playing with this thought, not sure what to do with it, she faced Dee, both of them still kneeling, the black candle's flame between them. The stereo was quiet, Fleetwood Mac having come to an end; the only sound came from the wind in the trees and a car going by in the alley.

"Andy was the one who took off screaming," she said, cradling admiration in her voice. "I like the knife in the door. Nice touch."

Dee's hands moved compulsively, molding the soft wax at the candlewick's base. "I practice knife-throwing at the dartboard in our basement," she said, her voice edgy, as if reluctant to reveal much. "I'm better than Andy and he knows it. Sometimes I just aim for the walls. Daddy likes to show the knife marks to his clients."

Jez tried to imagine her own father proudly displaying a wall full of his daughter's knife gouges to visitors. "Why don't you keep the jackknife in the door permanently?" she said. "Come in handy if you ever need to use it."

"You're not mad about Andy jumping you?" asked Dee, her eyes flicking past Jez's. "I thought you'd freak. He always jumps my friends. Sometimes he goes further, sometimes not."

"You mean this was supposed to be some kind of a date?" said Jez, stunned.

Dee took a deep breath, and the hand holding her

cigarette shook. "Most of my friends *like* Andy," she mumbled. "Usually they're in his room with the door closed." Shoulders slumped, she sat staring at the candle flame. "D'you like him?" she asked hesitantly.

Jez tasted contempt. "Like I said," she grunted, "keep the knife in the door."

Dee's eyes darted to her face. "Would you use it?" she asked.

"Would you?" said Jez.

Wordless, they stared into the long search of each other's eyes.

"If I had the guts," Dee said finally.

Getting to her feet, Jez crossed the room and took hold of the jackknife. It slid easily out of the door, then sat in her hand—balanced, a necessary fact. Many of the chosen ones had used a knife in the service of the Lord, she thought, studying the jackknife's contours in the room's dim light. Most important, of course, had been Abraham, in the moment when he had leaned over his altar-bound son Isaac, sacrificial knife in hand. This scenario was never pictured in children's Bibles or Sunday school papers—it was usually a gaily colored drawing of Abraham pulling a ram out of a nearby thicket as a wide-winged angel hovered overhead. But what about those frantic heartbeats that must have taken the patriarch as he stood over his only son, holding the knife to his throat?

Faith is a knife, Jez thought slowly, *its edge pressed to the pulse of everything you know, everything you think you know.* Lifting the black sheet tacked to the inside of the door, she studied the jagged hole the jackknife had made of Farrah Fawcett's face. "Poor Farrah," she said, placing the knife tip onto the arced neck and slicing downward through the hard nipples, the flimsy red swimsuit. "Poor, poor Farrah."

Still kneeling beside the coffee table, Dee gave a startled laugh.

"Poor Farrah," repeated Jez, disemboweling the actress's image. "If you still had a face, you'd be smiling at me right now. I could do anything I wanted to you and you'd keep smiling. A murderer could buy this poster, a rapist, a fucking cannibal, and you'd still be smiling."

In the pause that followed, she observed the gutted poster, her breath slowing and lengthening, changing the mind of the room and inviting a deeper darkness. Gradually, almost imperceptibly, a hazy presence began to take shape around her—an underground cavern that opened onto several tunnels. From the mouth of one of these tunnels came the distant rustle of robes and the glow of handheld candles; then a row of gray-robed figures filed into the cavern, silent except for their breathing. Surrounding Jez, they slid a similar robe over her shoulders, raised the hood onto her head, and placed a bone-handled knife into her left hand.

"So how come you're wearing my clothes?" asked Dee, apparently oblivious to the arrival of The Chosen Ones. "How come you let me put makeup on you?"

Disoriented, Jez stared at the solid jackknife in her right hand and the transparent ceremonial knife in her left. *Knife of flesh, knife of spirit*, she thought, trembling with intensity. Before her, still silent, stood The Chosen Ones, a transparent row of gray-robed figures, and beyond them knelt Dee, clearly defined by candlelight. What had brought The Chosen Ones *here*, Jez wondered dizzily, into *this* room, after so many years? If they had come to fulfill last night's dream and slit her disobedient throat, why place the killing knife directly into her hand?

For the first time, The Chosen Ones were acknowledging her. Jez could feel the weight of their gaze, invisible under those shadowy hoods and staring directly at her as if waiting for something—something that needed to come from her. Some kind of signal. A secret sign.

Uncertain, she shrugged at Dee. "Who wouldn't want to look like Farrah Fawcett?" she asked. "I just wouldn't want to turn into her. Smile-baby poster chick."

"That's what guys'll think of you if you dress like that," said Dee.

"So I'll carry a knife," said Jez. "Surprise them like you did."

"Can't hide it in those jeans," said Dee. "They're licked on."

"They'll think it's a mascara bottle," Jez said.

Tilting her head to one side, Dee studied her. "You're different," she said, "than when you came in."

"So are you," said Jez.

"My ass got bit," Dee said pointedly.

Hesitating, Jez glanced around the room, then asked, "What's with all the black?"

Dee's voice warned her away. "Just something I felt like doing," she said.

"So it wasn't for me?" asked Jez.

"Why would you think that?" asked Dee.

Another shrug from Jez, echoed by Dee. Delicately, their eyes met. *Equal footing*, Jez realized. Dee was watching her straight on, as if assessing her for the first time.

"What do you believe in, Jez?" she asked hoarsely. "*Really?*"

Jackknife in hand, Jez stood, Farrah's paper guts dangling from the blade, the gray-robed Chosen Ones waiting silently around her. "You mean God?" she asked.

"More than God," said Dee. "More than the Devil. More than your parents, or your boyfriend, or anything anyone's ever told you. They'll run you any way they can—fuck, they'll try to tell you how to come." She shuddered violently, then added, "Coming's your soul, man. If they take that, they've got everything."

Eyes fixed on the candle flame, she sat, shoulders slumped, her voice the empty shell of what got left behind. "Okay, so it's just you and me, Jez," she said. "Everything else is gone." Vaguely, she gestured at the black shapeless room. "This is a nothing place we're in here, nothing but what we think. We're starting over; our brains are completely free. We run the entire universe; we align stars and planets; whatever we decide happens." Raising her eyes, she looked directly at Jez. "So," she asked, "what happens?"

A nothing place, thought Jez, glancing around the room: Darkness. Genesis. The Chosen Ones waiting in the shadows, Dee's tear-smeared face over a candle flame. Knife of spirit, knife of steel. As she stood pondering, she felt the room pulling at her thoughts, throbbing with the power of a mind coming into being—the dark energy of planets, the slow intention of shadow galaxies dreaming themselves toward solid matter. Kneeling, she placed the jackknife onto the coffee table, where Dee picked it up and passed it through the candle flame; tranced, they watched the quick slant of smoke that rose from the blade.

"I don't know what happens," whispered Jez, "except for me. *I* happen." Hot tears stung her eyes. "I *want* to happen."

"We'll do a ritual," Dee said dreamily. "A seeking ritual. You don't know what you really believe, and I don't know, either. We'll be like monarchs—lift up off everything we know and fly toward what we dream." Pausing, she circled the flame counterclockwise with the tip of the jackknife blade. "From now on," she added slowly, thinking her way word to word, "we do whatever we want. No rules—their power over you starts when you believe in their rules. Everything's open—wide open—and we're on the hunt. Seekers."

"Seeking what?" asked Jez.

Unfocused, Dee's eyes seemed to fix on something beyond Jez's head, and for a moment Jez thought the other girl had seen The Chosen Ones standing in their transparent half-circle, waiting for whatever it was that had brought them here. But Dee's expression remained neutral, dreamy, lost in thought.

"Whatever we want," she said finally. "Seekers seek; they find out for themselves. They seek because they *don't* know. People who *know* are assholes. People who *know* believe what they're told. When you *know*, you're conquered. We're seekers—we're still free."

Pausing, she sat, letting her thoughts pass into silence, then handed the knife to Jez. "Seekers," said Jez, holding the blade to the candle flame and watching light play across steel. Without warning, she was visited by a memory of her mother sitting with *My Answer* in hand and reading in a breathy, high-pitched voice. Even now Jez could feel that hiss-whispering voice reaching for her, trying to surround and lift her up into those high, bright places, and seal her in. All those years she had been held prisoner by her mother—sealed against her own mind, her own body. What had been lost?

"Seekers," she whispered, letting the murmur of her voice sink deep into herself. "To seek and to find. Finding out is what they never let happen. Finding out is what they're most afraid you'll do. Finding out is the biggest sin, the darkest evil. Finding out is a part of you, a part of every person—the part that gets stolen away and locked up because it's what's closest to sin. Finding out is the part of you that never gets through church doors; it'll be left behind when you rise to Heaven; it *wants* the Apocalypse; it *wants* to win the war against God."

Suddenly, behind her, The Chosen Ones were keening, their voices shredding the air. Turning, Jez saw that they had taken up a whirling dervish dance, their curved knives rising and falling. *The sign*, she thought giddily, *the secret password—it's Apocalypse. Yes, Apocalypse.* A word that had always belonged to the other side—it was a meaning to fear, to guard against. Yet here it was, the Logos that had risen, unbidden, out of her deepest depths—the Word that belonged not at the end, but at the beginning of things.

"Apocalypse," she whispered. "I am seeking the Apocalypse."

"That's the end of the world, isn't it?" Dee asked hesitantly.

"The end of everything," said Jez. "Everything we know."

Dee's eyes narrowed and she nodded. "We must give blood," she said. "Seal our souls to this quest."

Their eyes met, then drifted to Jez's bare forearms. Jez held the knife; it was up to her to choose the place where blood would be released from skin. Pensively, she traced the blade along her left forearm. Nothing spoke to her; nothing called it in. Gently, she touched it to her throat, her chin. Again nothing, but unexpectedly her tongue flicked out, tasting the flat of the blade.

Behind her, The Chosen Ones keened louder, their robes rustling feverishly as they danced. *Apocalypse*, thought Jez, *Apocalypse*. Turning the jackknife, she ran the tip of her tongue in one swift motion across the blade—the first word was thin, fiery pain, blood birthed into space. Quickly, Dee reached for the jackknife and drew her own tongue across its edge. Then, grimacing, she leaned forward. Jez knew what was required—she had heard of pressed fingers, joined wrists. Also leaning forward, she touched the slashed tip of her tongue to Dee's as The Chosen Ones whirled about them in frenzied epiphany.

Abruptly, the robed figures were gone, their rustling silenced, the dream cavern vanished. In the black-sheeted room over the garage, two girls drew back from one another, their breathing harsh and frightened, their tongues vivid with pain. Tears sparkled in Dee's eyes; she drew her bloody tongue over her lips, releasing a dark line of drool that ran down her chin.

"Fuck, this hurts," she muttered. "Why didn't you pick fingertips?"

And so the Apocalypse began.

FOUR

Before the advent of the Tongue of Fire, before the Waiting for the Rapture End Times Tabernacle, before the house on Quance Crescent, I had a different mother—one not living in constant anticipation of the small white stone that would reveal her secret name. This mother had a casual theology, based on the salvation of laughter, and her favorite version of the Creation myth was one in which the Lord God Jehovah woke one morning belly-laughing so long and hard, the earth rolled fully formed from the tip of His tongue.

"Monday to Sunday," she would say firmly. "It's all there together—the fishies, the birdies, you and me." Discussions regarding the conflict between theology and science left her with little patience. "Darwin, Shmarwin," she would retort dismissively. "Leviticus, Shmiticus." And to all those who claimed a special dispensation from God, she replied simply, "Chosen, Shmosen."

This mother saw the Creator's touch in everyone and everything, and she saw it everywhere—vibrating among the peonies, dropping slow and leisurely from autumn trees, sighing the color of dusk as it crept across the backyard. "There, can you see it, Mary-Eve?" she would whisper, her breath hollowing a warm cave inside my ear. "Those purple petunias, the way they're dancing in the breeze—that's God humming to Himself. The whole world is God's song. It's all one big Sunday morning hymn He's humming to anyone who'll listen."

This mother summoned no glowing figures of light, nor did she wake at night and prowl the house, seeking otherworldly realms; it was the death of my seven-year-old twin, Louisie, that triggered these dramatic changes; until Louisie died, the song of our mother's body was enough for her. Few among our parents' social circle, however, approved of Rachel Hamilton's approach to the sacred. Every August, for instance, she volunteered to teach Sunday school at our neighborhood Presbyterian church (in order to get out of listening to the weekly sermon), and every September was once again refused on the basis of a particularly unorthodox lesson she had once given about Jonah and the Loch Ness monster. My father, who came from a long line of Presbyterian ministers, often tried to improve her theological attitudes with pointed discussions concerning the sermon on the drive home from church, but she usually ducked him with comments like "Lawrence, that sounds interesting, but could we stop at the Dairy Queen? I know it's Sunday and all, but I would *so* love a soft ice cream cone."

This mother loved to play. One of the earliest children's games that she devised was the Flannel Graph Board Story Game. It began with a flannel graph kit from the local Christian store, which contained a flannel graph board, a stand, and a multitude of flannel-backed paper dolls, including brightly robed men and women, shepherd boys, and the Christmas ox, ass, and sheep. Each paper doll wore the obligatory look of wonder, even the animals, and every human had pinkish-white skin, except one of the three wise men, who was a chestnut brown. To round things out, an Adam and Eve had also been thrown into the mix, Eve with foot-length blonde hair to cover all the trouble spots, and Adam with a robust cluster of fig leaves growing between his thighs. A host of angels was also represented, most of them apparently singing "O Little Town of Bethlehem," and every one of the bunch had blond hair, blue eyes, a white robe, and a close-fitting halo.

"You watch yourself, girls," warned our mother upon seeing them for the first time. "You get to be too well behaved, and God'll put a giggle around your head. That's what a halo is, you know—the head of a goodie goodie with a God-giggle around it."

Our mother encouraged Louisie and I to play with the flannel graph set and create our own plotlines. To expand the possibilities, she created extra paper dolls, searching through a wide variety of magazines—from *National Geographic* to *Maclean's* and *McCall's*—and cutting out children from every country and race, then backing them with cardboard and flannel. We also had a number of Billy Grahams, scrounged from the covers of *Christianity Today*, a few Diefenbakers and JFKs,

Snow White and several of the dwarfs, Annette Funicello in her Mickey Mouse cap, Snap, Crackle, and Pop from the Rice Krispies box, one serenely fluttering Tweety Bird, the Littlest Hobo, Flipper, and two Lassies, not to mention the Breck girls and our favorite models from the Eaton's Christmas catalogue—more than enough to round out any manger scene, since the latter came bearing carefully wrapped gifts.

The flannel graph board game that Louisie and I most liked to play was called Sunday Morning Church. At Louisie's request, our mother had drawn a looming pulpit with red Magic Marker flames erupting from both sides, behind which Louisie would set a Billy Graham paper doll (one with an upraised hand and a particularly pleading look), then give long, decorous speeches about being polite, saying your bedtime prayers, and *always* putting a nickel into the Sunday morning offering plate. I, on the other hand, preferred to channel through one of the Virgin Marys—her downcast eyes looked so subversive—and got an admittedly fiendish delight out of making her say words like "poop," "fart," and Woody Woodpecker's "That's all, folks! Ha-ha-ha-HA-ha!"

The flannel graph kit also provided a Michelangelo-type Jehovah, a single white dove to represent the Holy Spirit, and a Jesus for every occasion. Satan was depicted by a snake, but it was such an overwhelmingly unimpressive garden-variety type that when Louisie and I played Heaven and Hell, I deputized Eve and Tweety in his place, and had them lead the sinners down into the fiery furnace. While I spent the rest of the game devising all manner of eternal torment for the damned, Louisie handled Heaven, bossing everyone through Billy Graham, to whom she had taken quite a fancy—so much so that she began to carry one of his flannel-backed paper dolls everywhere, keeping it in a small, white purse that she slid under her pillow for after-school naps. At breakfast, she even propped Billy against her milk glass and talked to him as she ate, sometimes falling into long pauses during which she would stare at the paper doll as if listening to its reply.

"That's stupid," I would scowl, watching her whisper giggly secrets to the paper cutout.

"Shh," our mother would whisper back. "She's just playing. Soon she'll get tired of Billy, and another giggle will come along."

But to everyone's surprise, Louisie's infatuation with Billy Graham lasted a full year, during which time everyone else took second place to his beatific paper face. Whenever we played Heaven and Hell, she immediately snatched all the Billys for Heaven, which sat atop some flannel-backed cumulonimbus clouds and several sunsets that our mother had delicately removed from library books and our family set of the *Encyclopedia Britannica*. I, of course, ran Hell—a brilliant collage of forest fires and barbecue flames that snapped, crackled, and popped along the bottom of the flannel graph board.

"Hello, down there!" Billy Graham would holler from atop a soaring cumulonimbus. "Hear ye, hear ye, all ye sinners! Are ye getting hot yet?"

"Not too bad," one of the Breck girls would unrepentantly reply. "But I must wash my hair, and there's no water down here."

"That's what ye get for sinning!" scolded Flipper, riding a particularly lovely sunset. "But maybe I could send you a

Popsicle. Mom!" yelled Louisie, switching to her human persona and running to the doorway. "Can we have a Popsicle? Hell is thirsty today."

"Yes, yes!" I cried, waving the beseeching hands of a Billy Graham that I had quietly confiscated for Hell when Louisie wasn't looking. "I'm getting thirsty from all this preaching down here."

"Hey!" yelled Louisie, returning rapidly to the flannel graph board. "Billy Graham's got to be in Heaven. He's got no sin in him."

"But I like him in Hell!" I protested vigorously. "All those flames make him preach better!"

"No!" yelled Louisie, making a grab for the paper doll. "Give me that Billy!"

"You already got three!" I bellowed back, clutching Billy to my chest. "You can't have *all* the Billys!"

"Mom!" shrieked Louisie, lunging at me. "Tell her it's a sin to put Billy Graham in Hell!"

"Now, why is that a sin?" asked our mother, coming into the room from the hall, where she had probably been stifling her giggles as she listened in.

"Because he's the big church guy! He was on TV!" shouted Louisie, her face contorted with intensity. "He's God's best friend, and God wouldn't let him go to Hell."

"Eve would," I interjected slyly, just as I saw her start to calm down. "And Tweety thinks he's a thilly little puttycat."

At this, Louisie's eyes grew huge and her lower lip trembled. "Billy's going to Heaven and I am too," she whimpered. "And when we get there, we won't let *you* in." Pointing dramatically at me, she pronounced, "You are the Abomination!

God will spit you out of His mouth and you will be damned for all eternity!"

"Louisie, Louisie," coaxed our mother, adopting a soothing tone. "Billy just needs a holiday for a couple of days, and then he'll come back to Heaven. Mary-Eve will let him come back up, won't you, Mary-Eve?"

Louisie's sobs quieted and they both looked at me expectantly. With an exaggerated wink, our mother gave me the thumbs-up signal, and I reluctantly pulled the crumpled Billy Graham from my chest, straightened his beseeching hands, and handed him to Louisie. "You can have him," I said sulkily. "Heaven is for sucks, anyway."

Our personalities were obviously polarized; nevertheless, Louisie and I were as close emotionally as our faces were near-identical. Even so, I was caught entirely unaware when she died during our seventh summer. Though she had always been physically weaker, she had not displayed signs of pronounced illness. And while the autopsy revealed a weak heart that had suddenly given out, it had been a summer of record-high temperatures, and complaints of mild sunstroke, dizzy spells, and headaches were common. Not once had Louisie mentioned chest pains, and her only unusual behavior had come the week before she died, when she began getting up at night and prowling the house. It was one of the few activities of her short life in which she did not invite me to share, but because we slept in the same bed, all she had to do was turn over and I came awake. So when she began getting up in the middle of the night and slipping out of the room, I followed close on her heels, thinking she intended a midnight foray into the pantry cookie jar.

Instead, I found her wandering window to window, pausing every now and then to stand with both hands on a sill and look out as if expecting someone. At intervals, she turned to face the room, her eyes fixed midair as she whispered excitedly to her favorite Billy. Finally, without showing the slightest interest in the cookie jar, she headed back to bed, where she fell immediately asleep.

Puzzled and hurt by the secret she was apparently keeping from me, I followed her about the house for several nights. Each time, she kept to the same pattern—whispering and staring through various windows and then returning to bed to fall swiftly asleep. On the fourth night, weary of tiptoeing around after her, I hid behind the living room couch and leaped out at her in an attempted surprise attack.

"Hi, Louisie!" I rasped, prancing about in my best hissing cat imitation.

A paper Billy clutched to her chest, Louisie stood in the center of the room, facing the window, her white nightie an eerie glow in the dark. Without looking at me, she said reprovingly, "You should go back to bed, Mary-Eve. This isn't for little girls like you."

"I'm the same old as you!" I replied indignantly.

She did not respond, simply continued to stare through the living room window, and gradually I became aware of something invisible but tangible in the room—a quick, soundless pulsing, vibrations that filled the air.

"Oh!" I whispered, stretching out my hands to touch it. "It's God singing all over the place, just like Mom said. Louisie, can you feel it?" Excited, I grabbed her free hand, then dropped it as I felt the humming pulse that emanated from her body. "It's you!" I whispered, taking a step back. "You're the one making the air go funny."

Face radiant, Louisie turned to me and said, "I'm an angel, Mary-Eve. Just like the angels that are standing all around us. You can't see them because you're The Abomination, but it doesn't matter because they didn't come for you. It's me they want, not you. I've been waiting and waiting for them, for days and days and *days* now, and finally they're here to take Billy and me to Heaven."

Fear exploded through me then, and I stared around the room in horror. "You're lying!" I accused. "There aren't any angels, and they aren't taking you anywhere. Anyway, you can't go to Heaven without me. I'm your twin, and twins are stuck together for life."

"Uh-uh," Louisie replied calmly. "Not when it's time to go to Heaven. Besides, you like Hell better. You said Heaven was for sucks, remember?"

Not knowing what to say, I merely gaped, and she turned from me, giggling and waving at something I could not see. Abruptly, she gave an odd cry and stumbled forward, clutching at her chest. As the paper doll Billy dropped from her hand, I darted forward and grabbed her arms, pulling her body in against mine. That close, I could feel her heart pounding, hard and irregular—different from the evenly racing thud in my own chest—and it terrified me.

"Let me go, Mary-Eve," she whispered, pushing against me. "Let me go."

The air's soundless pulsing deepened; I felt a roaring in my ears; strange flickers of light flashed through the room. Then Louisie's body jerked once, she gave a quiet grunt, and her soul shot out of her body like a star seeking the heavens. Before she got there, however, she had to escape my clutches—the arms, legs, and soul I had wrapped so desperately around her. The struggle that followed was vivid and blurred—I remember radiance too brilliant for flesh to endure, sensations of heat, panic, and trapped wings. Visions rolled through my head—confused images of glowing figures, reaching hands, and the sheer white light of Louisie's soul caught somewhere inside my chest. A shudder passed through me; deep within, something shoved and heaved; then came a vast inner tearing as Louisie's soul broke free a second time, escaping my body and leaving me standing alone, clutching her corpse.

Slowly, my arms loosened and I sank to the floor, allowing Louisie's lifeless body to collapse beside me. At a sound from the doorway, I turned to see my mother standing open-mouthed. To this day, I do not know how much she witnessed of Louisie's passing over, but without my telling her anything, Rachel Hamilton seemed to know there was nothing that could be done. Kneeling beside me, she sat statue-like, one hand resting on Louisie's chest.

On my knees beside her, I whimpered, "She said she was going to be with Billy Graham in Heaven. She said there were angels all around, and they came to take her home." Frantic, I wormed against my mother's shoulder, waiting for her to tell me that I was not The Abomination and that angels would return to take me too. "Why couldn't I see the angels?" I asked pleadingly. "Why didn't they take me to Heaven? I want to be in Heaven with Louisie too."

In lieu of replying, my mother fell into an abyss of silence that lasted for months. When she resurfaced, she had transformed into someone utterly unfamiliar. Gone was the unrestrained laughter, the references to God-giggles and Chosen-Shmosen. Instead, my mother had become consumed with the urgent need to know God's will—to understand His exact directives for each and every moment of her life. Edgy and fretful, she sought constant change, continual rebirth. Also in search of rebirth, my father requested a transfer at work. Within a year of Louisie's death, we moved to Eleusis and Quance Crescent, where we visited several nearby churches, but my mother remained restless, wanted to keep looking, said she had to find the true house of the Lord.

Then came the Sunday we first attended the Waiting for the Rapture End Times Tabernacle, the Tongue of Fire descended onto Rachel Hamilton's head, and she heard a sweet, angelic voice announce, "I was taken from you as a blessing, Mommy—a blessing to make you look inside your soul and repent from your wickedness. Now someday *maybe* you can come live in Heaven with Billy and me." There was no more earth for my mother after that—only Heaven, the Promised Land, and the small white stone that contained her secret name. As for me, I became the leftover child, the one of the lower understanding, trapped in the flesh and representing the lifetime of suffering she would have to endure until she could rise to live with Louisie—child of spirit, the innocent who had loved God with her whole heart and now lived in the land of light, waiting for her mother to join her.

And so I spent the years between Louisie and Dee following my mother on her nightly prowls about the house and dreading the moment I would find her standing in the middle of the living room, her tranced eyes turned toward me as she whispered, "I'm an angel, Mary-Eve. God has finally come for me, and I'm going to Heaven to live with Louisie and Billy Graham." This vision gave me no respite; I was haunted by it for a full decade, and only later did I regain memories of an earlier time, Eden before the fall. Of these, the earliest is this: Several months old, I am resting on the full comfort of my mother's bosom. Her palm cradles the back of my head, startlingly warm, and Louisie is nowhere near—it is just my mother and me, her breath whispering across my bald head, caressing it the way the wind susurrates among the trees. Back then, her murmur was simply the texture of breath and soul, the sound of love, but as I return now to this memory, I can make out my mother's actual words: *You are so beautiful. You are so beautiful.*

And I was.

•••

Slow thighs, earth and sky shifted along the long ache of the horizon. In every direction, trees sent their October-golden nerves adrift across a vast afternoon blue. Spinning in that blue, breathing air veined with autumnal light, the high school smoking crowd moved like gods. Slouched, leaned, or sprawled, their communal nervous system wrapped itself around newcomers, measured their pulse, then pulled them into a collective brain wave that was always on the edge of a tease, a collective tease—a girl ran her fingertips up someone's arm and everyone was suddenly skin on skin; a guy swiveled to ogle tight breasts in a tube top and the entire group turned slack-jawed and heavy-lidded, licking the same dream.

The smoking crowd's fantasies rarely varied and they were addictive as slow smoke. Dressed in Dee's clothes, wearing Dee's makeup, Jez learned to translate herself into the expected—a shade paler than the goddess, perhaps, definitely a tone quieter, but familiar enough to be immediately absorbed into the swirl of smoke, laughter, and wandering gypsy leaves.

"Hey, Dee, who's your lapdog?" was the first official acknowledgment of her presence, accompanied by a domino effect of turning heads.

"Isn't that the Jesus-girl?" came the second as she shadowed Dee's movements, hesitant and cautious, along the periphery of the group.

"*Ex*-Jesus-girl," corrected Dee, edging Jez and herself deeper into the crowd. "Well, maybe a double agent, eh, Jez?"

Without replying, Jez blew mysterious smoke and tapped her ember free of ash.

"Hey, Jesus-girl," sneered a pair of Jagger lips, leaning in. "You ever rode cock?"

"Hey, wise guy," Jez shot back, forgetting that discretion is the better part of survival. "You ever rode brain?"

A snicker ran through the surrounding group and they shifted en masse, turning slightly to keep her in their sights, but covertly, sort of like espionage. Being seen with Dee was like putting out an OPEN FOR BUSINESS sign, except no one was certain what kind of business the ex-Jesus-girl was in. Neither was Jez; her Christian grope-and-grunt experiences were a far cry from the Rolling Stones T-shirts and woodies that currently encircled her. And so she made Dee her reference point, memorizing the other girl's exact method of tapping out a cigarette, the way she cupped her hands around that signature moment of fire or jitterbugged her fingers up a guy's back—all of it a kind of code, meaning carefully inscribed into pressure and stroke, which part of the body was touched, when, and how.

Dee touched a lot of guys; only the chosen few touched her. That October, the person she touched most was Jez—leaning against her, hip to hip, as they talked, draping a casual arm around her neck, or pulling the double agent Jesus-girl onto her lap for a quick lunch-hour smoke. Sometimes, on especially golden-giddy days, she brushed a lipsticked smooch just inside Jez's collarbone to add another layer of tease for their hungry watchers to absorb; the smoking-crowd wolf pack was constantly on the prowl, eyes narrowed and watching for anything that looked like prey. Knowing this, *breathing* it in, both girls reveled in the display as Dee played Jez like bait—fiddling with her belt loops, stroking her arm, even nibbling her hair as they kept up their ongoing banter regarding the sex lives of Old Testament prophets and every biblical act of violence Jez could remember. Jez wasn't fooling herself; she could feel the game singing in Dee's fingertips, but she also knew herself to be without resistance—a single live nerve caught on a hook, the blind arc of a worm awaiting that epiphanic moment when the smoking-crowd goddess leaned through the taut communal breathing system that surrounded them and their tongues touched. Jez's body shuddered sweetly and invisibly open then; she knew full well she gave off signs—a dusky perfume sighing from her skin, a soundless moan that broadcast in stereo as she and Dee separated into tranced eyes and murmured laughter, their mutual refusal to explain.

Mornings, Jez woke to a sultry cat purring in her groin. Pulling off her nightgown, she twisted deep into the bed-sheets and wrapped herself in the memory of Dee's throaty laughter until her mother had returned several times to knock on the door. Then, rising, she pulled a midi carelessly from its hanger—checked, striped, paisley, or plaid, it no longer mattered; she was now free to slide into those voracious darts without anguish. Safe within this disguise, she joined her parents for breakfast, and listened blank-faced as her father read sonorously from *The Daily Bread*. At her mother's request, she fetched the small box of Trust and Obey verses sitting atop the fridge, and all three selected a well-fingered card—each with a TRUST verse printed on one side and an OBEY on the other. Reading both sides aloud in turn, they then bowed their heads and humbly asked God to keep them marching, that day as every other, along the ever-narrowing, never-meandering path of righteousness.

Each of these rituals Jez performed as she had always done, her calm, even-paced voice reciting Bible verses and praying over oatmeal and cinnamon toast—familiar words that now held entirely changed meanings, like The Chosen Ones who had stepped over with her onto the other side of God. During these breakfast deceptions, she sometimes felt them about her, The Chosen Ones silent and watching—not in judgment, but simply bearing witness. She wondered then if her mother could sense the transparent gray-robed figures, but Rachel Hamilton showed no sign of it—her mind tuned to a different pulse, the bright, high faraway. Every morn-ing, the war against God began at the breakfast table and Jez's mother did not notice, did not question her daughter's demure double-agent kiss good-bye, nor her breathless, nonstop nine-block dash to the 7-Eleven on Dundas, where a VW Bug idled in the parking lot and a sulky eighteen-year-old girl perched on its roof—an earthbound goddess riding her personal powder-blue catch of sky.

Dee was always the one to touch first—a quick brush against Jez's shoulder, a tug at her hip pocket; with this, Jez's day truly began. When they had driven to a nearby alley, Dee punched in an eight-track and slid over to straddle Jez; and Jez, letting her head fall back, prepared herself to receive the smooth, stroked-on gleam of iniquity—aqua blue across the eyelids, cherry red on the lips, the lolling, languid scent of Chanel No. 5 fingerprinted into the hollow of the throat; all of it a kind of rebirth, a soul's slow becoming, the rescue made over and over, each and every school morning, of a lost and drowning heart.

Sometimes Dee went further, playing with Jez's face, running a finger along the slant of her cheekbone or scooping back her hair and tracing the lines of her neck. She never talked then, and Jez kept her eyes closed so there was only their breathing to speak for them, dialoguing their bodies—the girls in sync, quick and deep, breaking out together into a warm sweat. One morning Dee whispered, "You're so beautiful, I want to kiss you," the words quiet, unbelievable. Jez wanted to breathe them in, lick them tongue-tip delicate from Dee's mouth; instead, she shuddered the thought away, turning her flushed face to the window—for a moment she had seen herself naked and broken open under Dee like a wound.

"What's the matter?" asked Dee, leaning her forehead against Jez's. "Don't you like compliments?"

"Not used to them, I guess," mumbled Jez.

"Not used to compliments?" murmured Dee, nuzzling her nose.

"Not like that," said Jez.

"Or not used to kisses?" whispered Dee.

A flutter-winged panic hit Jez; she shifted between the heated trap of the other girl's thighs. "I've been kissed," she muttered.

"Oh yeah," said Dee, snickering into her hair. "Summer camp."

"Christians have lips," said Jez.

"Yeah, I noticed," grinned Dee. "Pucker. Let me see a Christian pucker."

"Christians don't pucker," said Jez. "They kiss like angels slowly descending onto the earth. Each kiss is like two wings touching."

They watched each other's slightly parted mouths.

"And then," Jez added, swallowing, "there's Heaven."

"Heaven on earth?" cooed Dee.

"Heaven wherever you want it," said Jez.

"You're a tease," said Dee, "but you're good."

"*You're* good," said Jez. "And I'm training to be your twin, aren't I?"

"Your hair's blonde," said Dee, "your eyes are brown, your mouth's an *angel* kiss. Hardly my twin."

Hesitant, Jez touched a fingertip to Dee's cherry-red upper lip. "Same lipstick," she said. She paused to stroke the blue vein that pulsed at the other girl's temple. "Same eyeliner, shadow, and mascara." Tentatively, her finger followed the curve of Dee's cheek. "Same blush. Add us together, we're Chanel No. 10."

Dee's eyes tranced. "I like that," she said dreamily. "I like thinking of your face over on the smart side of school, looking like mine." Carelessly she shrugged, then added, "I'm giving myself to you, okay? It's like giving blood, only different."

Curving out the tip of her tongue, she waited as Jez touched it with her own, submerging them both into that original moment of blood-pain, darkness, and candle fire. Dee's eyes shone, drugged with some kind of ecstasy. Unease shifted through Jez and she muttered, "I'll say, *different*."

Absurdity hit them and they giggled through a shared cigarette, Dee still straddling Jez's lap as they blew smoke through the open window. "You're doing all right, y'know," she said thoughtfully, staring off. "I think you're ready to party."

"Party?" gulped Jez. Lunch-hour banter was one thing— wordplay and the odd questing hand could only go so far on the school front lawn. But a *party*...now that was a concept straight out of one of Dee's album covers—black leather, colored lights, acid, and hash. Sticky fingers. Rooms *full* of woodies.

"Well, yeah," said Dee, eyeing her. "Joking about cock is one thing. You want more than a word, don't you?"

"Yeah, sure," muttered Jez, avoiding her gaze. "There's just one small problem, you know."

"I started the pill years ago," said Dee. "Mom took me to the doctor and gave her permission."

Jez rolled her eyes dramatically. "My mother is *not* giving her permission for such heathen activity, I can tell you that!" she said.

"Okay," said Dee, looking thoughtful. "Mom'll be home after school. Maybe—"

"Maybe *what*?" demanded Jez, panicking. "Maybe if you tell your mother, she'll tell mine. And *then* maybe my mother will lock me in my room until Armageddon."

"Uh-uh," said Dee, a small smile twitching her lips. "No maybes on this one, babe. Yeah, today after school, I think you are going to receive the privilege of meeting my mother."

It was an ominous promise, full of portent, and Jez's initial glimpse of Mrs. Eccles as she entered the family home for the first time did little to dispel her sense of foreboding. Leaning against a kitchen counter, Dee's mother was a slender, dark-haired woman dressed in a black pantsuit and loaded with cleavage and so much jewelry, entire galaxies flashed as she moved. The only completely non-Christian mother Jez had observed up close, Mrs. Eccles was definitely on the pagan side of things—her Playboy Bunny eyes professionally wide and startled, her lips slightly pursed so they took on a bruised, fleshy quality. Both Dee and Andy had inherited her large blue eyes and angular face, but even with this rock-solid evidence, it took faith for Jez to visualize the woman standing before her as somebody's *mother*.

Dropping into a chair at the kitchen table, Dee explained the situation in a bored, very compact nutshell. "Mom," she said, her face expressionless, "Jez wants to start fooling around. She needs the pill, but her mom's a Jesus-freak and so is their family doctor. Got any ideas?"

"Shhht!" hissed Jez, slumping into the chair beside her and

covering her burning face with both hands. In the Hamilton residence, the crotch lived in sacrosanct silence. Everything that linked biology to ecstasy was to be discovered on one's wedding night; before this, even language was restricted to a form of waiting. When Jez was nine, her mother read her a book about the sex life of gerbils. Mr. and Mrs. Gerbil were married on the first page; soon afterward, Mr. Gerbil's sperm met up with Mrs. Gerbil's eggs and a batch of baby gerbils was born. Vague particulars were given regarding gerbil vaginas and penises…*very* vague; to Jez's nine-year-old mind, the infant gerbils' conception seemed to have taken place the way all divinely ordained miracles occurred—in splendor and mystery—and Jez had known better than to question *that*.

Several years later, when she had gotten her first period, all she had said was "Mother, it happened." Gerbils menstruated and so did she. What else was there to say? Her mother had given her a tiny gerbil-like smile, taken her to the linen closet, and pointed to a skyscraper-size box of sanitary napkins. "It will come once a month," she had said primly. "Make sure you wrap the dirty ones in toilet paper before you throw them into the garbage, so your father doesn't have to look at them." For the past five years, Jez had been shrouding the incriminating evidence of her connection to gerbils and burying it at the bottom of a bathroom garbage pail. Now here was Dee's mother, casually sipping a late-afternoon martini and assessing her daughter's new debauchery-destined friend while she scanned her Bunny-fucked brain for *ideas*.

"Jez," murmured Mrs. Eccles, the purring undertow in her voice belying her startled Bunny eyes. "Short for?"

"Jezebel," said Dee, cutting in. "Did you know the first

Jezebel was a queen that got tossed out a window by a creep named Jehu, and wild dogs licked up her blood?" Sprawled in her chair, she was fiddling with a sugar bowl shaped like a naked woman's body—the lid a pair of breasts, the bowl a crotch and buttocks. "Check it out," she said to Jez, lifting the lid and tipping the bowl so the sugar slid to one side, revealing an impossibly large cock inside the ceramic belly.

"Jez," repeated Mrs. Eccles, pulling Jez's startled gaze back to her face. Even the ceramic cock was no competition for this woman's voice. "Let me ask you a few questions."

Jez nodded, swallowing convulsively as she fought off various shades of red.

"Have you had sex before?" asked Mrs. Eccles.

"Yeah," mumbled Jez. Then, thinking better of it, she straightened, folded both hands neatly on the tabletop, and added, "I mean, yes."

"Can you say yes without blushing?" purred Mrs. Eccles.

"Uh, maybe," said Jez, losing out to yet another wave of red. No two ways about it—this woman's questions felt like a vaginal exam.

Thoughtfully, Mrs. Eccles stroked her generous cleavage with long red fingernails. "Tell me, Jez," she said. "Did you experience this sex *before* you met my daughter?"

Dee's body went into minor convulsions and she hissed something indecipherable.

"Uh, before," said Jez, glancing at Dee's stony face. "Yeah, definitely before. More than once too."

"At summer camp," Dee interjected heatedly. "*Bible* camp."

"I don't need to know the details," said her mother.

"It was *Christian* sex though," said Dee, her hard, bright eyes pinning her mother's. "Does *Christian* sex count?"

Suddenly, overwhelmingly, and without question, Jez wanted to go home. She wanted war that was restricted to her mother's polite Biblical crusades. She wanted to devote herself to interminable celibacy and listen to Billy Graham for the rest of her life.

"What counts, Jez," Mrs. Eccles said coolly, swirling the contents of her martini, "is whether or not you enjoyed it." Delicately, she sipped from her glass. "It's just that you look so angelic, honey. You have to want this for yourself. I don't want Dee pimping you."

"Oh, for fuck's sake!" exploded Dee.

"Just an expression, sweetie," purred her mother. "I know how you can be when you get going."

"Yeah, everyone tells me we are so much alike," muttered Dee, spinning the sugar bowl so violently, its contents scattered across the tabletop.

"Would you like my help or not?" asked her mother, her tone ominous.

"Um, *yeah*, actually," said Dee, slumping downward until her hips rode the edge of her chair.

"Fine," said Mrs. Eccles, finishing her drink in one swallow. "Dee, dear, your prescription is with Dr. Blakely. I'd suggest we get another one from Dr. McCormack, and that you fill it at a drugstore across town. This is illegal, you understand? Jez, I need your word that you won't tell any of your friends. Or your mother. Dee, I know I can count on you."

Dee sighed heavily. "You betcha," she mumbled.

"I absolutely promise," Jez added fervently. Now that the

ordeal was over, she felt like leaping to her feet, hand over heart, and reciting the Pioneer Girls Club creed, or displaying her Red Cross volunteer badge—anything to prove to Dee's mother that she could be *responsible*.

Mrs. Eccles's brief smile cooled to ice. "No sex for a month," she said sternly. "It takes a while to kick in. You'll just have to fend them off until then."

"Thanks, Mom," said Dee, her expression clearing as she picked up the almost empty sugar bowl and licked the cock clean of sugar. In a parallel motion, Mrs. Eccles ran a quick tongue around the sunlit rim of her empty martini glass. Then, without looking at each other, mother and daughter gave identical slide-through smiles—the split-second kind that come and go like a prowler at a bedroom window.

"Come on," said Dee, slapping Jez's knee. "I'll show you my knife marks downstairs before I drive you home."

Getting to her feet, Jez glanced one last time at Mrs. Eccles, but the woman, her back turned, was setting her martini glass into the dishwasher, the conversation and its subject matter apparently dismissed.

FIVE

At every corner, Louisie anchored our Eleusis home in the spirit world. My initial glimpse into this realm came not through my mother, but in the ghostly mirrors the former owner had left hanging on the second floor. As I first ran through those empty rooms, mysterious portals seemed to open in walls and closet doors, allowing what appeared to be my twin to repeatedly step toward me—a hazy welcoming figure edged in dust and blurred light. Words could not describe this resurrection of my heart. A grave had opened, releasing the other half of my life, albeit one that remained separate and beyond, the antique glass yet another membrane dividing the split atom of self.

Immediately following Louisie's death, I had been placed in the care of our minister's wife so my father could focus on funeral arrangements and my mother's collapse. The minister's wife was an austere, italics-hissing woman who considered it unseemly for children to interact with corpses and refused to take me to the funeral home to view *the body*. Although I had no clear idea as to a funeral home's function, I learned through intensive blank-faced eavesdropping that my twin had been *laid out* at McAllistair's Funeral Home, a building I had seen often enough from the local Dairy Queen directly across the street.

All roads lead to the Dairy Queen when you are seven; blindfolded, I could have found my way to it from any direction. And so it was entirely predictable that, midway through what was supposed to have been my second afternoon nap at the manse, I was instead to be found tearing along Dover Avenue toward the familiar ice cream cone sign, then crossing the street and lugging open the front door to McAllistair's Funeral Home. Inside the lobby's dense, carpeted silence, voices could be heard from an adjoining office, discussing "the little girl's viewing," which further eavesdropping revealed was scheduled to take place shortly in Room Two. Several doors opened directly off the lobby, and Room Two was easily located, along with its small white coffin and bouquets of lilies. Dragging over a nearby stacking chair, I climbed onto the seat, leaned into the open coffin, and hissed, "Ha! Just joking, huh? Didn't fool me, but you sure got everyone else praying for you."

Bright-cheeked and red-lipped, Louisie lay demurely, both hands folded over her chest. Her hair had been curled and tied with a bow, she wore our best matching Sunday dress, and the lower half of her body was covered with a white satin sheet. Despite the dull chemical smell that emanated from her skin, she could have been merely asleep, with me awake beside her and listening to her breathe, as had so often been the case. From birth, Louisie had possessed the knack of falling quickly and deeply asleep, and many had been the night that I had laid my head on her chest and ridden the cadence of her breathing steadily into dreams. So that afternoon, without thinking, I followed my longing into the coffin and laid half on, half beside her body, as I twisted a lock of her hair around my finger.

"Louisie," I whispered hesitantly. "What's it like in Heaven? Do angels sing boring old hymns all the time? Do they ever fart or burp?"

When I touched her cheek, it was as cool as the varnished surface of our bedroom dresser. What gave me pause, however, was not the blush that smudged my fingertip, but my twin's lack of response to my blasphemy—the complete absence of scorn or prediction of eternal hellfire blasting from her ruby lips. A kind of knowing descended upon me then, a cold animal shifting in my bowels, and I began the slow rotation toward fear.

"Hey, Louisie," I hissed, pushing that fear desperately aside. "Did you know the minister's wife picks her nose when she's on the phone? She's always blabbing on this big red phone they got in the kitchen, and the whole time, she's pulling another goober out of her nose. She always checks to see how big it is too, before she rubs it on the wall."

No disgust twisted my twin's face in response to this information, no petals of breath floated from her mouth. Fighting the terror that now fish-hooked my gut, I burrowed into her hair and hung on. "Hey, Louisie," I whimpered. "Don't you think you're tired of Heaven yet? Maybe just a little? Don't you think God's got enough souls up there already to keep Him company? I only got one twin, you know, and that's you. And yesterday I heard the minister's wife say Mommy took a fit over you dying, and I ain't seen her for two days because I got to stay with the nose-pickin' minister's wife, and you took it all away, Louisie. You took it all away."

At this point, someone entered the room and turned on a vacuum cleaner. Startled, I sat up, causing a young woman in a McAllistair's Funeral Home uniform to shriek loudly and flee through the open doorway. With similar haste I executed my escape, making it back to the manse before the minister's wife came to wake me from my nap. In the half hour that I had been gone, my absence had not been noted, and no one ever learned of those desperate whimpering minutes spent clutching my dead twin in her coffin. The following day, I was allowed to attend the funeral and watch as she was lowered into the ground, part of me still trapped inside the casket, arms wrapped tightly around her silent form and begging for a resurrection.

So, one year later, Louisie's rising into my mirrored reflection was an answer to my prayers. For weeks after we moved into the house on Quance Crescent, I stood before those mirrors, fingering the flowers and horned beasts carved into their frames and whispering into the glass. For the first time since my twin's death, I had someone to talk to, and each time my parents called me away from my reflection, I felt myself grow numb and distant as if I were losing something—something that was internal and at the same time entirely *other*.

Neither of my parents noticed my sudden obsession with mirrors, my mother still staggering under a monumental burden of grief and my father forced to divide his attention between his own sorrow, keeping my mother functional, and fitting in at his new workplace. As a result, when, several months into our attendance at the Waiting for the Rapture End Times Tabernacle, my mother received a revelation concerning the abomination of vanity, my father did not think twice about taking down every mirror in the house and storing them behind several steamer trunks in the basement. This presented somewhat of an inconvenience with regards to my ongoing dialogue with Louisie, but nothing insurmountable; I simply took my quest underground. Day after day, I descended the steep basement stairs into the furnace room, where the mirrors had been leaned against the back wall and covered with a tarp. Crawling under the tarp, I then spent hours seated cross-legged in a musty between-worlds kind of place, holding a flashlight dimmed by a pillowcase and whispering to my shadowy-faced twin. To further encourage her cooperation, I would hold up one of several flannel-backed Billy Graham paper dolls that I had rescued from the trash before the move to Eleusis; its presence never failed to bring Louisie's high-pitched voice to mind, full of remonstrations concerning Jesus and the rules of Heaven, thereby allowing me to take on my accustomed role as her opposite, an identity familiar and defined.

For weeks, I descended into this underworld while my parents went on above me, distant muffled voices and the reassuring creak of floorboards. Then one afternoon, I discovered the tarp tossed carelessly across the steamer trunks, and nothing but bare wall where the mirrors had been stored. Immediately, I understood that the mirrors had been thrown out with the trash; just as quickly, I realized they could not be retrieved, the garbage trucks having already completed their weekly rumbling journey along the crescent. Panic was a moth over a candle, its wings on fire. The mirrors had been my link to Louisie, and I was certain she lived inside them. If they were gone, she was too, taking with her some ephemeral hoping part of myself…but there was no point whatsoever in pleading my case with two fully committed Waiting for the Rapture parents.

"The mirrors loved me," I was reduced to wailing. "The mirrors saw me. I'm all gone away again. I'm all gone away."

"Vanity, vanity. All is abomination," was my mother's response, but she must have sensed Louisie's second departure on some level, for it was soon after the mirrors' banishment that photographs of my twin began appearing all over the house. The supply of these pictures was extensive—before Louisie's death, our mother had been an avid photographer, and an entire living room bookcase was crammed with her photo albums. Now, feverish and distraught, she piled these previously beloved albums onto the kitchen table and ransacked them. Scissors in hand, she rifled through images of her lost daughter, lifting snapshot after snapshot out of its four corner pockets and cutting Louisie free. If the picture contained other figures, they were unceremoniously lopped off, their black and white Kodak remains scattering across the tabletop, and I watched in growing horror as my mother's pink-handled scissors edged me out of birthday parties and pillow forts, the shared grins of my first seven years.

Having reduced each photograph to Louisie's solo image, my mother would get to her feet and walk slowly through the house, eyes half-closed and humming until inspiration struck, then abruptly whirl and tape the picture fragment of my twin onto a wall, door frame, or running board. Soon into this process, she began to add wings to the tiny Louisie figures, and spent hours cutting insect and angel wings out of magazines or creating them from colored construction paper. Significantly, these winged figures initially appeared in the positions the antique mirrors had originally hung, but they spread quickly throughout the house, and I returned daily from school to find new versions of my twin hovering in diapers, bathing suit, or Sunday best on the wall above my bed, on the side of the fridge, even next to electrical outlets.

Gradually, the house filled with these flitting, flying images. Wherever I went, they rose from floorboards, manifested inside opened cupboard doors, and circled overhead light fixtures. At first I was delighted, exulting in the discovery of another Louisie angel taped to the front of the de-mirrored medicine cabinet or gazing out from the center of the telephone's rotary dial. In spite of the disappearance of the antique mirrors, my twin had found her way back to me, and was stepping out of every angle of wall, ceiling, and floor. Transfixed by this merge of internal and external worlds, I shifted naturally into a state of nonstop communion, and poured myself in an unguarded river toward the legion of Louisie angels that drifted about the house.

As time passed, however, and the number of angels increased, I grew disoriented, unsure if I was walking floor or ceiling. Home had become a veritable house of mirrors, splintered into a multitude of tiny-winged reflections, each a near-replica of my own face and body. To make matters worse, I was not allowed to contribute to the Louisie collage. If I drew a picture of my twin and taped it to the fridge, it was summarily removed and placed on my bed. And if, by accident or design, I happened to shift one of the Louisie angels, several stinging slaps were applied to my hand with the wooden spoon. Furthermore, nothing was explained, the meaning of my mother's actions left to reverberate like invisible electric wires in my head. As a result, my confusion grew daily. Whose soul was it, in the end, that had been entrapped in winged points of light all over the house—Louisie's or mine? And where was I supposed to locate myself—within the wave field of angels that vibrated soundlessly in the house walls, or in my numb, increasingly hopeless child's flesh?

After their initial appearance, the Louisie angels were not acknowledged by my parents, and, over time, decreasingly by myself. We seemed simply to live our physical lives within the dream of their ethereal wings, oblivious to the part of our consciousness that had escaped us to fly at greater and greater heights. Not once did we discuss what it was that actually hovered about us, what sort of otherworldly awareness might have been drawn to such displaced yearning. Silent yet keening, a high-frequency anguish vibrated like invisible string art between the angels and our bodies. Each Kodak cherub was a tiny nerve prick of pain, sent out and away. Gradually, as we continued with our anesthetized lives, the Louisie figures began to curl at the edges; then, as the tape holding them in place loosened, their long, silent fall began. Gently, they spiraled downward; catching them midair, we pulled them from our hair and stared numbly. Unvoiced was the knowledge that the angels held something that belonged to us—something we needed to recover but could not. Without sadness, without even seeming to notice, my mother swept the withered forms into the garbage, but their high, white current of grief remained trapped in the house walls, each angel's previous location like a gate that had been fixed into position, waiting for the Divine Sister's night prowling to call it open to the other side.

• • •

It was the following Saturday night, with a huge rain coming down in sheets that transformed Sinbad into a muffled shell of sound. Huddled in the front passenger seat, Jez fished in her jacket pocket for her lighter and cigarettes. The time was 12:15 a.m.; she had been waiting under the 7-Eleven's overhang since midnight, and her lime jacket and red and white checked midi, even her oxfords, were bone-chillingly damp.

"Got any dry clothes?" she asked, lighting up.

"Uh-uh," said Dee, shaking her head. "I checked out the party and it was a bust, so I figured you wouldn't need any."

It had been easier than Jez had thought it would be to sneak out of the house. The evening had gone as usual—a Young People's meeting at the church, which had involved a Bible study and a floor hockey game. Her parents had been at a prayer-cell meeting at another church member's home; when it had ended, they had picked her up, and all had been home and in bed by a quarter after eleven. Because her mother generally slept heavily until one, and her father never stirred until forced awake by his morning alarm, the only difficult part had been the guilt—sneaking out the back door had felt tantamount to sneaking out of the womb.

"So…if the party's a bust," asked Jez, surveying the empty parking lot with studied casualness, "what d'you want to do?"

The car's interior was full of the small come-and-go shifts of Dee's perfume. In the dim streetlight, her face was a series of shadows, contained within the sleek fall of her shoulder-length shagged hair. "I dunno," she said, putting the idling car into gear. As she drove out of the lot, she seemed pensive, moody, her mind on another planet. Reaching for Jez's cigarette, she dragged deeply. Abruptly, she asked, "You ever been in a backseat?"

Startled, Jez ransacked her brain for possible responses. The last thing she wanted right now was to be forced into an admission of innocence. "You mean a *car* backseat?" she hedged.

Dee gave a slight hiss and rolled her eyes. "Yeah, a *car*," she drawled. "With a *guy*."

"Not exactly," muttered Jez, turning to look out the side window.

Dee laughed. "You mean *no*," she said.

"Okay," Jez said, growing irritated. "So, *no*."

"That's what I figured," said Dee, her face grim. "Okay, lesson time coming up. Keep your eyes peeled for the first available groping alley."

Chin resting on the top of the steering wheel, she drove slowly through the downpour, then turned onto a residential side street. Here and there, a post-midnight window could be seen glimmering in the rain, but most of the houses were dark. Killing the engine, Dee coasted in to the curb beside a small park and the two girls sat in edgy silence, outlined faintly by streetlight as they passed Jez's cigarette back and forth.

"So what's with this lesson business?" Jez broached tentatively.

Without responding, Dee leaned toward her and Jez jerked away, bumping into the car door. "Lesson number one," Dee said coolly as she opened the glove compartment. "Don't act like you're on electric shock."

"Yeah, okay, fine," mumbled Jez, her cheeks burning.

Dee pulled out a beveled glass bottle and unscrewed the cap. "Gin," she announced. "I diluted it so you could drink some. I figured we could both use a shot. Just don't drink too much or you won't be able to concentrate."

After two expert swallows, she passed the bottle to Jez. Holding it with both hands, Jez sat for a moment staring at it. Her hesitation wasn't due to a lack of alcohol consumption experience—Waiting for the Rapture was certainly a teetotaler denomination, but teenagers of every stripe could be counted on to sneak booze to summer camp. Rather, it was because none of the beer, scotch, or rum that she had drunk to date had felt like a condemned man's last drink before facing the firing squad. Cautiously, she raised the bottle to her lips and took a sip. Gin was new to her, its taste like dull fire; not great, she decided, but not *too* bad. As she took another sip, an image flitted through her mind from earlier that evening—the face of her church's youth pastor, desperately sincere as he waited for someone, *anyone* among the bored adolescents staring back at him to respond to his question regarding Paul's instructions to the church at Ephesus. There was no way on earth or Heaven, Jez thought suddenly, fiercely, that she was going to end up like him. Upending the bottle, she took a deep swig.

"Okay, okay, girl. Enough!" exclaimed Dee, grabbing the bottle.

"Geez," burbled Jez, feeling the warm fuzzies start to percolate. "Don't *you* act like *you're* on high voltage."

"Sure, no voltage," said Dee, taking an audible breath. "Look, Mom and I talked, and for once I think she's right. You've got to know more. Guys are dogs, man—I can't just throw you to them."

"Gosh, golly, darn," said Jez, sliding down in her seat until she could barely see over the dash. The warm fuzzies were really going now. "Thanks tons, man."

Dee waved a dismissive hand. "You should hear them talk when you're not around," she snapped. "I knew it'd be bad— like Mom said, you're the angelic type. But they're foaming at the mouth to be the first to thrust into you."

Jez's warm fuzzies went into an unmitigated fizzle. Stunned at Dee's bluntness, she stared at her. "You are worse than your mother," she said finally.

"I am *just* like my mother," replied Dee. Taking a doomsday gulp of gin, she screwed the cap back onto the bottle. "Okay," she said, letting out a whoosh of air. "Backseat." Without another word, she opened the door and ducked through the downpour into the back of the car. There she shrugged out of her black leather jacket, revealing the long bare slope of her shoulders and the plunging neckline of a halter top. In the murky streetlight, her skin ran with the shadows of the rain that coursed down the windshield. Sprawled onto the seat, she lay with her head back, staring at the ceiling. "C'mon, Jezzie baby," she sing-songed. "I'm waiting for you."

Mouth open, Jez sat staring at Dee's reflection in the rearview mirror. Never, *never*, she was certain of it, had her heart thudded this hard or her knees come so close to complete dissolution. Again the Technicolor memory of the blushing youth pastor flashed through her mind. The guy, she thought savagely, had looked ready to pee himself. Reaching for the bottle of gin Dee had left lying on the driver's seat, she took her own doomsday gulp, then shoved open the passenger door and stepped through the harsh curtain of rain into the back of the car's uneasy silence. With a distinct squelching sound, she edged onto the seat beside Dee's sprawled form. Further squelches followed as she pulled off her soaked jacket.

"Well," said Dee, looking out the side window. "So, okay. These are the basic rules. You can block moves, but you can't call them. Which means you have to wait, basically, for the guy to decide what he wants to do or you'll wither his dick. It'll shrivel right up on you. Dead dick. Guys are like that. Pathetic. If they can't get it their way, they turn off, and what you want is a turned-on guy, right? Believe me, a turned-off guy is one complete and utter waste. So, like I said, you can say no, maybe you can say how far or how fast, but you can't say what. Got it?"

"Seems basic," said Jez, pulling at the front of her dress. A determinedly practical blend of polyester and acrylic, the damp fabric lifted off her stomach with a distinct sucking sound.

"Yeah, it's basic," muttered Dee, still staring out the window. "It's all pretty basic, isn't it?" Then, without warning, she was moving—one hand snaking around Jez's shoulders and grabbing her breast while the other covered her mouth, muffling her startled yelp. Astounded more than humiliated, Jez pushed to get free, but Dee hung on tightly, continuing to squish her breast painfully as she spoke low into her ear.

"That first move's called the One-Hander," she said. "This one's Pin-the-Bitch." Without hesitation, she swung a leg over Jez's lap and straddled her, pressing both hands onto her breasts. "And this one," she added hoarsely, "is called Riding Double. If there are two guys back here with you, the second guy'll grab your knees, pull you open, and start whamming you." Curved over Jez, she breathed quickly and intensely. Strands of wet hair fell into her eyes and plastered her cheeks.

"Take your hands off," mumbled Jez, her eyes downcast, the blood pounding everywhere through her.

"*They* won't," said Dee. With a calculated thrust of her knee, she separated Jez's legs. "Thirty seconds and he's into you, baby," she mocked. "You're a fucking open door, you're that easy."

"Oh yeah?" said Jez, heat shooting through her, a gut-pulsing flame. "And what's *that* one called?"

"Open Sucker," said Dee. "And this—"

With a cry, Jez wrenched her arms free and grabbed the hand going for her crotch, the two girls grappling in grunting silence, a chasm opening beneath them, one of them about to go down. Sharp-edged, Dee's nails dug into Jez's wrists. Jerking a hand free, Jez clawed frantically at whatever was within reach and half of Dee's halter top came loose, drifting downward like a slow-floating leaf. The sight peeled Jez of all resistance. Slowly, gently, Dee levered both Jez's hands onto the top of the seat, then sat motionless, her eyes closed as she calmed the half-sob in her breathing. Bewildered and trying to mend the violence in her own breath, Jez felt the sweet-sighing inevitable descend upon her as the other half of the halter top slid down, riveting her gaze and trapping her in the song of her skin.

"So where's your jackknife?" Dee taunted softly, her face filled with absolute knowing. "The one you were always going to carry?"

"I didn't think I needed it," mumbled Jez, closing her eyes, "with a *girl*."

"You're such an innocent," said Dee.

"I am not *stupid*," hissed Jez, incensed, her eyes flying open.

"You're beautiful," Dee said sadly, ignoring her anger. "They're gonna tell you that, and it's true. You'll forget all about knives, you know."

Releasing Jez's wrists, she traced her lower lip, and Jez stopped breathing. "All that time," Dee whispered, touching and touching her mouth. "Watching me from windows. What were you looking for, Jez? Were you looking for me?"

They stared, the fear huge and delicate in their faces, and then Dee leaned through God, the Devil, and the Apocalypse, and brushed her open-lipped mouth across Jez's. Siren nerves chorused, tongues touched; Jez's hands slid like a groan up the wet slope of Dee's back as they kissed. From somewhere a whimper sounded; rain splashed full against the outside of the car; another chorus of nerves washed all externals away, leaving only lips, tongues, and a deep-beating sweetness— that inner drum of softness reaching deeper, deeper, until gently, irrevocably, it opened into a peach-pink luminosity that rose through Jez and partway into Dee, the two girls together shuddering and crying out as each lip of a glowing orchid unfurled, joining them within its radiance.

"Holy fuck!" Dee whispered into Jez's damp hair. "Fuck, *never* let that happen with a guy, you hear me? You let your soul out like that, he'll suck it right out of you."

"That was my guardian angel," Jez said fervently. "Something sent by God, I'm sure of it. I've never seen it before, but that must be what it was."

"Your guardian angel?" said Dee, incredulous. "That was no angel, baby—that was you. *Angels!*" She gave a short laugh. "That's cute."

"Angels aren't cute," Jez said stiffly. "I'm not talking cupids here."

"Jezzie," said Dee, licking her nose. "That was your one-and-only deep-down soul. You keep it to yourself. Don't give it away *ever*—not to anyone. Believe me, that's the most important lesson of all."

It was a silent drive back through the rain. Arriving at Quance Crescent, Dee parked two doors down and they sat without speaking, observing the Hamiltons' darkened house.

"Looks Christian all the way from here," muttered Dee.

"The Rapture will start on our doorstep," said Jez. "My mother will be first in line."

Hands abruptly fidgety, Dee played patty-cake on the steering wheel. "Look," she said carefully. "I hate to tell you this, but I don't think you're ready for guys yet."

"Open Sucker, eh?" said Jez.

"Yup," agreed Dee. Their eyes met and she grinned hesitantly. Since returning to the front seat, they hadn't touched—even their knees were tucked tightly and primly together. Now Dee sat, one hand on the gearshift, her leather jacket zipped shut. The lonely voice of Jez's skin sang to no one.

"Dee?" said Jez, forcing herself to look directly into the other girl's face. "Why'd you do that—tonight? Why?"

Head tilted against the side window, Dee stared into the rain-falling dark. When she finally spoke, it was so quiet Jez had to lean forward to catch her words. "Just something girls do when guys aren't around," she said dully, almost mechanically, as if reciting something she had heard many times. "What girls do together is just practicing for guys, that's all. It doesn't count, not really. *Everyone* knows that."

Alone in the middle of the street, Jez stood in the rain, watching the wet blur of Sinbad's taillights travel away from her. At the corner, the Bug paused without turning, as if in that instant Dee had decided to light a cigarette before going on, or was perhaps rethinking her words, rewriting them, *regretting* them…the two girls waiting out that single stretched moment of forever, and then the car turned.

SIX

Being the Divine Sister's only child had its drawbacks. If Louisie had been there to share the experience, perhaps the imprint would not have gone as deep—less would have been stolen. As it was, I stood alone in my mother's reflected glory, the only child who could follow in her footsteps and haunted by what I lacked. Each and every Sunday, the eyes of the congregation settled onto my head, searching in vain for a Tongue of Fire; each and every Sunday, the divine flame failed, yet again, to descend upon me. Still I burned, and for years my bedtime prayers were a variation on a single theme—pleas to the good Lord to send any available Tongues of Fire my way: "Jesus, please make me a Divine Sister like my mother, with a holy burning Tongue of Fire, and please make extra sure there's some good, loud glory-talk coming out of me that doesn't sound like English or no one'll listen. In Jesus' name, amen."

The good Lord, however, continued to turn a deaf ear to my requests, so one Saturday morning, I decided to try out the sackcloth-and-ashes approach. Carefully setting fire to a copy of the *Eleusis Tribune* in our basement, I smeared the cooling ashes onto my nine-year-old arms and face, then crawled up and down the basement stairs in a potato sack, reciting the best mad-prophet, Tongue of Fire Bible verses I had been able to find: "Now it came to pass in the thirtieth year, in the fourth month, in the fifth day of the month, as I was among the captives by the river of Chebar, that the heavens were opened, and I saw visions of God...And I looked, and, behold, a whirlwind came out of the north, a great cloud, and a fire infolding itself, and a brightness was about it, and out of the midst thereof as the color of amber, out of the midst of the fire. Also out of the midst thereof came the likeness of four living creatures. And this was their appearance; they had the likeness of a man. And every one had four faces, and every one had four wings. And their feet were straight feet..."

The detail of the straight feet particularly impressed me, sidetracking my fervor, and I pondered it strenuously as I crawled. Didn't everyone have straight feet? I wondered. But maybe four-faced angels were different. Maybe some four-faced angels had crooked feet and some had amazingly, *astoundingly* straight feet. And maybe—here I stopped crawling, struck by the thought—maybe *astoundingly* straight feet were a sign of being sent by God, of being chosen.

Removing one of my shoes, I examined every aspect

of my foot. It looked straight enough—except for the fifth toe, which angled off to the side. With a scowl, I pushed the fifth in against the fourth and examined my foot again. Now everything looked quite straight, in fact *very* straight, and that, I decided with enormous satisfaction, would give me bonus points in the Tongue of Fire request department. Quickly, I got back onto my hands and knees and resumed my crawl up and down the basement stairs, repeating my original recitation but throwing in a few pointed reminders in case the good Lord had missed the obvious: "And their feet were straight feet *like Mary-Eve Hamilton's two very straight feet...*"

Straight feet or no straight feet, God made no apparent response to my sackcloth-and-ashes attempt, and the congregation continued to send resigned glances my way as, week after week, the Tongue of Fire shunned my head. "Crying shame, isn't it?" came the church members' whispers. "Mary-Eve Hamilton *didn't get the Gift.*" Strangers, however, who made the pilgrimage to our church to hear my mother prophesy, were oblivious to my shortcomings, and often held cosmic expectations of the Divine Sister's one-and-only daughter. Murmuring in anticipation, they would surround me—the women heavy with perfume, the men sagging over silver-buckled belts as their tobacco-stained, nail-bitten hands stroked my rag-curled ringlets, lace collar, and white-leather King James Bible. I lost buttons and barrettes to them, strands of my hair, even my Jesus-on-the-cross necklace, and learned to survive their peppermint- and pepperoni-scented kisses by pretending I was John the Baptist calling the unwashed throng to repentance, even Jesus Himself giving the Sermon on the Mount. All it took to get me going were a few *Hear ye, hear ye*'s and *I say unto you*'s and I was launched into a fairly good mountaintop sermon, replete with at least one *You may now kiss the bride.*

It was as close to speaking glory-talk as I got. Inspired by the pilgrims' devotion, I waxed loud and prolific, but no matter how stridently I proclaimed, I could feel their desperation and it frightened me. Voices were at war inside their heads, and their souls leaned out of their bodies like ships' figureheads; it was as if these people could not bear to remain inside their own flesh. Though these perceptions were clear to me, I never discussed them with my mother, and I doubt she ever picked up on the distress they caused; instead, she and my father chose to focus on what they called my "attention-grabbing dramatics." To solve the problem these "dramatics" presented, a sales booth featuring autographed photographs of the Divine Sister was set up in the church lobby. As time went on, the list of purchasable items expanded to include greetings cards that featured the Divine Sister in a variety of poses, as well as photographs of the church, Pastor Playle, and the deacons, plus picture frames, Christian coloring books, T-shirts and knickknacks, and devotional tapes featuring the Divine Sister's voice. Most pilgrims were satisfied with trinkets, and the booth functioned as an effective decoy. Some, however, continued to corner me and ask for "a little bit of the glory-talk" or a demonstration of the Tongue of Fire—"Just a quickie, love. That'll do it." Others requested a blessing, but after my mother caught me standing on a pew with both hands on a woman's head, calling angels into her soul, I was placed on "Deacon Watch," and for months following, a deacon and his wife were assigned to supervise me at all church functions.

Deacon Watch was nothing compared to Mother Watch. Soon after her transformation into the Divine Sister, my mother began to monitor all aspects of my play. Before this, she had taken a vivid but mostly hands-off interest in my activities; now, if she saw me drawing wings, fire, or tall glowing creatures, she would rip my picture in half and demand, "Draw Mother a cat." I was allowed to build houses, cars, and people out of Lego or Plasticine, but when I formed a body with its spirit rising out of it and explained, "The body's sleeping, so the soul's going visiting to see what it can see," my mother pounded it flat with her fist. Around this time, I developed a habit of hanging out of my bedroom window and watching the dusk rise slowly from the earth as I talked to angels that I claimed flew "everywhere that the air moves, Mother, but like love." She never argued, simply formed her arms into a circle around my head and lowered them, pulling down an invisible hood of forgetfulness so dense that I stood momentarily confused, not remembering where I was or what I had been doing.

Gradually, as she maintained this constant patrol around my activities and thoughts, my ability to see and talk to "angels," even my recollections of seeing them, began to fade. What did not fade, however, was my memory of *losing* the ability to see into other worlds—a sense of the way my mind had slowly been narrowed until I could only occasionally catch sight of my mother's high-frequency apocalyptic landscape. For years, my favorite reading material remained the books of the Old Testament wherein loin-clothed prophets covered in boils snatched glimpses of forbidden places—those tingling invisible realms of the chosen ones that gave the air its electrical charge—and when I crept about at night, watching my mother commune with other dimensions, I understood full well that the distance between us was not spatial but vibratory, that she communed with a higher plane and I with a lower; she had been chosen and I had not.

Still, there were moments when consciousness broke open for me and I was able to fly past my mother as if it was *her* mind and memory that had been trapped within a mundane lower order. During my tenth year, the winter solstice fell on a Sunday. As was its custom, the Hamilton family was in attendance at the evening service, seated in the third pew as the choir sang and Pastor Playle pontificated for the elect. Suddenly, and entirely without warning, the air quivered as if a great wave of energy had passed through it, and the sanctuary lights flickered off and on. Gasps and cries sounded all around, but I found myself growing quickly distant from the panic, standing separate and alone within a silence that seemed to be deepening inward and shifting toward another level of reality. Desperately, I reached out with my hands, and small whimpers formed in my throat. Some kind of presence appeared to be drawing nigh—a realm that felt both familiar and completely unknown, its electrical charge so tangible, it could be physically sensed.

Again the air quivered and the sanctuary lights flickered off and on. What followed then is difficult to describe in human terms—a vast ethereal crescendo of voices and the rippling of a translucent light throughout the sanctuary, this light dancing and shifting like waves on the surface of a prismatic ocean. As I watched, open-mouthed, the waves of light took on the shape of tall glowing figures that separated from one another and began to walk through the congregation—figures that looked human but were transparent and appeared to pulse through a variety of forms, so that church members later insisted, *They were as tall as the ceiling. They were tiny and small like the fairy people. They had wings and wore robes. No, they had no wings but were covered in eyes like in Revelations, and they carried scrolls to announce the end of the world.*

Whatever their true form, these angels walked for one diaphanous moment among the congregation, touching each member somewhere on their person—forehead, mouth, or chest, for each individual it was different, but always spirit blessing flesh, welcoming contact. Across the sanctuary, people cried out in wonder, their wordless singing like yipping or laughter, so caught up in ecstasy that they did not appear to notice the angels circumvent my father, the Divine Sister, and Pastor Playle, refusing to lay hands on them. At least I never heard anyone speak of it—only I seemed to be given this awareness, the angels making me also wait untouched between my parents as they made contact with every other member of the congregation. Then, coming together into a single brilliant pulse, they swept toward and directly through my body, returning to whence they had come and filling me with such unboundaried joy that I gave utterance in gut-raw sounds, roaring and dancing until exhaustion laid me onto the floor.

For several days following, I was consumed with the memory of this event, but to my bewilderment, neither of my parents would discuss it, directing me instead toward the usual Christmas activities. At the same time, my mother's nightly prowls intensified and she seemed always to be touching me; whether it was my shoulder, arm, or cheek, I sensed that she was thereby drawing something from my body to hers—a force, tangible but invisible, was leaving me. This process was so imperceptible, I did not notice that my memory of the solstice angels was also fading, and it was only when Pastor Playle launched into a joyful description of the incident the following Sunday evening that it came back to me, but vaguely, like reflections scattered across a watery surface.

It had been a long sermon and the good pastor stood slumped at the podium, his tie loosened and his strained voice cracking as he raised an open Bible. "And the glory of the Lord came down among us!" he proclaimed huskily.

"Amen!" shouted my reliable father.

"It was the night angels walked among us!" cried Pastor Playle, rocking back onto his heels.

"Yes, brother!" called my father, rocking in counter-rhythm.

"And the Divine Sister!" sang Pastor Playle. "The Divine Sister called them to us! It was her faith, her example—"

About me rose a great chorus of "Amens" as people stood to clap their hands and sway, but in the third pew I remained seated, weighed down by a sudden knowing: Pastor Playle was lying. Though my memories of the solstice visitation were now vague, I could still pinpoint the exact moment the angels had swept toward and through me, ignoring my parents, who stood to either side. Whoever had called them, it had not been the Divine Sister, and Pastor Playle knew it. And if the good pastor was lying about this, he had lied about other things.

That liar was my mother's only translator.

The next day marked the beginning of a three-day provincial Waiting for the Rapture retreat at a rural conference center. Placed in a cabin of ten-year-old girls, I rarely saw my parents except at evening services, when they were involved with Scripture reading, song leading, and prophecy. One of my cabinmates had brought along a book she had received for Christmas called *Codes of the Ages*, and I borrowed it, sneaking it into services to read during the sermons. One of the chapters described methods for creating a secret language, and my cabinmates and I went into typical ten-year-old contortions of delight as we inserted the word *fuck* between the first and second syllable of every multi-syllable word and claimed the result as an ancient Mesopotamian language. One afternoon during quiet time, when our counselor temporarily stepped out of the cabin, I asked the other girls if they thought speaking in tongues was actually a kind of code.

"You mean like speaking backward?" one girl asked eagerly.

"That's how Satan talks, idiot," said another.

The girl who owned *Codes of the Ages* was scrutinizing me. "You think your mom's a fake," she accused.

"No, I don't," I protested. "It could be that the code is in there, but she's so carried away with her revelations that she doesn't know. I mean, it makes sense that God would be using a code so we could figure it out. Because..."

Heart pounding, I paused, then blurted out, "What if a

false serpent became her translator? That could happen, you know. And if it did, God would want to give us some way of exposing him, wouldn't He?"

"You think Pastor Playle's a false serpent?" someone demanded excitedly.

"I don't know," I said, backing off from a direct accusation. "But what *if*?"

"I bet the Divine Sister's been sticking 'fuck' into her revelations all over the place, and we never even noticed!" yelped someone.

"I think it was God's will that this book about codes ended up in our cabin so we could decipher the Divine Sister's code and figure out if Pastor Playle is telling us the truth," I announced.

Everyone agreed that we should begin work at once on decoding my mother's glory-talk. Solemnly, we accepted our assigned lists of syllables, swearing on our mothers' graves to keep a record of how often they occurred in the Divine Sister's glory-talk and to track any discernible patterns. It was a tough job for a group of ten-year-olds, hunched in a pew and trying to take surreptitious notes on the occurrence rate of a particular vowel within the speech of a babbling un-miked woman located on the opposite side of the room while everyone in the immediate vicinity clapped and shouted out with joy. In fact, it took approximately two minutes for our plot to be uncovered—we were all hunched shoulder to shoulder in the same pew—and then we were led to the front of the sanctuary and forced to confess the sorry scheme in front of the entire congregation.

One by one, we knelt before the Divine Sister and she

placed her hands on our heads, praying in tongues while Pastor Playle translated, so that all might hear what the Lord had to say regarding the individual forgiveness of each remorseful girl. I was the last to kneel and make my repentance. As the Divine Sister placed her hands on my head, I felt something heated and bright, like an invisible fire, tighten around my scalp. Instinctively I cringed, then glanced up at my mother, and in that moment I saw a white-winged creature, transparent and ethereal as the solstice angels but with altogether different intentions. Instead of pulsing within a great prismatic ocean of knowing, this creature manifested alone, vibrating inside my mother's body like the wire in an electric lightbulb, and the expression on its face was entirely remote, as distant from the experience of flesh—its joy and pain—as it was possible to be. In a flash, I realized that I was seeing the Divine Sister in her true form: She was not human but a hostile vibration from another realm that had invaded my mother's body and taken up residence, with or without her consent.

As the circle of fiery white pain tightened around my head, I pushed against it, rising halfway to my feet and trying to press through the Divine Sister to my mother—that mother who, years ago, had been stolen from me along with Louisie. But I was not strong enough. Even as I resisted, a heaviness came over me, and a darkness; I was pushed back down to my knees and the Divine Sister prayed over me. Then I was led to the portable baptismal tank for a spontaneous baptism, where Pastor Playle held me under so long, I was truly born anew.

• • •

Jez's first party could be heard from a block away; the earth moved under her feet as she and Dee came up the front walk. The surrounding neighborhood had been claimed decades earlier by university students, and the dilapidated two-story clapboard house they were approaching was typical to the area—the windows draped with national flags and the front porch stacked with cartons of empties. As the two girls started up the porch steps, a pair of naked buttocks appeared in an upstairs window, mooning Planet Earth. Giving it an ear-splitting whistle, Dee pulled Jez through the crowd of stoners on the porch, their acrid smoke and *M*A*S*H* T-shirts, all of them several years older and murmuring, "Hey, lovelies, where ya goin'? I've got somethin' here—"

The doorway loomed, electric with the press of bodies and high-pitched laughter, and then they were penetrating deep into the inside of a headache—Deep Purple pounding in the room to the right, Jimi Hendrix resonating from the left. Smoke, sweat, and perfume layered the air, guys dancing bare-chested, girls in their bras; underfoot, the floorboards pulsed like a blood throb. Farther down the hall, the crowd divided as the upstairs-window mooner came streaking down the stairs, one more hallucination in a long, party-hard trip.

As the streaker disappeared out the front door, Jez found herself being hauled in the opposite direction—along the crowded hallway and into a kitchen lit dimly by strings of flashing Christmas lights. Confiscating two beers from the fridge, Dee popped both tabs and handed her one. Then, reaching under her skirt, she slid a small foil pouch out of her garter, opened it, and tipped several yellow and red capsules into her hand. "One for you, two for me," she grinned, dropping one into Jez's palm. "Pop it quick. We've got some catching up to do."

Without waiting for Jez's response, she swallowed her two capsules, then chugged half her beer and returned the foil pouch to her garter. "Take a look," she yelled over the music, pointing through the open back doorway to several semiconscious bodies lolling on an outside staircase that led to the second floor. "Stairway to Heaven. If you want to actually talk to someone, you've got to get here early."

It was the weekend following Jez's "lesson" in Sinbad's backseat, sometime into the wee hours of Saturday morning. Her parents had also slept soundly through tonight's escape, but this time Dee had shown mercy, parking the idling Sinbad in an alley half a block from the Hamilton residence. A change of clothing had awaited in the Bug—a red spaghetti-strap stretch minidress, black lace underthings, black nylons, black heels. No bra. "A true Jezebel," Dee had said approvingly after completing Jez's face. "Maybe you're not *quite* ready for guys, but you'll still be a mother of fun."

Dee was an *I Dream of Jeannie* wet dream in a black push-up bra, loose brocaded vest, and black miniskirt. As Jez closed one hand uncertainly around the capsule she had been given, Dee shut her eyes, raised both arms toward the kitchen's high ceiling, and began to snake her body to the Deep Purple/Hendrix sound fusion. Within seconds, an audience started gathering in the hall doorway, their gaze predatory, their comments loud and appreciative. Seemingly unaware, Dee continued to snake and swivel, absorbed by the energy of her own movement, but Jez found herself stepping back into the room's shadows, arms crossed over a braless chest and trying to calm a growing sense of panic. On and off the Christmas lights flickered as the music throbbed through the floorboards and Jez's heart thudded body-wide. The sensations pounding through her were extreme, composed in equal measure of fear and the most savage turn-on she had ever experienced, and she didn't know whether to pop the yellow and red capsule in her hand and throw herself, wide open, at whatever was coming, or hold onto the tiniest shred of sanity and wait it out.

Arms still raised, Dee continued to curl her body in, under, and around the beat. Somewhere nearby, Hendrix came to an end and was replaced with AC/DC. Concentration broken, Dee opened her eyes and assessed the audience in the doorway, then glanced over her shoulder at Jez, laughing as if the whole thing were the punch line to a joke shared only by the two of them. But before Jez could react, a voice called "Dee baby!" and a tall guy with a closely clipped beard stepped through the packed doorway and enveloped Dee, kissing her neck and sliding one hand under the back of her skirt. Still swiveling, she pressed against him and he stripped off her vest, flinging it over the heads of the watching crowd. With a laugh, Dee pulled his face to her own and kissed him hard, and Jez realized that whatever the reason she had been brought here tonight, she had just been erased from the shifting terrain of her friend's brain and was now completely alone—a stranger in a *very* strange land.

Without further ado, the bearded guy upended Dee over his shoulder and pushed into the hallway crowd, Dee drumming her hands unevenly on his butt. Quickly, Jez shoved her way after them, jumping frantically to keep Dee's upside-down body in sight as it turned into Deep Purple and flashing red floor-lights. Reaching the doorway, she saw Dee once again on her feet, momentarily dizzy and wobbling, then close-dancing with the bearded guy, their hips pasted. A knowing grin on his face, the bearded guy spoke into her ear and stepped back, and Dee exploded into movement, transformed into a twisting red-lit vortex that everyone turned to watch, their approval pounded out with hands and feet.

Pressed between a bookcase and a large potted fern, Jez huddled bug-eyed and hugging herself. On all sides, a sweaty half-dressed throng stood cheering Dee on, the floor shaking under the collective stomp of their feet. Never in her life had Jez been so relieved at being unnoticed. She had been in this house for under a half hour, and already the constant adrenaline rush had her on the verge of the shakes. Opening her hand, she let the yellow and red capsule fall into the potted fern. A year ago, in a fit of innocence, she had read *Go Ask Alice*. The novel hadn't put her off chemical euphoria entirely, but if she ever swallowed a completely unfamiliar get-happy pill, she knew it wouldn't be in a room of stoners like this one—all of them on the edge of fornication and probably sporting multiple cases of VD.

Someone turned up the volume and "Child in Time" began eating up the floorboards. Partway through Ian Gillan's screaming chorus, the streaker entered the room, his head tilted back in a parallel shriek as he zoomed through the crowd and took his personal nightmare back out the door. Closing over his wake, several guys surged toward Dee and hoisted her onto a nearby table. Whistles erupted and the horde pressed close, circling the table and banging it with their fists. Someone began clapping, and others eagerly picked up the rhythm. Clearly visible above everyone's heads stood Dee, her eyes half-closed and arms outstretched as if surfing the group's energy, reading its intent. Abruptly, her head came up, her nostrils flared, and she began gyrating in quick, sleek movements.

The zipper was at the back of her skirt. She made a slow job of it, laughing through the hair she let fall across her face, the story of her hips telling itself forever as the mini-skirt dropped to her ankles, leaving her ass-naked with a tiny black thong outlining her crotch. Mouth agape, Jez stared, her heart in a stereo beat as she finally realized why Dee was on the table—what she was about to do. Across the room, the horde let loose with a roar as several girls were lifted up to join Dee. Others began climbing onto various chairs, collecting their own spectators and leaving Jez enough room to wedge her way through to the central table and break out into the front line.

Five girls had joined Dee on the table; already they were bare-breasted. But the focus of attention remained on Dee—her heels, nylons, and garters now discarded, her hands sliding languorously under her thong. As Jez watched, swallowing and swallowing her panic, she knew she had never seen Dee this beautiful—an exquisite scattering of butterflies rising along the arched arc of her spine, spilling over the heartache of her breasts and into the proud thrust of her hips. Slowly, the thong began its downward slide, and the air shredded into wolf whistles and cheers. Tears running down her face, Jez reached out and grasped Dee's ankle, seeking some kind of contact, something known, *knowable* in this utterly incomprehensible scene. Instantly, Dee's eyes flicked toward her, their bright glaze dissipating as she took in Jez's shattered face, and then something entirely alien twisted through her expression—a brief awareness, equally feral but savage and trapped...an animal backed into a corner, hissing and choking on fear.

Startled, Jez released her ankle just as the bearded guy moved in, wrapped his arms around Dee's legs, and carried her out of the room. Behind him he left a crowd actively fermenting—girls being pulled off the table and chairs, the orgy in full swing. Ducking the hands that reached for her, Jez dove toward the nearest possible sanctuary—under Dee's dancing table. Out of sight she was out of mind, and the first thing she did was ditch the high heels Dee had given her to wear. Between the table legs stretched a vision of undulating bodies and throbbing red floor-lights; anything she had ever wondered about was describing itself in full detail for her now. On all sides, cries of ecstasy mingled with cries of pain. Somewhere out there, thought Jez, was Dee, stoned out of her mind and rotating on the axis of abomination: Pin-the-Bitch. Double Whammy. Open Sucker. The possibilities were endless; she agonized through each one.

Like a message from God, a butterfly flit-flitting into her mind, a voice came to her then—Dee's voice, asking, *Would you use it?*

If I had the guts, her own voice replied, mocking her now, taunting. Helpless, Jez stared at her empty, useless hands. Where was the knife she had vowed to carry at all times? she thought bitterly. What was she good for except shredding

Farrah Fawcett's paper neck and cutting the tip of her own tongue? With a cry, she shot out from under the table, lifted off everything she knew, and flew over the room's moaning, heaving panorama. At the doorway, she turned left, darted around a few more whimpering bodies, and headed toward the kitchen. To her relief it was empty, no one having submitted to the urge to copulate on its cold, cracked linoleum, and she was free to yank open each and every cupboard drawer until she had found a bread knife with a blade large enough to reflect an entire string of winking blinking Christmas lights—a knife Abraham could have used to kill Isaac, a knife with which Solomon could easily have sliced a baby in two. In short, a knife that would merit The Chosen Ones' approval.

As Jez headed back along the hallway, no one paid her any notice; she was no more than a foreign brain wave tripping through their skulls. Oblivious to the bread knife in her hand, couples traded off against the walls, and several giggling guys coordinated a collective piss over the stairwell railing. Giving them a broad berth, Jez started up the steps. All she could think was that Dee had to be on the second floor—it wasn't likely the bearded guy had carried her out of Deep Purple to have his way with her in AC/DC. At the top of the stairs, Jez found herself standing at one end of a hallway of closed doors; doggedly, she opened each one and switched on the lights, flinching at yells of protest as she scanned the unfamiliar faces in the beds. At the far end of the hall stood a single door with a large crack near the top, carrying the message of someone's fist. It was the last unopened door in the house; either Dee was in there, Jez thought grimly, or she had been taken out of the building. Without pausing, she tried the knob, but the door was locked. Rattling the knob, she threw her hip against the door and called Dee's name; no response came back to her.

"Hey!" called a voice behind her. "What ya doin' at Dinky's door?"

Turning toward the sound, Jez saw a guy approaching. Mustached, long-haired, and wearing a *M*A*S*H* T-shirt, he looked like something that could have risen directly out of the blue and orange psychedelic carpet under her feet. Bread knife clutched to her thigh, Jez backed in against the locked door. In spite of all the other doors she had opened in this hallway, none of the various rooms' occupants had come out after her, and she and the stranger were alone in the corridor. Lean and lithe, the guy looked as predatory as a hunting cat. Sweat trickled into Jez's eyes, blurring her vision; as she raised the bread knife and pointed it at the *M*A*S*H* T-shirt, her arm felt sluggish, a dead weight.

"Whoa!" said the guy, his eyebrows taking a hike. "Where'd *you* come from, chickie?"

Gripping the knife tightly, Jez felt her fingers slip on the sweaty handle. "Do not come near!" she ordered, forcing the words past the quaver in her throat. Once upon a time, long ago, Sodom and Gomorrah had received fair warning—this abomination deserved one too. "Do not come near and you will be spared!"

"Oh man!" groaned the guy, his eyes traveling carefully between the knife and her face. "You sound like my mom. This is God stuff, right? We don't usually let God in here, babe."

Quickly, he shifted to the right and Jez shifted with him,

following his movements with the knife. In the pause that followed, she could feel him poised on the tip of an edgy silence, assessing her. When he spoke next, his voice was quieter, more conciliatory. "What's that you got in your other hand?" he asked.

Glancing at her left hand, Jez saw Dee's thong dangling from her wrist. For the life of her, she couldn't remember picking it up. "It's not mine," she said.

"Too bad," said the guy. "But you gotta go home now, chickie. Dinky don't like no Jesus-freaks hanging around his door."

Jesus-freak! thought Jez, staring at him in amazement. *Fine, let that be my disguise.* "Does this Dinky have a beard?" she asked cautiously.

"He does indeed," confirmed the guy.

"Dark and closely clipped?" pressed Jez.

"Dark, and indeed closely clipped," agreed the guy.

"Is he in this room?" she asked, turning slightly and pointing the knife at the locked door.

"Try the secret knock," the guy said immediately. "Three quickies, two longies, and one scratch straight up. If Dink's in there, he'll open to that knock."

A secret knock! thought Jez. Codes of the ages—they never seemed to wear out. Keeping the knife tip trained on the guy's chest, she raised her other hand to knock on the locked door. Instantly, the guy ducked to one side, wrenched the bread knife from her hand, and lobbed it down the hall. Then he lunged at her, carrying her body into the locked door with a resounding thud. Trapped by his weight, Jez punched; she kicked and bit, but was forced to the floor and her legs shoved apart, *Open Sucker*. Still she fought, arcing her spine and thrusting her body upward, but in one swift motion the guy grabbed her head with both hands and slammed it against the floor. A wave of dark-light shot through Jez's brain and she was useless, rolling with the pain in her head. Vaguely, she felt the skirt of her dress pushed up and her panties torn off—all of it happening as if from a great distance, on the other side of far, far away.

Out of that distance then, traveling toward her like a tendril of smoke, came a vision of a scarlet shape radiating pain. Difficult to define within form, the image flowed in and out of itself like a gaseous cloud, though it seemed to have a core—a long, narrow face that jutted like a ferret's. Because of its color, the apparition looked to have been skinned alive, and it was sniffing the air like one of Tolkien's Dark Riders, its eyes fixed directly on her.

At the same time, a voice above her grunted, "Come on, chickie. Come *on*." Though she clenched herself against it, pain erupted between her legs and rolled through her—cataclysmic, catastrophic; choking on her sobs, Jez thought she could actually see the fear-lit fibers of her flesh splinter and begin to disintegrate. Then, as pain continued, huge, unboundaried, she found herself lifting up and away from it, through what appeared to be a network of veined neuronal light—a membrane of molecules that stretched like a radiant onionskin across the outer edge of consciousness. Finally, with a roar of white light, that onionskin split open, and she was rising directly out of its gaping wound, spilling out of the trapped and choking body beneath her like a butterfly emerging from its cocoon.

Somewhere beneath and yet also above her, a heavy weight rolled aside and the brilliant pain started to recede. Half in, half out of her body, Jez hovered uncertainly, then sank back into her sweaty, stinking flesh, the gutted hole between her legs.

"Jez?" whispered a voice. Gently, a hand touched Jez's face and she cringed. *More pain*, she thought. *Not more pain. No, no more.*

"Shh, baby, it's me," continued the voice—Dee's voice, Jez realized. But when she opened her eyes, she was met with the sight of the blood-red ferret's face directly over her own, still sniffing as it shifted in and out of its gaseous cloud. Terror ripped through Jez and she screamed, the fear pouring from her in raw gushes of sound.

"Shh, Jezzie, cool it. Cool it, okay?" pleaded Dee, using the full length of her body to keep Jez down. "Come on, it's me. You're okay now, you're okay."

Slowly, Jez's fear began to dissipate, leaving her with a sharp pain tunneling her gut. "Watch out," she whimpered, hot tears slipping from the outer corners of her eyes. "There's a guy, he's bad. He'll hurt—"

"Jezzie, it's all right," said Dee, pressing her hand lightly over Jez's mouth. "I knocked him out with a brick from Dink's bookcase. He's out cold."

"Cold?" whispered Jez. "You mean dead?"

"Just out of it," said Dee. "You want him dead?"

Jez flinched. "I was looking for you," she moaned. "Trying to—"

"I saw, Jezzie," Dee assured her. "I'm here now, aren't I?" As she hovered over Jez, her face continued to shift in and out of itself—sometimes human, sometimes narrow and jutting, a skinned bloody ferret's. "Shh," she said softly, her face peeled and bleeding. "Shh."

"Dee," quavered Jez, staring. "You're red—"

"Baby, it's my demon," said Dee, kissing her nose. "My guardian demon, that's all you're seeing. Don't be scared."

Guardian *demon*—the word roared through Jez's mind and once again she was split wide open, reality spinning on itself like a child's toy. Demons were the ultimate unholy whited sepulchers, the stench that rose from rotted flesh. Closing her eyes to escape the tortured shifting of Dee's face, Jez discovered the same apparition filling the inside of her head, its blood-red face turning to look at her dead on.

"Dee, it's looking at me!" she shrieked, slamming the back of her head against the floor in an attempt to force the demon out. "Sniffing at me like the Dark Riders. It'll smell my evil and pull me into Hell. I'll be stuck down there for—"

Grabbing Jez's head, Dee kissed her hard, sealing her mouth and closing her into a small wet cave of tongues, whimpers, and sucking flesh. Head rocked with pain, the absolute crescendo and crash of it, Jez fixed on the second tongue in her mouth and sucked, sucked, *sucked* it.

"Okay," she sighed, releasing it as the apparition faded from her mind. "But I can't...I can't..."

"Can't what?" asked Dee, her face now fully human but intent, watchful.

"...can't be *like* you, Dee," confessed Jez, keeping her gaze lowered. "I keep trying, but it's too hard. I'm not..."

Dee waited her out, tense and still, and Jez shifted under the heavy weight of her silence. "...*like* you," she repeated finally, the words desperate and true.

Breath harsh, Dee pushed up and away, and Jez saw she was naked. "Yeah, well, fuck you," Dee snapped, then broke off and picked up Jez's hand. "What are you holding?" she demanded. "My *thong*? Why are you holding my thong?"

"I was looking for you," mumbled Jez. "I had a knife. I was—"

"A knife?" said Dee, staring at her. "Where'd you get that?"

Jez was crying freely now, the tears a gushing stream. "The kitchen," she gulped.

"Did you *use* it?" demanded Dee, bug-eyed.

"That guy threw it somewhere," said Jez.

Lifting her head, Dee peered intently down the hall. "Jesus!" she said softly. "It's a bloody *ax*!"

A groan sounded and Jez turned her head to see the *M*A*S*H* rapist splayed next to her, pants down to the knees, shrunken rubbery dick resting on one thigh. Wincing, she reached for the skirt of her dress, but Dee pushed her hands away and gently worked it down over her hips. For a moment then, the two girls paused, looking away from each other as if anything more would be too much, even the air rubbed raw. Downstairs, it was quiet—the music turned low, a few voices talking. The party seemed to be over.

"How far did he get?" asked Dee.

"Pretty far," mumbled Jez.

"Can I look?" asked Dee.

"No!" cried Jez, cringing back from her.

"To see if there's damage," explained Dee. "Mom's a nurse. If you need help, she could—"

"Your mother's not looking at me!" shouted Jez, covering her groin with both hands.

"Fuck, Jez! Stop yelling, would ya?" said Dee, stroking the hair awkwardly from Jez's forehead. "I'll get my clothes and we're outta here, okay? Don't worry about that asshole—he's passed out bad as Dink."

Disappearing into the room with the punch mark on the door, Dee left Jez huddled with her back to the wall, staring at the carpet's blue and orange paisley pattern. *Paisley is sperm*, she remembered. *Christ, you're a sperm whale.* Listless, almost without intent, her gaze drifted from the prone shape of her attacker to the bread knife, its tip stuck in a baseboard fifteen feet down the hall. Curiously light-headed, she got to her feet, walked over to it, and picked it up.

"What the—?" said Dee, coming through Dinky's doorway.

On her knees beside the M*A*S*H rapist, Jez had pulled out the neck of his T-shirt and was shoving the tip of the bread knife through the cloth and into the floor, embedding it so the blade rested against the skin of the exposed neck. "Don't move, baby. Don't move," she rasped directly into the sagging, oblivious face.

Beside her, Dee clutched herself, choking on awed giggles. "Jezzie, come on," she gasped. "We've got to get out of here before someone sees this."

"Okay," said Jez, wincing as she got to her feet. For a moment, she stood staring at the splayed figure on the floor. "One good kick," she murmured. "I'll dream about it for years."

They came gingerly down the stairs, Jez hanging onto Dee's arm and hissing whenever a sharp tearing sensation told her to slow down. Once they reached the first floor, she started crying again, tears pouring from her eyes like an upended box of Smarties. Cautiously, she stepped over the bodies sleeping off chemicals in the hallway, cringing when her foot touched a naked arm or thigh. As she limped through the front door, cold air came at her like a slap of consciousness, pulling her out of a muffled, shattered haze. Arms wrapped tightly around herself, she waited, shivering, at the curb as Dee ran off to fetch the Bug, then crawled warily into the front seat, pain sideswiping her each time she moved.

Reaching into the back, Dee picked up her red and white checked midi and draped it across her lap. "Need some help?" she asked.

"No," said Jez, blowing her nose into the midi's skirt. "I'll do it."

As she changed, Dee drove in silence, her eyes fixed on the street ahead. "Look," she said hesitantly as Jez struggled, hissing with pain, to do up the midi's back zipper.

"Yeah, I know," said Jez, cutting her off. The shakes had really taken over now, her thighs giving off quick, ugly shudders, throbs of self-contempt. There simply was no escaping the overwhelmingly obvious—she had been a complete and utter fool; Dee had never been in danger; there had been no apocalypse, and all she had managed to do was get herself raped. No one in her right mind would want to hang around with someone that dense. On top of everything else that had gone wrong tonight, this was kiss-off time for Jezebel—return to Mary-Eve, *exile*.

Face shifting between thoughts, Dee continued to drive silently, then ventured, "I remember the first time I got raped."

Still braced against what she had expected to hear, Jez fumbled toward Dee's actual words. "Who raped you?" she asked, startled.

"Who cares who?" replied Dee. "It was years ago. I was spaghetti for a long time afterward, okay?" Grabbing a pack of Player's from the dash, she dug out the last cigarette. "That's when my demon was born, see?" she said, lighting up. "My *first* demon. She came out of me while it was happening, and she's been with me ever since—outside of me, but always near. Always watching. She sees things I can't see, things far away or maybe in the next room—like you with that guy in the hall. I saw it happening in my head while I was with Dinky. My demon showed me."

Again, the vision of the peeled-raw ferret face flashed through Jez's mind. Grimacing, she made herself look at it straight on. "So that's what it was," she muttered. "Just before that guy started…Your demon—it was watching me while…"

"Yeah," said Dee.

Jez stared through the side window into darkness. A *demon* watching over her? she thought wonderingly. *A demon born out of a rape?*

"If that's how they're born," she asked haltingly, "do I have one too?"

"No," Dee said immediately. "You went back in. At first, when I ran out of Dinky's room and that guy was whamming you, I could see a fuzzy light starting to lift out of your body. But then when I hit him with the brick, the light went back in. It didn't leave and take on its own life. That means no demon was born."

"So you're telling me," faltered Jez, "that creepy red thing is you? *You're* a demon?"

"Not exactly," said Dee, dragging on her cigarette. "But my demons came out of me, and I know that's how they were born." Taking another drag, she paused, then said carefully, "Look, thanks for trying to save me, but you need to know— this is the way I am at parties. I'm the spark that gets the fun going. It's like pulling the trigger on a sex gun—see how many people you can shoot."

Lifting the skirt of her midi, Jez cleaned the mess of tears and snot from her face.

"None of it's personal," added Dee. "None of them are my friends. At least, not like you are." Falling silent, she drove, her fingers stroking thoughts onto the steering wheel. "A lot of girls get jumped," she mused. "Hell, all the girls I know have been jumped some time or other. None of them ever picked up an *ax* over it." Slightly awed, her eyes flicked across Jez's. "You gonna be all right?"

Gingerly, Jez shifted around the tunnel of pain in her gut. It was the same pain Dee carried; if she was to give it a shape and a name, it sure wouldn't be *angel*. And after years of watching the false serpent Playle parade around as God's right-hand man…well, this wouldn't be the first time she had seen something manifest as its opposite.

"I need a smoke," Jez said gruffly, lifting the cigarette from between Dee's lips.

A hesitant smile crept into the corner of Dee's mouth. "Sure, take my last one," she complained.

Their eyes met, and Jez realized she had passed some kind of test. "Cerro Pelon," she said quietly. "Some day, I really want to see that place."

"Jez," said Dee, "you *are* that place. Or you're no place."

The darkness took them home.

SEVEN

It was during an Easter weekend retreat that I saw Pastor Playle and my mother having sex. God presented me with this revelation during the wee hours of Sunday morning just before the Resurrection originally took place, when Waiting for the Rapture believers were supposed to be worshipfully asleep, burying the old self in dreams so they could wake reborn into the morning light. At least, these were the instructions Pastor Playle had given us during Saturday evening chapel, after which we had devoured juice and cookies and retired to our conference-center family rooms—narrow cells of concrete and linoleum furnished with several sets of bunk beds. My parents had immediately selected lower bunks, my father's next to a window that overlooked the grounds and my mother's (significantly) nearest the door, while I took an upper one, preferring to sleep afloat above their heads.

It was the year I turned thirteen, the year I watched other girls turn doe-eyed and stupid, pluck the wings off thought and ground themselves. It was also the year the Eleusis and Eastbrook Waiting for the Rapture congregations decided to combine for their Easter retreat. The Eastbrook youth group was twice our size and considerably more worldly—the girls were allowed to wear makeup, and some of their skirts had inched above the knee. Just before Good Friday dinner, I overheard several of them in a washroom making plans to sneak off later that evening during a scheduled stargazing activity. So after night snack, when everyone began pulling on sweaters and heading outdoors to listen to the two pastors' competing oratories about stars, wonders, and the end-times, I kept my eyes steadfastly ground-level, monitoring the furtive figures that were edging out of the upward-gazing group and into the nearby trees.

Slipping stealthily after them, I followed their giggling whispers to the conference center's rec room, where a large collection of old sofa cushions had been stacked in one corner. Quickly, the twelve Eastbrook teenagers headed for the pile and paired off. Odd girl out, I huddled in a nearby corner, maintaining a careful analysis in the dark, though it didn't seem as if those vague huddled shapes could be doing much— they were all grouped close together, so quiet that there was only the odd sucking or giggling noise, and the pillows barely moved. Every now and then, partners seemed to be switching, but what with the frequent trips the girls were making to a nearby washroom, it was difficult to be sure. Either too much lemonade had been consumed at night snack or the girls were spending a lot of time comparing notes. Whichever it was, with so much traffic tiptoeing in and out, I figured no one would notice if I subbed in.

Cautiously, I crawled among the whispering bodies and waited, and soon enough someone rolled toward me. I didn't have a clue who he was—couldn't remember a boy who reeked of the odd combination of Vicks VapoRub and Esso Supreme—but since I wasn't looking for anyone in particular, I allowed his mouth to bump tentatively against mine as he worked his way into a hesitant pucker. The girl beside us must have been allergic to dust—she kept sneezing and complaining because the pillows hadn't been vacuumed—and I could hear other couples bargaining back and forth.

"Come on, let me," mumbled a guy.

"Not if you do that," demurred his partner.

"You did it with Garth last year," protested the guy.

"I didn't do it like that," hissed the girl.

The Vicks-Esso boy had gentle hands, but an odd kissing style that involved puffing out the wet insides of both lips, then plastering them in all their gooey glory across his partner's mouth. All in all, the experience could only be described as wormlike, and did little to inspire desire. In addition, he kept pausing to trace his fingers over my face and whisper, "Renita, is that you? Joanie? Sylvia?"

Afraid my identity was about to be discovered, I decided the best defense was a good offense. A recent junior-high gossip session had aroused my curiosity as to the merits of French-kissing, and since this boy's lips had turned out to be a complete loss in the passion-incitement department,

I resolved to bypass them. That I might thereby be setting new standards for the mores of the Eastbrook youth group's female members did not occur to me; I simply waited until Mr. Vicks-Esso had whispered his nervous way through several more girls' names, then sent my tongue energetically into his hovering mouth.

The results were electric. Jerking back with a loud gagging noise, he yelped, "What was that?" I froze, and in the seconds that followed became aware of a surrounding stillness so deep, *nothing* was breathing. The entire room literally ached with the intensity of listening, and it was then that I realized the reason the stack of sofa pillows had not disintegrated, but remained intact against the wall—the Eastbrook Waiting for the Rapture youth group's idea of sin in the dark was a two-button-down hickey. Sliding out from under Mr. Vicks-Esso, I felt for the pillows anchoring the bottom of the pile and pulled hard. Pillows and bodies cascaded everywhere, and in the ensuing melee, I took off without a backward glance.

The next morning, I rubbed some of my father's aftershave under the collar of my dress then ventured casually among the Eastbrook youth group, intent on sniffing out Mr. Vicks-Esso and secure in the knowledge that he would not be able to identify me. I need not have worried—Eastbrook's older teenagers were busy giving each other speculative glances, but no one appeared to have considered the possibility they had been infiltrated by an alien thirteen-year-old. Careful sniffing led me to a tall, pimply fifteen-year-old who wore a READY FOR THE RESURRECTION T-shirt and played guitar during sing-alongs. All day I studied him, trying to decide if knowing what he looked like was an out-and-out deterrent to the possibility of future passion. The memory of his wormlike kissing technique almost tipped the balance, but in the end I resolved to return to the rec room that night to see if the Eastbrook youth group managed to pull off a repeat performance—one that got some pillows moving.

After evening snack I retired, hoping this would encourage everyone else to similar aspirations, then lay awake counting heartbeats while members of both congregations engaged in hearty games of Snap and Monopoly. Eventually I drifted off, and woke some time later to the sound of my father's snoring in a lower bunk. Still wearing my midi dress, I slipped inch by creaky inch down the ladder at the foot of my bed, then out the door and along the dimly lit hall.

Several turns along darkened corridors brought me to the rec room door, which I found slightly ajar. Edging through the doorway, I crept into the shadow of an old upright piano and stood a moment, letting my eyes adjust to the darkness. To my disappointment, the youth group was nowhere to be seen, but this was quickly forgotten as I realized that not only had the stack of sofa pillows finally disintegrated, it had scattered madly in every direction. At the center of this chaos, I could see two bodies undulating—a man on top, his arms cradling the head of the woman beneath him. Her hands appeared to be gripping his buttocks, both her flabby legs had risen into the air, and the sounds they were making could have called anything to them, could have raised the dead. Until that moment, I had never seen my mother look beautiful, her pin curls released, her usual hooded expression vanished, and the gift of tongues claiming her so completely, her voice and body burned as one flame.

I do not know how long I stood watching. Pastor Playle seemed to last forever inside my mother, and she clung to him as if he were her life. Soaked with sweat, they swore wildly as they came, collapsing so completely I thought they had died. Without speaking, they began again, kissing deep inside each other's mouths, but I was trembling, my mind blown by what I had witnessed, and stole quietly from the room. Still trembling from shock, I made my way back to our family room and lay in my bunk, trying to recover the mother I had just lost—a mother who spent her afternoons reading Billy Graham, baking brownies, and waiting for my father and me to come home.

Or did she?

Pastor Playle had a paunch and training-bra titties; his cock had slid in and out of my mother in a long, hard line. He had called her *Magdalene darling, my most beautiful whore.* For the rest of the weekend, I watched them, but they gave no sign of what had occurred in that feverish pillow-wild room; I fell asleep that night before my mother returned to her bunk, and when I woke, the memory seemed entirely distant, removed from me as if a dream.

• • •

It had been a week of rain and gusting wind. Long shivers of yellow left the trees, and the sky collected every shade of gray, pouring its sadness down upon the world. Huddled under dripping umbrellas and in school entrances, the smoking crowd's lunch hours were a bust, a string of sodden butts whirling along the gutter. By Thursday noon, Dee Eccles was more than ready to blow that Popsicle stand, and waylaid Jez as she came through the school's main entrance with a hollered "Jezzie, babe, get your ass over here!"

Standing under the damp archway at the top of the stairs, Jez poised in that moment of stillness that comes before a long fall. Across the street she could see Dee leaning through Sinbad's window, heedless of the downpour—a flash of color and sound beyond the shifting vibrations that rode the smokers crowded around the school door. The last week had been a major buzz. Since the assault at Dinky's party, Jez had been continually sliding in and out of her own head as she watched a world that seemed to have divided itself into twinned dimensions—one solid and one of glimmering shifts of energy, like a radio and its song. Perhaps reality had always broadcast itself like this and she had only just tuned in, or maybe it had something to do with the feeling that she was constantly emanating out of her body in a silent, unending moan—one version of the way loneliness presented itself when reality got too big and started pushing mind out of body into the electric scream-world of thought.

Jez didn't know what to call the scene vibrating in front of her—its mix of Eric Clapton and Emily Carr—or the fact that she could see Dee's demon manifesting as a slight red halo around her head. It had been five days since the assault. The ache in her groin had since disappeared and the back of her head had lost its throb, but sudden sounds and movements continued to make her flinch and her mind stubbornly clutched the live wire of memory, refusing to let go. Everywhere she went, scenes from the party replayed remorselessly inside her head, so vivid she could smell, even taste, the experiences, yet the world that surrounded her remained oblivious—carrying on with the mundane, everyone sailing their paper boats across life's surface while she drowned in silence below. Never before had she been made so painfully aware that forgetting made one functional. Since dropping her off after the party, Dee hadn't once mentioned the rape, and every subsequent lunch hour had been the same—a wild car ride, Jez crowded into the back with two or three others while Nazareth boomed from the dash, Dee in high gear and allowing no pauses, no waiting moments, no way for Jez to hold up her hands, their cupped fluid pain, and say, *There is no shape to this. My cup runneth over; I am pissing fear.*

Hiking her sweater over her head, Jez darted down the stairs into the downpour and across the street. As she climbed into the Bug, Dee pulled out from the curb so quickly Jez found herself slamming the door onto moving pavement. An immediate sharp-shouldered quiet moved in on them—Jez sprawled sullenly, Dee staring blank-faced and dead ahead as she drove.

"Where is everyone?" asked Jez, watching the rain stream down the windshield.

"Everyone," said Dee, "bores me. Hungry? Chips and dip in the back."

Obediently, Jez hauled a bag of groceries into the front seat, then braced her knees against the dash and placed an opened package of potato chips and container of sour cream on her stomach. Crunching methodically through chip after chip, she listened as Nazareth poured out of the dash, Dee pushing Rewind every time "Love Hurts" hit the final chord, and playing it again.

"Don't you know any other songs?" Jez asked after the fourth time.

"Better than listening to you," snapped Dee. Silently, they waited out the whirring rewind, Jez sprawled low on the seat, her head tilted back as she watched the tops of trees whirl aimlessly past. She had no idea what street they were on, if, indeed, they had any specific destination. The pulsing pushed-out-of-her-body sensation was on her again, and when that happened, everything solid faded and she became a song leaving the radio, a vibration quivering along the earth's magnetic grid as it guided thousands of monarch butterflies south—she would get to Cerro Pelon someday, given enough sky.

The whirl of passing trees took a jarring tilt to the left, and Jez felt the car turn onto gravel and grass. Suddenly, a willow tree loomed straight ahead, brilliant yellow in the gloom. Without stopping, Dee coasted directly toward it and Jez gave a hoarse shout, bracing herself for a crash as the windshield was engulfed by the tree's countless trailing tendrils. But no crash came. Instead, there was stillness as Dee cut the engine and "Love Hurts" bit the dust, leaving them with the thick, wet scent of earth, the muffled far-off grief of rain, and the radiant inner mystery of an autumnal willow tree.

"This is incredible!" whispered Jez, staring at the curtain of yellow that had completely surrounded the Bug.

"I found it last night," Dee said casually. "Part of the park fence is down. You can come in off the road, so I drove around a bit."

"Oh yeah?" said Jez, trying to keep obvious interest out of her voice. "You with Dinky?"

"Just driving," said Dee. "You don't want to overdo Dink. He's an asshole unless you're fuckin' him."

Switching the engine back on, she let it idle, and the car was once again flooded with "Love Hurts." Almost in a trance, Jez listened to the haunted lyrics, her gaze fixed on the wealth of branches that crowded the windshield, traveling their every twist and turn. Unexpectedly, her body gave a convulsive jerk and the bag of chips tilted on her stomach, threatening to spill its contents. Swiftly Dee grabbed it.

"Just stop it, okay?" she hissed, catching the container of sour cream, which had also begun to slide. "*Stop* it!"

"Stop what?" asked Jez, hypnotized by the willow branches, their vivid curves of pain.

"Stop stopping breathing!" snapped Dee. "You're like a corpse—you sit there staring and then you stop breathing. You make me want to check your pulse."

"You stare too," Jez said sulkily.

"Yeah, but I *breathe*," said Dee. "My heart beats, all the vital signs are there."

"Bully for you," said Jez, and went back to staring at the willow branches. Except this time she also noticed it, the way her breathing backed inch by inch up her chest and throat until it ceased and she was nothing—not breath, not thought, not being. Just a fixed, long, ongoing stare.

"Fuck!" muttered Dee. Then she was silent, but Jez heard it loud and clear—the smoking-crowd goddess's tight-lipped unvoiced judgment: *Basket case.* Sudden breath returned to Jez, deep, gulping caves of it. Pushing herself upright, she punched Nazareth into oblivion.

"Wha*t*?" demanded Dee, turning to glare at her.

"This is wha*t*," said Jez. Shoving her face into the other girl's, she opened her mouth and screamed—no vapid sob-story words like "love" and "hurts," just a great gut-digging, raw-clawing banshee shriek. Then she turned, the entire world in a slowed, blurred tilt turning with her, and slammed her fist against the closed passenger window. A second time she pounded and a third, the cracked glass now smeared with blood, and still she was drawing back to pound again, but Dee was on to her, had launched herself swearing over the gearshift and was scrabbling for the door handle. In the small enclosed space, bodies thudded and grunted, the door lurched violently open, and the two girls rolled out through the wet slap of willow strands onto cold, hard ground and on into the downpour, Jez choking on huge chunks of sound, earth and sky wrapping them tight as pigs in a blanket as bit by bit they slowed, coming finally to random dizzy rest. Head spinning and soaked to the skin, Jez dug her face into the sodden grass and gave vent to empty desolate sound.

"You knew it would happen," she whispered.

Silent and unspeaking, Dee pressed down upon her, the wet sky above them immense with falling, word by word.

"You dressed me like that," Jez rasped, forcing herself onward. "You took me there. You got them going, and then you left me alone."

Still silent, Dee lay over her, breathing, just breathing. Finally she spoke, her voice low and tremulous. "You wanted to know what I knew," she said.

Jez's body contorted, one long jackknife of agony. "So that's it?" she cried. "This is one long lesson plan? What's it going to be next week—murder? Heroin? Syphilis?"

With a hiss, Dee scrambled to her feet. "What d'you want from me, man?" she snapped.

"No," said Jez, following her up. "What do *you* want?"

Dee's face was all nerves, twisting across the surface—all the endings and beginnings of nerves. Whirling, she took several strides toward the car before forcing herself to slow and turn back. Then she simply stood for a moment as if emptying herself, letting the rain wash intensity from her face.

"You're different," she shrugged. "I'm not bored yet."

"What's that supposed to mean?" shouted Jez, helpless with disbelief. "I'm the fucking *Muppet Show*? D'you get a kick out of watching your friends get raped? How long did you stand there and watch?"

Dee's face contorted and she took a step back, both hands raised as if fending something off. "I came as soon as I knew," she protested. "I jumped him...I got him off you. What the hell are you talking about?"

Meaning splintered like pick-up sticks; Jez began to shake uncontrollably. "I'm not me anymore," she wailed. "I don't know who the fuck I was, but that's gone now and I don't know what's left. Is this the nothing place I'm supposed to be seeking? Well, I don't *want* it."

Retreating into the cave of her hands, Jez shrank into loneliness—a thin, rib-shivering sound she couldn't believe she was making, couldn't believe the way she ached to make it, to press deeper into it, find the wound, the *first* wound, the original hidden truth.

"Jez," said Dee, her tone distressed, urgent. "C'mere, okay? Would you just c'mere a minute?"

What were the options? Jez wondered wearily. As the rain continued its random pattering of nothingness, she turned like a compass needle toward the girl who sat slumped on a nearby picnic table, black leather jacket soaked, hair plastered to her head. In one hand, Dee held the red-handled jackknife that she had thrown at her brother; as Jez stared, wide-eyed, she made two quick incisions, cutting into the skin of her other wrist.

"What are you doing?" screamed Jez.

"Shut up," Dee said tersely, wiping the blade on her socks and snapping it closed. "There has to be blood."

"What the fuck for?" cried Jez.

"It's the way it works," said Dee. "The way it comes to me." Shoving the jackknife into a pocket, she fell silent, her eyes lowered as if focused on some inner shift. Balanced on a knee, her upturned wrist pulsed with blood and rain; drawing near, Jez saw the two incisions curved together into the shape of a fish.

The secret sign! she thought, glancing startled at the other girl's face. *The sign of the fish!* But how would Dee know of it? How could she possibly have encountered The Chosen Ones' secret, most inner-sanctum code?

A sigh shuddered through Dee, and she stood and reached for Jez's injured hand, turning it to expose the bloody scratches left by the cracked window glass. "This here," she said, nodding at her own cut wrist, "is the Eye. The *true* Eye." Bringing their damaged wrists together, she sealed them with her free hand. "Blood and pain," she added gruffly, leaning her forehead against Jez's, "open this Eye. All you have to do now is close your outside eyes and watch."

Together they stood in the falling rain, eyes closed, foreheads touching, and pulsing with the pain in their joined wrists. *Blood bleeding into blood.* The thought came to Jez, and she didn't know if that thought was hers or Dee's. *Blood knows.* Then, for a while, there was nothing—just the coldness of rain and the regular soft puff of their breathing. Gradually, a sensation of denseness crept over Jez, and a heaviness, and darkness that pulled downward. Thickness rushed her mouth and dizziness; she felt so exhausted she could barely breathe. This dissipated, and she found herself lying on a bed in a dark room, her body naked and small. *Young*, Jez realized, bewildered. She was young—maybe three or four. And she was crying—her lungs, every part of her, filling with panic as a great weight pressed down on her, trapping her so she couldn't move. Pain began then, much worse than that which she had experienced at Dinky's party—the kind a steamship would bring into a rabbit hole. And with her mouth and nose jammed into the soft flesh of the stomach above her face, she couldn't scream, couldn't breathe, couldn't *breathe.*

But what was most different this time was the hatred she felt—only three or four years old and already she knew it like an old friend, a confidante who realized how much she detested her own skin and so peeled her out of it, inch by raw inch the way a carrot is peeled except feeling the screams, all of her now red gore and uglier than anything she had ever seen but free, she was *free*, and *nothing*—not love, not revenge, not hunger or need—would ever pull her back into a body that could be done to like this.

Again, briefly, Jez found herself looking directly into

the skinned-raw ferret's face of Dee's demon, those haunted glints of eyes, as it rose before her inner vision, blocking the image of the rape on the bed from further view. Then, like an exhaled sigh, the entire experience slid from her mind and she felt herself being returned to the mundane world. With a low moan, Dee pulled away, releasing her wrist, and Jez opened her eyes to a gray-raining world that somehow seemed lit by an inner glow.

"It's...so full of light," she said, looking around herself in awe. "Everything."

Dee nodded. "It's like that when you come back," she said. "Because it's so dark inside, maybe."

Jez hesitated, swallowed, then asked, "Was that...how you got your first demon?"

"No," said Dee, turning toward the car, her face like a door slammed closed. *Too much*, Jez realized, watching her. *Too much, too fast.* She had to walk carefully here. And yet, she thought, awareness humming through her like a cold little ditty, Dee hadn't walked that carefully with *her*. And it was obvious, in spite of her casualness, that the smoking-crowd goddess had planned this entire episode—from the willow tree and her cut wrist, to the Eye and all that Eye had revealed. Just as she had intended the lessons learned at Dinky's party—not the exact events, perhaps, but, like she had said, she was the sex gun that shot it all into motion. She had known all the possibilities.

"I'm sorry that happened to you," said Jez.

Dee nodded and kept walking. Running to catch up, Jez took enough breath to keep herself going. "I still want to know why you took me to that party," she added hoarsely.

Dee stopped, her back to Jez, motionless in the gray glow of the rain. "Because," she said finally, her words quiet and bleak, "I didn't want to go alone."

For a moment all Jez could do was stare, her brain numbed by the rain, its constant dull fall. Then, slowly, she began to get it, the meaning of *alone*—that it included everyone else who had been at the party, even Dinky; with all of them, Dee had been alone. Only Jez was excluded from the word; only with Jez was Dee not alone, because theirs was a friendship that was seeking beyond the flesh—a friendship that wove minds, *spirits*.

But that kind of seeking, Jez realized, her mind leaping thought to thought, took blood and pain, as Dee had said—shared agony—and the smoking-crowd goddess had known it. Knees buckling slightly, she stared at the other girl's unmoving back.

"You weren't alone, Jez," said Dee, as if reading her mind. "I came, didn't I? I didn't leave you alone. I won't," she added, turning slowly so Jez could see her profile, "ever leave you alone."

I'm right, thought Jez. *It* was *an initiation*. Astoundingly enough, her rape at Dinky's party had been a kind of sacrifice. Through it, her body had been split open and shoved full of terror, in order to teach her something about the spirit. Before the rape, she hadn't known the first thing about the spirit. It had been all words, pronouncements and pontifications, contemptible to The Chosen Ones. Now, *finally*, she understood those gray-robed figures—the pain and fear they had endured in their rites of passage, and the way it had opened them to the realm of spirit so that they stood with one foot locked in the world of the flesh and the other in dimensions of utter possibility.

"My mother," Jez said haltingly, "does this too. Different, but still the same—blood, pain, the Eye. Her demons are white, your angels are red."

"Angels," said Dee, her mouth quirking. Hesitantly, her gaze flicked across Jez's. Without blinking, Jez met it dead on.

I don't believe you, she thought straight at the other girl. *At least, not everything you said. But you're not alone, either. I won't ever leave you alone, Dee, even if I get bored.*

She waited, testing it out, and was rewarded by the slow understanding she saw creep across Dee's face. "Okay," sighed the smoking-crowd goddess, her shoulders straightening as if this time it was she who had passed a test. "We'd better get moving, unless we want a late slip."

Without warning, Jez was rushed with exhilaration, broadsided by it. "Nah, no late slip," she sang, getting her stiff legs into gear. "No late slip for this baby." Putting on a burst of speed, she passed Dee and ducked into the watery strands of the willow tree. "Come on!" she called, opening the Bug's passenger door. "Step on it, eh? I've got English in ten."

"So?" asked Dee, getting in opposite and turning the ignition.

"So," said Jez, leaning into the backseat and grabbing the opened bag of chips. "We're reading *The Diviners*. I happen to like it."

Dee gave her a knowing smile. "My class finished it last week," she said. "You get to the cock part yet?"

"Huh?" demanded Jez, cramming her mouth full.

Dee backed the Bug out of the willow tree, then cut across

a small park and out through a gap in the surrounding fence. "Should've seen everyone's faces the day we were supposed to have that chapter read," she said. "It's about a third of the way through the book. Teacher was grinning her fool head off; the rest of us were in shock. I hadn't started the book yet, but Pierre Chartrand showed me—the word 'cock' right there on the page. I couldn't believe it—a school textbook that actually knew what one was. I figured maybe I should read it."

"The page or the whole book?" asked Jez.

Dee's lips wavered, but her eyes remained thoughtful. "Yeah, that book was okay," she mused. "The river runs both ways. You got a river running both ways, Jez?"

"You mean up and down?" teased Jez, reaching for the pack of Player's on the dash.

Dee accepted the lit cigarette slid between her lips. "I mean lost and gone," she said quietly.

"You're not lost and gone," protested Jez. "You can't be lost when you're with me—it's a simple matter of geography."

"Guess not," murmured Dee.

Leaning back against the seat, Jez stretched into the luxury of ordinary conversation. "How come you get to read *The Diviners* in grade twelve and I have to wait for grade thirteen?" she complained.

"You academics are so pure," said Dee. "They probably thought you needed an extra year to matuuuuure."

Jez rolled her eyes. "Manuuuuure," she replied. "Man, they probably won't even let me into the classroom. The only dry part of me is this cigarette."

"So tell your English teacher you fell into Morag's river," said Dee.

"And the river took me both ways before I could get out!" hooted Jez.

They giggled, impressed with the literary quality of their joke.

"Baby," said Dee, "you tell her whatever the Manawaka you want."

EIGHT

My father held a shadow position in my mother's life, carefully manufactured for public consumption. To the average Waiting for the Rapture attendee, he was no more than the amenable balding man who escorted her to Sunday services, stood in the aisle passing the offering plate pew to pew, and lingered, chatting in the lobby with anyone who would bother, long after most of the congregation had gone home. Only the two who knew him best recognized the tension underlying his Sunday morning smile—that smile an uneasy weight like a Charlie Chaplin mustache, and part of me always on the alert, waiting for it to fall off.

Watching that smile come into being was an equally covert activity. Hidden behind an upraised Bible and ostensibly memorizing my Sunday school verse, I would sit in the

Valiant's backseat as we drove to church and track every stage of the Sunday morning transformation taking place on my father's face. All down Lewis Street, along Catledge Road, and over Droney Bridge, he was familiar—my father, Lawrence Philip Hamilton, the gloom-laden salesman from Quance Crescent. But at the Royal Bank on Berkeley Avenue, his face began to change. Beset by small subterranean tremors, facial muscles loosened one by one, and the heavy weight of his eyelids started to lift. Then, at the Tim Horton's on Bernard Street, the hard line of his mouth trembled and gave way like a plea, and for a moment his face sat empty and vacuous—the face of someone who could become anyone.

It was at this point that my father commenced his grand deception—pulling a new face, detail by detail, out of the air. Observing the familiar process, I would wonder from what source he was getting these components—the free-floating spirits of the dead? Memories of happier times, before he had married and been saddled with a wife and daughter such as my mother and myself? Regardless of their origin, these facial specifics were stolen goods, I eventually concluded; the glimmer that appeared in his eyes, for instance, did not belong to him—he had to *ponder* it into being, part of a carefully planned ritual of self-determination that was so predictable, I could foretell the exact moment passing the supermarket on Conestoga Avenue when he would force up the muscles of his cheeks and quirk the corners of his mouth. Still, his face retained the look of a mere practice session, an only partially complete mask, until the instant we turned onto Fern Street, one block from the Waiting for the Rapture End Times Tabernacle. As the church came into view, my father's chest swelled and his face filled with joviality. Taking a deep breath, he swung the Valiant into the RESERVED FOR DEACON HAMILTON parking space, opened the car door with a flourish, and swaggered up the front steps into a flurry of handshaking and exclamations of "How are you, *Brother*?"

If my father was a marionette pulling his own strings, his body never fully accepted the disguise and could not seem to move fluidly; when he turned his head, his entire torso rotated, as if the vertebrae had fused, melding his neck to his shoulders. No one except me seemed ever to notice this stiffness, this armor of false joy—women fawned, children sat on his knee and accepted peppermints, and other men waited until he had bellowed his first "Amen!" into the sermon, and then the chorus of male approval began. To a lesser extent, this had also been the case at our previous church, but there Lawrence Philip Hamilton had been merely one of many Sunday morning men, with nothing to set him apart from the next husband and father. With the descent of the Tongue of Fire onto my mother's head, however, he achieved immediate prominence, it being assumed that the source of her spiritual fervor had to be rooted in her provider and keeper. My father, always quick to recognize a door with his name on it, also realized that my mother's transformation was the key to unlock this particular door; while I would guess he never glimpsed the Divine Sister's true visage or had much of an awareness of the high-frequency realms with which his wife daily communed, there is no doubt my father understood guilt—particularly the type of self-recrimination that my mother had been engaging in since Louise's death. Once he had identified this festering remorse as the cause of Rachel

Hamilton's transformation, he patrolled it the way a mother watches a sick infant, pulling every breath into its lungs with her own.

That first Waiting for the Rapture Sunday, the one upon which my mother received the Tongue of Fire, was the day she opened fully to her innate sinfulness and shed it, along with her earthly ways. Though she never explained exactly what occurred at the initial moment of contact, it was obvious that she had been brought into resonance with another plane of existence; from that day onward, the physical world lost all meaning, retreating into a vague shadowland as she focused her activities upon that invisible assembly of the elect known obliquely to the uninitiated as the chosen ones. Through her almost continually whispered prayers, I learned my mother understood her transformation to have admitted her into a select group that lived a hidden history—a secret lifeline that stretched from past to present like a glowing path breathed from the mouth of God, linking the individual minds of the chosen and lifting them into a realm of pure light. Mere centuries could not separate those who lived within this realm, for it was there that the Holy Spirit located Himself, speaking His coded truth in a high-frequency vibration that pulsed far beyond the consciousness of the majority of mankind. Tuned to this vibration, the eyes of the chosen were opened to visions and apparitions, signs and portents that had been concealed from their fellow men, and they came quickly to the understanding that they were the means through which the Holy Spirit acted upon the physical world—their very lives serving as a translation of one level of meaning to another, spirit to flesh.

And so it was that my mother lived among them in a realm invisible to mundane men, constructing a Biblical landscape of meaning about everything she did. Rising every morning at five, she would bake a single loaf of bread for the day's consumption, then scatter the uneaten portion that evening for backyard birds in order to fulfill the chosen's mandate of collecting only enough manna for daily sustenance. As she frequently admonished me, evil thoughts were washed away by doing laundry, sweeping the floor made the way clear for the Lord, and setting the table was an invitation to any angels that happened to be in the vicinity—the whole of my mother's physical life thereby shrunk into a low-level metaphor for the truer, brighter reality of the chosen.

To further shrink herself, she took to wearing a head covering and deferring in all matters to my father. Each act of submission was done with rabid intensity, including an evening ritual in which she went down on her knees before him, removed his shoes, and washed his feet. At meals, she kissed his balding head with a little humming sound, then served his meal first, letting her own grow cold while she peppered him with questions about his day. Only her expression held something back, and this only in part—a tiny obtuse smile that hovered about her mouth like a presence, as if something had come down around her, sealing her off from the rest of us. She wore it most often when she looked at my father, though it vanished if he happened to glance in her direction, her eyes darting sideways and one hand fluttering to her throat. An oddness would enter my father then, and he would lean forward, chin jutting, to stare in measuring silence while no one breathed and we all waited out the ticking of the clock.

Although I never engaged him on the topic, years of observation led me to conclude that my father regarded the Holy Spirit as little more than a fraction within the divine equation of God the Father. If Lawrence Philip Hamilton's wife had suddenly and dramatically been chosen as the Good Lord's mouthpiece, that was the extent of it—God came, spoke, and left; the woman herself constituted no more than a simple entry and exit zone. Certainly, it gave her no call to set watch on her husband—judging and holding her own thoughts as if she were more than a simple vessel, as if the Holy Spirit actually resided within her, holding private consultations that made her answerable to no one. At the Waiting for the Rapture End Times Tabernacle, my father stood in awe before the Divine Sister and her oracles as was required of every deacon in the congregation; within the confines of home and family, my mother answered to him.

She did her best to reflect his expectations—down to the meek hunch of her shoulders and the defeated shuffle in her walk—but that odd flicker remained in her eyes, and her mouth continued to curve into its mystery smile. During the first few months after the Tongue of Fire claimed my mother, I often came upon my father staring at her over the top of a newspaper or peeking around an open doorway, watching as she worked; but however much he prowled, she kept her truest moments from him. Instead she allowed me to discover her seated on the living room couch, moaning over the Bible in her lap and rocking with growing intensity until her hands abruptly shot upward and she began crying out in wild, beautiful sounds. For weeks after her initial Tongue of Fire, she spent hours each day crying out in a strange, glad voice, and when I tried to imitate her, dancing and flapping my arms like a bird, she laughed and drew me close. What followed then is difficult to explain—like quick spun gold, an essence or vibration passed from her chest into mine, filling me with such high-frequency bliss that I leaped about squealing until exhaustion collapsed me to the floor.

One afternoon soon after this, my father returned unexpectedly from work to find us, hands upraised and making incomprehensible noises as tears ran down our laughing faces. No Tongue of Fire burned upon my head—both my mother and I understood full well that I had been caught up merely in the echo of her ecstasy—but all my father saw was his little girl dressed in a bed sheet, spinning circles and squeaking gibberish. Without a word, he scooped me up and carried me to my room, where he locked me in. Then, returning to my mother in the living room, he launched himself, the sounds of his attack traveling muffled through my bedroom wall—the body thuds, my mother's repeated grunts, and the one odd cry that ended it.

Thus ended our daily ecstasy sessions, and from that time forth, if my mother caught me speaking gibberish or dancing alone in my room, she would shush me, saying, "Go talk to your father. You should spend more time with your father." But the Sunday following that beating, the Tongue of Fire descended upon her with startling brilliance, and utterances spilled from her lips in heightened rapture. My father must have taken note, for several days later, when this state of bliss faded, he took her into their room and beat her again. Violence was not new to their relationship, but until that point, his attacks had been erratic and rare. Inevitably, this changed as it became obvious that the worse the beating he meted out, the more fervently she called upon the transcendent the subsequent Sunday, and the brighter the Tongue of Fire glowed upon her head.

Wisely, my father chose never to compete with my mother in public. In spite of the fact that he was the free-walking deacon, the board member, and the man who cleared his thick bull throat to read Scriptures at Sunday services, he faded to insignificance in the Divine Sister's presence, reduced to little more than her escort. Behind the scenes, however, he kept my mother in a state of carefully pitched anguish—his beatings most vicious before the church's high holy days, when an especially grand display was required of the Divine Sister. Though I saw this process repeat frequently over the years, I was well into adolescence before I realized that my parents despised one another. For no matter what occurred between them, they continued to converse at meals as they had always done, my mother maintaining her suppertime ritual of washing my father's feet, kissing his head, and serving his meal before her own. And from the sounds that came to me after the house lights had been turned out, it was evident they continued to engage in sex.

At some stage, my father must have become aware of the affair between my mother and Pastor Playle, but the knowledge did not seem to anger him; instead, he grew more cocksure—a few words from him, and the mighty pastor and Divine Sister would topple from their blessed thrones. I do not know what kind of bargain the three of them struck, but over the years, my father's position at the Waiting for the Rapture End Times Tabernacle accumulated the type of power that directs from behind the scenes, where everything thrives on silence.

• • •

"He thinks his tongue is a cock," complained Jez.

"You wish," Dee said lazily.

It was mid-November during another one of Jez's midnight escapes, several hours into her eighteenth birthday. To celebrate her officially becoming legal, the two of them were consuming the obligatory Molson Canadian, along with a shared joint and half a dozen cupcakes, as they sprawled on the brown plaid couch in bras and jeans.

"All he can do with it is thrust," Jez finished triumphantly. Knowing she had scored a point, she settled against the back of the couch, waiting, and was rewarded by the small smile that slipped across Dee's mouth.

"Show me," Dee singsonged, the smile playing with itself, disappearing, reappearing.

"It'd wreck the ambiance," Jez replied mournfully. In one corner a lava lamp oozed out the perfect atmosphere, the room as vague and slip-sliding as the smile on Dee's lips; beyond the wall opposite, reality was a deep-shadowed dream kept at bay by the red-handled jackknife, which protruded from its storage site in Farrah Fawcett's face. Still, the place was gradually losing its resonance, a by now familiar sensation— over the last few weeks, Jez had become well acquainted with "bye-bye to the high." It wasn't the best omen for comparing notes on the kissing techniques of Eleusis Collegiate's male students, an increasingly frequent pastime; since October,

Dee had demonstrated the modus operandi of every point of interest on the senior football and basketball teams. Until this moment, however, Jez had been on the receiving end, and to contemplate reversing these roles was dizzying.

"No joke," she warned as she hovered above Dee's smirking mouth, choosing the moment, the *exact* moment to begin. "He thinks he's an elephant."

"C'mere, Elmer," teased Dee, slouching lower. "De-mon-strate."

"First kisses are usually good," Jez lied, leaning through the last second of anticipation into desire, double desire—lips that brushed and whispered, whimpered and wished.

"This ain't no guy," breathed Dee.

Without warning, Jez stabbed with a rigid tongue and Dee shrank back, grimacing. "The boy needs lessons," she muttered, wiping her mouth in disgust.

Straightening, Jez smiled grimly. "Who's going to coach him?" she asked. "First string?"

"The experts," said Dee.

"Sure like to meet *them*," muttered Jez, reaching for a nearby bag of barbecue chips and picking through the entrails.

The object of their discussion was a certain George Kovacs, a senior football player who had transferred to Eleusis Collegiate in his grad year due to its superior football program. New to Dee as well as to most of the student body, he lit up daily with the smoking elite—the jock smokers in their jock cars in the jock area of the student parking lot—and had only recently noticed Jez among the smoking proletariat. When he had asked the rest of the first string about her, they had assigned him the task of checking out her finer details. Every lunch hour since had been spent necking in his Impala, Jez insistent things be kept above the waist, and to her relief, while George pawed, groped, and made sounds like a drowning man, he didn't color outside the lines she drew for him; this wasn't Dinky's party—she could kiss for free, tease, and pull back. Or so it seemed until later, when she met up with George's school-hall grin and the grins of his friends—the way their eyes honed in as if they held some secret knowledge about her, a certain knowing of something that hadn't yet happened but would.

Across the walls, the lava lamp's glow slid through itself, constantly shape-shifting as it flirted with the room's shadows. Watching it, Jez felt herself begin to detach and lift out of her body—a sensation that was occurring less frequently now that the memory of the rape was retreating into the back annals of her mind.

"How many times have you made out with him so far?" asked Dee, her eyes closed as if in deep thought.

"Seven," said Jez, her cheeks taking on a faint heat. "You already know that."

"He get under your shirt yet?" asked Dee.

"Yeah," muttered Jez.

"*Details*, Jezzie," ordered Dee, opening her eyes.

"Why are you interested?" Jez stalled, balling up the chips bag and bouncing it off the other girl's forehead. "The last two times, okay?"

"You take off your bra?" asked Dee, perking up.

"No!" said Jez.

"He take it off?" asked Dee.

"Not yet," said Jez.

"What a polite young man," mused Dee. "How much d'you like him?"

Jez shrugged and Dee shrugged back, their grins effortless and light-headed. From the alley came the contented sound of a car idling past; slowing to a halt, it reversed until it sat with its headlights flush on the window.

"Midnight cowboy," teased Dee, her eyes fixed on Jez's. "Ready or not, here he comes."

Out in the alley, a car door opened and a male voice called, "Hey, Jez!"

Astonished, Jez sat up, her mouth soundlessly open as she stared at the brilliant window. Then the headlights shut off and the window went dark, returning the room to the dim ooze of the lava lamp. Again the voice in the alley called, "Jez!" but she remained glued to the couch, one hand necklacing her throat. Beside her, Dee's eyes were an unreadable glimmer, that indolent smile once again playing her mouth. Getting to her feet, Dee crossed to the window, opened it, and leaned out into the black November wind.

"You looking for the birthday girl?" she called.

George's voice paused, taking its time. "I think so," he drawled in reply.

It took all of two seconds for Jez to realize she had been set up. George hadn't been tipped off as to her after-midnight whereabouts by *her*—she hadn't known she would be here herself until a quarter after midnight, when she had heard Dee's coded horn honk down the block. So it was Dee who must have invited him, lured him over with promises of...*what?* Apprehensive, Jez mulled over the possibilities. With Dee

Eccles, those could include anything—nirvana, sticky fingers, the Apocalypse. Pushing up from the couch, she crossed to the window and leaned out beside Dee, who promptly pulled back, leaving Jez alone with the cold rise of her skin and the low-cut, ice-blue bra she had been given upon arrival. With an audible gasp, George stepped forward, his eyes widening.

"Coming up?" called Dee from deep inside the room. "Stairs are at the side."

Instantly, George lunged to the left, the staircase thundering under his charge.

"You invited him here!" accused Jez, turning to Dee, who was watching her, face inscrutable. "You—"

The door swung open, taking Farrah Fawcett's knifed face in against the wall. "Okay, so I'm here!" grinned George, stumbling into the room. "Birthday party's on now!"

Without missing a beat, Dee pointed at the bed. "All hands on deck," she said.

"No shit!" said George, diving onto Marilyn and rolling onto his back.

"Kissing lessons, Jez," said Dee, giving her a pointed glance. Then, crawling onto the bed, she leaned over George's wide-eyed grin. "Okay, George," she said. "This is the scoop. You're a lovely, well-bred boy, but you need expertise in the kissing department."

"What's the matter with my kissing?" asked George, his eyes darting toward Jez.

"Hey," teased Dee, straddling him. "Good kissers get *everything* they want in life. You want to get *everything* you want, don't you?"

"Oh yeah," George muttered agreeably, his hands sliding

up her thighs and hooking into the front pockets of her jeans. With a smile, Dee leaned forward, her purr almost audible, then pulled back at the very last second as George's tongue shot out, rigid and wiggling at the tip.

"Uh-uh," she said, her tone lightly scolding. "No tongue."

"No tongue!" said George, his entire body convulsing.

"And stick your hands under your butt," Dee added firmly. "You are going to spend the next while thinking about your lips, boy. *Just* the lips."

"Slave driver," muttered George, but he put his hands away.

"That's a good slave," purred Dee. "Now, we're going to take turns. No tongue for anyone until Jezzie says so. Jezzie's the birthday girl, and she's in charge here."

Again she leaned forward, then pulled back swiftly as George's tongue shot out and his hands jerked free. "No, no, no!" she scolded, slapping them off. "No dessert if you don't eat your din-din."

"Sorry," grunted George. "Habit."

Cautiously, Jez edged onto the side of the bed. The stunned rush that had hit when Dee had initially straddled George was now gone, and she was riding a wave of frank curiosity. *Seeking*, she sensed it in the air—two girls on the hunt, and the innocent, easily led boy on the bed had no idea. Eagerly, he tongued another foray into Dee's mouth and she nipped him sharply on the nose.

"Bad boy, George," Dee scolded, frowning down at him. "Bad boys have got to learn the hard way."

"Hard?" said George, grinning at Jez. "Did someone say 'hard'?"

Reaching under the pillow beside his head, Dee pulled out a pair of nylons, knotted one of the legs around George's left wrist, and tied it to the headboard.

"Hey!" he protested, but continued to grin as she tied his other hand.

"Hey nothing," soothed Dee, pushing his sweatshirt up his chest and over his head until it rode his wrists. "We'll make it worth your while. You know that, don't you, Georgie-Boy?"

"Yeah, I've heard," muttered George, quivering as her fingers ran his chest. "Okay, so this is the deal," he added gruffly. "You can tie me up, but no one's telling no one, or all the girls in Eleusis will think they can have their way with me."

"Deal?" questioned Dee, that unreadable glint back in her eyes. "Who's talking deal here? You're *already* tied up."

George's grin faltered. "You need me to play," he said.

"We have you," said Dee. Straightening, she unhooked her bra and teased it across his face. "You do want to play, don't you?" she asked liltingly.

Catching the bra between his teeth, George grunted, "Yeah, I want to play." Then he grinned, the weak grin of someone trapped in a turn-on nightmare, and the room began to breathe differently—shadows leaning in, the nebulous light of the lava lamp touching any which way it wanted. Taut and predatory, Dee leaned over the boy on the bed, a faint red glow haloing her head. For a moment it was all locked eyes and staring thought, everyone hesitating on the threshold of intent. Gingerly, Jez edged in beside George and slid her hand onto the leanness of his belly. He was at their mercy now, the knowing slurred in his eyes, but even so she couldn't pull back from the taunt of her hands—their delicate stroke across his nipple as he lay, mouth tightening, trying to hold sound in.

But nothing was going to hold sound in here—Jez knew this as she knew the animal in her skin that was opening its mouth onto the boy's throat and sucking his startled pulse, counting heartbeats, letting him know she knew the rapid thud of each one. Dee was again at his mouth; Jez could hear the give of their lips as Dee kissed, pulled back, scolded gently, and kissed again, George swearing, "It's a habit, a goddamn habit!" Leaving the shadowy beginnings of a hickey on his sweating throat, Jez journeyed the maze of George's ear on the tip of her tongue, whispering obscenities, all the soft obscenities she whispered only to herself alone in bed, because that was how alone this boy was now.

"Shi-shi-shi*t*," he muttered endlessly. "Shii—" Drifting a dreamy pulse across his cheek, Jez watched Dee hover above George's mouth, conversing in the endless monologue of loneliness that, was the game of her lips, and then the other girl was beckoning her in, George pulling convulsively at the nylons that bound him as Jez's hair slid down around his face and she began kissing him softly, so softly you would think she was barely there at all.

His tongue shot out to catch her—frog after a fly—but the tease was full in her, murmuring, "Uh-uh." Trapped and helpless, George grinned, begging for more, but suddenly she was filled with the thought of his left nipple and had to run her tongue over it, just *had* to, choreographing each of his whole-body shudders with her soft, sure licks. More obsessions followed, Jez flitting tangential as a butterfly from nipple to belly hair to the large chestnut birthmark just inside the musky-scented waist of his jeans. Once again at his mouth, Dee was still coming and going, but kissing longer now that the boy's tongue was staying put, learning its place under the whimsy of girls. Licking a languorous trail up George's chest, Jez paused, her face an inch from Dee's, and they observed one another through heavy-lidded eyes, their mouths puffy with kissing, their breathing sultry and sweet, exquisite with knowing.

"You slut," whispered Dee.

"You wish," Jez smiled, and the other girl retreated, leaving her the stretched-out boy. Sliding full onto him, Jez kissed and kissed his mouth with an abandon she gave only her pillow, slipping her tongue into his whimpering cries, both of them sucking and straining, wild to go deeper, deeper in. From behind, she felt hands tugging at her waist, pulling off her jeans and panties, and then a fully naked Dee was edging her off George and straddling his hips, laughing down at the quivering pulse that was his mouth.

"C'mere," she said, pulling Jez onto his hips in front of her so they both sat facing him, Jez taking the full weight of his stare as Dee hooked her arms and pulled them back, stretching her as taut as the watching boy, both of them an offering laid out and begging for mercy.

"Watch, George, watch," Dee whispered as she gathered Jez's hair off her shoulders and twisted it behind her back, cupped her hands under Jez's breasts, and stroked the blue lace bra. Placing a thumb in Jez's mouth, she let her suck, then circled a nipple, wetting it through the bra. "Like this, George," she sang softly, her bare hot nipples pressed to the skin of Jez's back as George rocked under them both, his eyes riveted to the thumb and its wet circling. Mouth gone slack, Jez arced backward against the other girl, her face buried in Dee's hair, her hands curved helpless with wonder at her sides. Between her legs beat a dense slickness; her face kneaded Dee's neck; slowly, *slowly* the blue lace bra came undone, George crying a single dusky "Duh!" as Jez's sobbing mouth found Dee's and they were kissing kissing kissing, George's hips insistent against them both.

"You want me to take this one?" asked Dee, and Jez pleaded at the raw knowing in her face. Swiftly, the other girl unzipped George's jeans and slid herself onto the full reddish-purple cock. "C'mere," she whispered again, guiding Jez through a half-turn on George's hips so the two girls sat facing each other. Reaching around Jez's buttocks, Dee pulled her in and they rocked in sync, quick jabs that had George gusting toward a wild climax, then a shuddering, gasping quiet.

"Shh," murmured Dee, "he'll be hard in a sec," and he was, the girls riding more deliberately this time, paying the boy no notice except for the way he anchored them together, their hands clutching each other's asses tight. "This is the way, George, this is the way," Dee crooned, the red halo darkening about her head as they started in on the third fuck, George grunting his repeated "Shishi*t*," everything going deeper, full of slow, fierce moaning. Briefly then, above Dee's head, Jez saw it—the skinned-raw ferret face of her demon, manifesting clearly and peering down at the three of them like a demented celestial guardian. At the same moment, Dee began to babble, her voice tiny and high, whispering, "Can you find me? Can you find me? Can you find me?"

Without warning, George started thrusting violently, the girls clinging so tightly, Jez found bruises the next day. After he had climaxed, Dee slid off him into a shuddery fetal ball, and Jez followed, wrapping the other girl's body with her own until Dee had moaned her way into a strange drop-off sleep. Slowly then, almost reluctantly, Jez turned back to the boy on her other side and saw his stretched-out body, cock again at full length. Their eyes met and she realized he had opened onto some new place; tears tracked his face; he stared as if her hands had dipped beneath his skin and stolen trinkets of his flesh.

"Ride me, Jez," he begged gruffly. "Would you just fuckin' ride?"

It was then that it came to her, finally, the gift Dee had laid out for her: the body of a boy wondering and helpless, a boy opened as deep as the rape at Dinky's party had opened her. No, deeper; this soft seeking, this gentle, merciless finding out had teased the two of them further and further into themselves, deeper than fear. Rising onto her haunches, Jez took his cock into herself and touched its tip to her inside place like a promise. Healing groans rose from her, the cries of the damned; she rode the boy like a resurrection—the end of everything, everything she knew.

After, she lay beside him, stroking the sweat from his upper lip as he breathed and breathed. "Jez," he whispered, his closed eyelids fluttering. "Cut me loose, would ya? Please?"

Rising, she pulled the jackknife from its guardian position in the door and cut the nylons from his wrists. Then, arms around her knees, she watched from beside Dee's sleeping body as George dressed and left without a backward glance for her, the bed, or the gloating depths of the cave-like room.

NINE

After the first several years, there was a period during which my mother's prophecies occurred less frequently. A visitation from the Tongue of Fire could no longer be expected weekly—indeed, it often materialized no more than once a month; the signs that foretold its coming, however, remained unchanged. Midweek, my mother's pupils began to swell and she would pace the house, stopping for long periods to stand staring into that high, bright kingdom visible only to her. By Friday, the trembling overtook her and she would sit by the living room window, her limbs consumed by small shudders, even her closed eyelids quivering as the thousand delicate wings in her skin struggled to lift free. This shuddering gradually increased, until by Saturday afternoon she was overtaken by major tremors, her eyes rolling back and spittle flying from her lips as my father tied her wrists and ankles to their bed with soft cloths to keep her from rolling to the floor. Curiously, each Saturday evening, her symptoms deserted her; as the moon rose, her tremors ceased and my father untied her, leaving her free to creep about the house, hiss-whispering as she pursued her divine nocturnal quest.

The following morning, she was generally still tremor-free, but based on the signs of the past few days, my father would call ahead to inform Pastor Playle that the Divine Sister looked ready to prophesy. The Hamilton family then made the crosstown drive to church, my mother wearing her best white felt hat and a pronounced quiet radiance. Upon arrival, my father would tell me to make myself useful distributing Sunday school papers to the various basement classrooms, and he and my mother would climb the stairs to Pastor Playle's second-floor office, a spacious room with windows overlooking the church parking lot but none in the door that faced the hall. At age eleven, this left me with no way to spy on what happened next—the door was unusually thick, and the walls conducted only vague sounds that could not compete with the grumble of cars in the parking lot and the bustle of church members arriving in the downstairs lobby.

In spite of these obstacles, on Sundays when the signs were clear, I settled myself resolutely onto the floor opposite Pastor Playle's door and refused to budge until my mother emerged from the office. Pleas made by Sunday school teachers and offers of Freshie or cookies were to no avail; if force was exerted, I returned it with such desperation that the well-intentioned deacon or Women's Auxiliary Prayer Group member admonished me with a flustered "Well, keep quiet and don't bother none of the classes," and left me with my eyes glued to the closed door. I could not have explained then why I felt the way I did—although I had witnessed the solstice angels pass over Pastor Playle, as well as the white-winged entity that had invaded my mother's body, no direct evidence yet implicated the good pastor in what I considered to be my mother's demise. Still, I knew that some kind of changing spell had been cast upon my family; since we had begun attending the Waiting for the Rapture End Times Tabernacle, my parents and I had altered greatly, and every difference in our lives seemed to point directly to Pastor Playle.

So on Sundays when the signs augured well, I hunkered down in the upper church hallway opposite Pastor Playle's office, convinced that nefarious deeds were being perpetrated upon my mother therein. Though only muffled undefined sounds came through to me, my suspicions were confirmed the moment the door opened and the good pastor and my father emerged with the stranger who had once again been installed in my mother's place—the Divine Sister, her face drawn and stricken, tremors haunting her limbs. As I rose to my feet, Pastor Playle and my father would glare, but my mother remained oblivious, leaning heavily on both men's arms and taking minute shuffling steps along the hall.

Several times I rushed after her, tried to take her arm and help lead her, but she did not even turn her head as my father tore my hand unceremoniously away. Once, however, Pastor Playle had to return to his office for something he had forgotten, and I quickly snatched up the Divine Sister's empty, twitching hand. Instantly, a current leaped between our palms, and I felt an energy shift inside the woman beside me as if some kind of struggle was taking place. Slowly, her face turned toward me and she knew me; my mother touched me on the cheek and whispered, "Mary-Eve. You are my lovely Mary-Eve."

But at that moment Pastor Playle returned, pulled her hand firmly from my face, and said, "Divine Sister, the Lord waits. We must not tarry." For one raw second, I watched fear rise up and sear my mother's face. Then distance fell across it, and she was again gazing into that faraway shimmering landscape that called to her alone. Without protest, she allowed herself to be led into a small room behind the sanctuary where a contraption known as the red velvet box was stored—a velvet-covered, wheeled wooden cubicle containing a bench that had been constructed after her first national-conference prophecy session, due to concerns over the unsightliness of the Divine Sister's convulsions. Alone in the hallway, I waited, and within minutes saw Pastor Playle wheel out the box, its red velvet drapes closed so nothing of its interior could be seen. Right on the good pastor's heels, I followed the velvet box's progress along the corridor and into the sanctuary, where it was positioned next to the podium. Here it remained, as it did every Sunday, drapes drawn firmly closed while my mother waited inside its cloistered darkness so no member of the congregation would be distracted by her facial grimaces and tremors until the moment of divine inspiration arrived.

For much of the service, the drapes remained shut. Hymns were sung, collection plates passed around, Scripture read, and all that was noted of the Divine Sister was an occasional thud from the box or a ripple passing through the velvet drapes. Each time this occurred, the congregation paused, their collective gaze fixing on the box as they awaited further signs, but when none came, they continued staunchly on, working themselves deeper into the customary rituals of faith. Morning could wear into early afternoon, the women halfway through packages of peppermints and the men trying for another chorus of "Amen!" and "Hallelujah, brother!" as Pastor Playle sweated and pounded the pulpit and I sat motionless in the third pew, stalked by fearful thoughts: *What if she's dead? What if she's lying cold and pale at the bottom of that box with a dead stopped heart? What if...*

Eventually, however, the red velvet box would begin to quiver and the drapes would draw slowly open. All eyes then converged upon the Divine Sister, displayed from the waist up by the box's front half-gate, her head banging erratically against the back wall and her body rigid and jerking. Finally, like a dove flown straight from the mind of God, the Tongue of Fire appeared above the box, its white fire beautiful and terrible to behold. Immediately, the Divine Sister called out to it, always at the same pitch, as if that note was its secret name, and the great light descended to rest upon her head.

With its coming, she lost all contact with the congregation seated before her, no longer seeing or knowing any of us. Sometimes at these moments, her face contorted with terror, her voice rose in a wailing cry, and she scratched at her arms as if covered in boils or insects. Other times, she was joyful, laughing as her eyes focused on something that seemed to hover directly before her. But, these moments of bliss notwithstanding, my mother's dry spells grew lengthier—so much so that by the end of my eleventh year they threatened to destroy her reputation as an inspired prophetess. What was most bewildering about these periods was the lack of divine illumination as to their cause or purpose; they remained a mystery as unexplained as the initial Tongue of Fire itself. Dissatisfied by the Divine Sister's reticence on the subject, members of the congregation began to come up with their own explanations. Rumors abounded, and in an attempt to curtail speculation, Pastor Playle started meeting with my mother daily. National elders were called in for healing sessions, even an exorcism undertaken, but to no avail—the Tongue of Fire decreased its appearances to every other week, then once a month, and it seemed paler, a paltry whimper of flame rather than the fierce burning core it had once been. In tandem, the Divine Sister's prophetic ability ebbed, and attendance at the Waiting for the Rapture End Times Tabernacle declined. Bible in lap, my mother continued to moan and call out from the living room couch, but nothing answered her, and at night the beings with which she communed seemed less luminous and the circuit throbbing in the house walls fainter, as if it were being called back to its source.

One evening, after a five-week dry spell, my mother stood at the kitchen sink washing dishes and staring out into a vast snow-falling dusk. As I leaned against the counter beside her, holding a tea towel, there came a moment when I felt her slow as if coming into a profound internal pause; the very lungs of the evening seemed to stop breathing. Then, without taking her eyes from the world beyond the window, my mother reached into the drying rack and took hold of a bread knife. Calmly raising it to her cheek, she slashed twice before

I was able to pull it from her hand. Bright blood streamed from her skin, and she sank sobbing to her knees as I ran, bread knife in hand, to fetch my father. When we returned, she was sitting quietly in a chair, staring straight ahead and showing no awareness of the bleeding gashes in her face.

Still holding the bread knife, I danced around my father in terrified steps, waiting for him to rush to my mother and stanch the blood flow, speak, do *something*...but instead he stood motionless in the doorway, watching intently as the pupils of her eyes dilated. A tremor erupted through my mother's limbs, followed by another, and still my father stood watching as thought crawled across his face. Finally, he turned without a word and fetched the first-aid kit, then cleaned and bandaged my mother's wounds and led her to their bed. Within minutes, he returned to find me standing where he had left me, my body caught in its own quick trembling and my eyes wide and staring, fixed on the opposite wall.

"Damn you," he yelled, "don't even think about it!" and slapped me hard across the face. Startled, I was knocked temporarily adrift, floating high above my body, but I was drawn irresistibly back by the harsh burn on my cheek and the sensation of gripping the bread knife so tightly that later my hand ached. As I descended once again into my flesh, a memory, almost forgotten in its two-year absence, returned to me, and I found myself standing between kitchen light and a dark, shadowy place, surrounded by robed chanting figures; in some deep, dream-laced trance, I raised the blade covered with my mother's blood and tilted its slow, strange meaning toward my father's throat. All of a sudden, he and I were struggling, his hands forcing the knife from mine. Only when it had been lifted free, when he had turned and thrown the bloody weapon into the kitchen sink, was I released from that dark inner place, and loud wails burst from my mouth.

"Go to your room!" he shouted, and I ran for my bed, diving into its warm cave and the all-around thud of my heart.

The following day, the signs were again upon us, and that Sunday, the Tongue of Fire rose above my mother's scabbed face like the pillar of light that led the Israelites through the desert darkness. No one, as far as I know, ever questioned my father's cover story about an attack by a neighborhood dog, and for a brief time the Tongue of Fire regained its brilliance, the Divine Sister recommenced her eerily accurate predictions, and attendance at the Waiting for the Rapture End Times Tabernacle surged. And so when the Tongue of Fire next began to fade, my mother knew what had to be done, and cut surreptitiously at her upper arms and inner thighs where the wounds could be hidden, until my father locked the household knives in his toolbox, fearing she would dig deeper than he could patch.

To compensate, my mother began throwing herself off the second-floor landing, allowing her body to crumple and slide down the stairs without making any attempt to protect her face or head. By this means, she circumvented potential dry spells—if the signs had not appeared by midweek, the staircase between the first and second floors became her solution. After her first few "tumbles," she started to protect her face, and my father eventually installed a thick carpet to prevent bone fractures. I do not know what other church members made of the dark welts that appeared on my mother's arms and legs; time and time again, I watched their gaze glaze over and slide across them without comment. I, however, never got used to seeing the purple-black marks on her arms, never reconciled myself to the red velvet box and its manufactured display.

One Sunday when I was twelve, the Divine Sister waited to prophesy until the very end of the service, and the hoarse and guttural message that spewed from her mouth left her drained and semiconscious. After the doxology, the congregation departed quickly to rescue simmering pot roasts; once everyone had left, my father and Pastor Playle together carried my mother's limp body upstairs to the pastoral office. Quite by accident, this unforeseen combination of circumstances left the red velvet box unguarded by the podium.

In the four years since its inception, I had never examined the box up close, for my mother's cage was treated like the Ark of the Covenant—kept in a locked room and wheeled into the sanctuary just before the service, then wheeled back out immediately afterward, as if a bolt of lightning would strike dead anyone who touched it without permission. That day, entirely alone in the sanctuary, I sat aiming vicious kicks at the pew in front of me as tears streamed down my face. Still aching from the loss of Louisie years earlier, I was being forced to live my life with only a small percentage of my mother available to me, and that box seemed to contain the rest of her. Slowly, knowing full well that what I was about to do was absolutely forbidden, I stood, slid myself out of the pew, and walked the center aisle toward the velvet box.

Gold script ran along the top, and images had been embroidered onto both drapes—an altar, a pillar of fire, Jesus standing with His right hand raised and a halo about His head. Circling the box, I ran my hands over the velvet material that had been stapled to the sides, seeking the presence of my mother there the way she felt out my bedroom vibrations during her nightly prowls. Close to the box's bottom, on the side that faced the podium, I found a tiny lightbulb that the Divine Sister obviously used to signal Pastor Playle when she was ready to prophesy, but I felt nothing of my mother, nothing that would even hint at her ever having been inside this contraption.

Kneeling in front of the box, I pressed my forehead to the ground and asked God's forgiveness for what I was about to do. Then I stood and pulled the drapes aside, opened the half-gate, and saw the well-padded walls, the braces and buckles, the harness meant to fit around the waist, and the soft shackles intended for wrists and ankles. Finally, I understood the reason the velvet box was always wheeled into the sanctuary with my mother already inside it—the congregation was never to see the Divine Sister tied up like a common dog, a marionette tangled in its strings.

Heart pounding, I climbed into the box and closed the half-gate, then sat staring out at the empty sanctuary, imagining my mother's view of the families who came, dressed in their Sunday best, to see if the Divine Sister would survive this week's visitation of the Holy Spirit. It was like a lottery—she had been chosen, my mother truly was a chosen one, bearing agony alone while everyone else got off scot-free. Next to my left hand, I noticed a small button that probably set the signal light flashing for Pastor Playle, and the lever that opened and closed the drapes. Carefully, I strapped myself into the Divine

Sister's harness, slipped my feet inside her shackles, closed my eyes as I imagined she must do, and waited.

For a second there was nothing—only an impression of vast restless emptiness—but gradually the darkness inside my head began to quiver, as if something was shifting the fabric of my mind, trying to make contact. Abruptly, I felt a sense of deepening, and a tilting and turning, and finally I thought I saw a glowing figure with wings take shape in the distance, then turn and start toward me.

At that moment, my father appeared at the half-gate, yanked it open, and pulled me out of the harness. "Blasphemy!" he screamed hysterically into my face. "You commit blasphemy! Don't you know you could be struck dead for this, Mary-Eve?"

• • •

The staircase was a long gray thought rising out of colorless earth, each step cracked and hollowed, the handrail filmed with frost. Alone with the late afternoon, Jez climbed slowly, withered leaves gusting in heavy breaths about her feet. At the landing she paused as she always did, poised in that moment scraped clean by wind and sky and gazing out over a collage of shingled rooftops and the stark arms of trees. *Empty*, the thought came to her, for no reason she could discern. *All of them empty and waiting.*

Within the hour, the horizon would flush plum and apricot, the trees darken to a black tangle of nerves. Gently, Jez tested the doorknob, then opened it without knocking. The note she had found inside her locker that morning had said the door would be unlocked and Dee would meet her here at four but had given no explanation for the other girl's all-day absence. Stepping across the threshold, Jez closed the door and looked around the room. At 3:40, she was early—had rushed out of her last class wanting the chance to stand alone in this place and soak in the gray slanted light.

Outside, the wind let out a long December moan, a sound that seemed to ooze directly out of the garage's walls, and not for the first time Jez felt the cold sadness that darkened these corners—the kind felt while drawing a finger across a damp windowpane, realizing touch was the only truth that could give a clear view of the world. As usual, the room was teasing her mind, pulling it into a between-thoughts kind of realm, the air floating with dust motes, bits of the lower brain surfacing to touch light. And, Jez realized, bringing with them the shadow heartbeat that found her at moments like these—a soft, slurred pulse that followed her own so closely, it seemed to envelop her with each beat. It had been a while since she had heard this second heartbeat—*months*, she thought, listening carefully—and it came to her now like a forgotten scent, lost tendrils of the mind. As if in a trance, she blinked, sleepy and deep-awake. Each time she came to this room she felt it more clearly, a shadowy inner landscape that was texture rather than image—a dark pulsing cave like that of The Chosen Ones, but deeper. Much deeper.

Like a womb, she thought, gazing around herself. *But empty, always empty. As if*— Flinching from the thought, she hesitated, then forced herself back to it. *As if it's always been empty. As if there never was another. As if others are just a game, a trick of the mind, and aloneness the true way of things.*

The true way of things, she thought, the phrase repeating itself bleakly inside her head. *Waiting, always waiting for the aloneness to change.*

From the alley came the sound of the garage's ground-level door; glancing out the window, Jez saw Dee's father lift open the door and disappear inside. Instinctively, she pulled back. Her contact with Mr. Eccles to date had been limited to brief hellos, nods of the head, and one prolonged encounter. The latter had taken place in the Eccles' kitchen a few weeks earlier, Jez seated across the table from the brawny fifty-something gentleman while Dee perched on his knee, giggling and cooing, almost... *Well, flirting with her dad!* Jez had thought, taken aback. Over by the sink, Mrs. Eccles had stood witness, flashing jewelry and ominously silent as she took in every smirking detail. Including the moment, Jez recalled uneasily, when her husband had glanced directly at Jez and given her a wink unmistakable in its meaning—unmistakable, that is, if it had come from a stranger staggering out of a late-night bar or a hotel called the Babylon Arms.

The episode had given Jez the unmitigated creeps, and she had avoided Dee's father ever since; now, as he backed his '72 Ford out of the garage, then got out to close the door, she pressed herself to the window frame's outer edge and watched, tracking his movements until he returned to his car and drove off. Even then she stood motionless, observing the deserted alley and wondering what it would be like to live in a household where everyone walked around constantly carrying knives—visible and invisible—the way this one did. As far as she knew, no one had yet drawn blood from anyone else, but collectively the Eccles family left Abraham and Isaac in millennia-old dust.

At that moment, footsteps started up the outside staircase, the wood absorbing the sharp kick of high heels. Coming out of her thoughts with a start, Jez dropped onto the couch and slid a cigarette from the half-empty pack on the coffee table. Then, assuming a casual pose, she dragged in heavily and exhaled a sultry tease-line of smoke just as the door opened… and Dee's mother walked in.

"Jez!" she said in her throaty drawl, giving the jackknife an amused glance as she closed the door. "I'm so glad you got my note."

"*Your* note?" gulped Jez, staring in astonishment. Then, realizing she was in the presence of an adult, somebody's *mother*, she straightened, stubbed out her cigarette, and placed both feet on the floor.

Another amused smile slip-slid across Mrs. Eccles's face. "I asked Andy to tape it to your locker on his way to work," she said lightly, "but I'm never sure if he *quite* hears what I say. You know boys." With a swipe, she cleared the love seat of laundry and sat down. "I think it's time we had a little chat, don't you?" Leaning forward, she slid a cigarette from Dee's pack and lit up.

"About what?" Jez asked guardedly. Over the last few months, she had learned to be wary of extended conversation with Mrs. Eccles, and today's chitchat promised more than the usual hazards—apart from their shoes, she and the woman opposite were dressed like identical twins. When Jez had opened her locker earlier that morning and discovered a sequined denim shirt, Levi's 501s, and a gold chain necklace, she had assumed they had been deposited there by Dee, who knew her combination. Apparently, however, Andy knew it as well. Faintly, Jez wondered if she and Mrs. Eccles were wearing matching underwear.

"Oh, *well*," said Dee's mother. "I got you that prescription, so I thought I should be responsible and check up on you, that's all." Coolly, she ran her gaze over Jez's outfit. Not a flicker of surprise crossed her face.

"I'm fine," mumbled Jez.

"Oh, I *know* you are," Mrs. Eccles assured her. "But I thought...Well, if you have any questions...about the pill, sex, men—*anything at all...*" Looking like a low score on a *Charlie's Angels* IQ test, she smiled dazzlingly. "Well, just feel free to ask."

Eyes narrowing, Jez ran her gaze in turn over the woman across from her, then simply shrugged and allowed an uncomfortable silence to swallow the room. In the ensuing pause, Mrs. Eccles's smile faded. Lifting her cigarette to her lips, she inhaled briskly, the sound of the smoke's inner progress clearly audible in the lengthening quiet.

"I see," she said finally, a carefully sharpened edge replacing her earlier drawl. "Dee underestimated you. You're no beginner, are you, Jez. My guess is that behind the scenes, you're quite an expert. That's a compliment, believe me. I admire a girl who can pull strings, handle what she gets, so I'll give it to you straight. I have a proposal to make. I know of certain gentlemen who would be interested in getting to *know* you, if you take my meaning. They're prepared to pay handsomely for your time, and the money would all be yours. Clothing and makeup would be supplied. The only commitment they would require of you is your silence. And that you're clean, of course."

"Clean?" stammered Jez, her mouth opening slightly.

"No VDs," said Mrs. Eccles, smiling.

Pain laced Jez, delicate and soundless. "Are *they* clean?" she asked hoarsely.

Mrs. Eccles's eyebrows lifted. "Of course," she replied.

Rigid, Jez sat encompassed by a body-wide heart thud as she was swamped by realization after realization: Dee, table-dancing at Dinky's party; the way she had taken on George so easily...*like a pro*; the identical slide-through smiles she and her mother had given after the kitchen-table discussion about Jez's birth control prescription.

"Why don't you discuss this with Dee?" continued Mrs. Eccles, apparently oblivious to Jez's stunned expression. "She can explain it so much better than me. It's really nothing like the stories you hear. A girl can make herself a lot of money for very little trouble, and Dee thinks you have so much potential."

So much potential, Jez repeated silently to herself, staggered, the pain this time anything but delicate. Every time she and Dee had kissed—every touch, every teasing comment...all of it being assessed as *potential*.

Blinking back tears, she squinted at the woman across from her; neither she nor Mrs. Eccles had turned on the lava lamp, and the window light was growing dim. Grimly, Jez peered through the gloom, determined to meet Dee's mother's gaze head on—get a fix on her, figure out the fundamental *lie* she exuded—and let loose a startled gasp. For directly opposite, hovering around Mrs. Eccles, was what appeared to be some sort of dark emanation. Not visible seconds before, and distinct from surrounding shadows, it could have been taken as a murky upper-body halo except for the fact that it shifted continually, like smoke or mist. Hair rising on the back of her neck, Jez tracked the dark outline's fluctuations. Whatever the *thing* was, it appeared to be able to manifest or conceal itself as it saw fit, like Dee's demon. Was that what this was then—a part of Mrs. Eccles that she had sent out of herself at some point in the past... perhaps when she was being raped?

Inside the room and out, dusk deepened, blurring surfaces, boundary lines, thought. Blank-faced, Dee's mother now sat motionless, as if shut down by an inner switch. Gradually, as Jez watched, the presence emanating from Mrs. Eccles took on a defined outline—hunched and multiheaded. At the same time, it began to speak, not in sound but with a kind of resonance that seemed to well up from inside Jez's mind.

You carry a wound, don't you, it sighed, its voice somewhere between a breath and a moan. *A wound that twists and groans, a secret private wound no one knows except you. You've buried it so deep that most of the time you're able to forget its hunger, but sometimes, sometimes when you're passing through doorways or looking into mirrors, it's here again—your lost part staring back at you with your own face. It's that part you long for, you long for...and it's still alive, haunting you from the other side and waiting for you.*

As Jez stared open-mouthed, Mrs. Eccles's stilled face became a miasma of darkness, the unfamiliar voice speaking through her many voices that whispered and overlapped. *It can be yours again*, murmured the shadowy weave of sound. *All you need do is find the place within you where the lost part passed through. That place is a gate. Approach and open it, call back what is yours, and it will bring with it all the power of the other side—more than anything you can imagine.*

Whisper-weaving and intense, the dark presence leaned toward Jez, enveloping her mind and making it difficult to think. *Open the gate*, it hissed. *Open; let the power through; become one of the few who join both worlds. Mysteries will be revealed; all things will come when you call; none will resist. All you need do is open the gate. Open the gate. Open…*

The few…the chosen *few…the lost part, the gate*: somewhere within herself, Jez had always known these were connected—her mother's life contained more than enough evidence to prove this. But the vibrations that ran through the Hamilton household, she thought, bewildered, were composed of light, not darkness. Was it possible there was more than one set of chosen few? Like the gray-robed guardians that had revealed themselves to her, did each chosen few inhabit a different plane of vibrations that contained its own gods and mysteries?

Still, regardless of the dark emanation's frequency, Jez understood immediately which wound it was targeting. Mired this deep in her own pain and loss, she could see it within herself—the gap Louisie had torn open during her tumultuous exit from the physical plane, shadowy and pulsing like a grounded butterfly. Just as Mrs. Eccles's emanation had said, that inner wound, hole, *gate* was still there. Did it lead to Louisie? After all these years, would it be possible now to pass through that wound and seek out her sister's soul, that sweet lost light and happiness, the certainty she had never been able to achieve on her own?

Louisie, Louisie—the name resonated through Jez, an ache, a longing she could taste and smell. Without conscious intention, she lifted a hand, as if reaching toward an invisible gate that she was about to unlatch and open. But before she could complete the gesture, a dense humming sensation pervaded her; then, to her astonishment, a semi-transparent gray-robed figure stepped directly out of her body. On its heels came the rest of The Chosen Ones, their curved knives raised in warning as they formed a protective half-circle about her and stood, humming low in their throats.

With their presence, Jez woke to the truth: The dark emanation opposite was not a lost part of Mrs. Eccles, but something from that other side of which it had spoken—an entity that had beguiled the woman into opening herself and inviting it in, just as Jez's mother had surrendered to similar deception…as Jez herself had been about to do, she realized, chagrined. Breathing deeply, she took on the same stance as the gray-robed figures that surrounded her, raised her left hand, and watched a curved spirit knife take shape between her fingers; as she brandished its tip at the dark entity, the presence emanating from Mrs. Eccles began to retreat. Then, as Jez stared, the murky haze around Dee's mother shrank and vanished, taking The Chosen Ones with it, and leaving only a woman and a girl sitting at dusk in an unlit room above a garage while withered leaves gusted the window.

A gasp sounded as Mrs. Eccles came back to herself, and she leaned forward, blinking rapidly while she stubbed out her cigarette. "Like I said, sweetie," she gushed. "You discuss it with Dee. *Think* about it. We'll certainly make it worth your while." Getting to her feet, she swept another amused glance around the room, her demeanor so cool and collected, so determinedly *suave*, Jez wondered if the woman remembered—even knew about—the entity that possessed her. "I do *so* like the way Dee lets her imagination run wild in here," Mrs. Eccles simpered. "Toodle-oo." With a flirty little wave, she let herself out the door.

Alone and sunk deep into her breathing, Jez sat, once again listening to the shadow heartbeat. "Louisie," she whispered, but all she got in response was that distant echo coming back from the other side, a vague answer to her own ongoing question, replying thud for thud. Longing flickered through Jez, multi-forked lightning along a horizon. Something had been left unfinished between Louisie and herself, and her twin seemed to sense it too. But how could they connect now, especially after The Chosen Ones, *her* Chosen Ones, had so obviously warned against reopening the death gate?

From outside came the sound of footsteps taking the stairs two at a time, and then the door swung open with such force, it was carried into the wall. Oblivious, Jez remained slumped and staring at an overflowing ashtray as Dee dropped her Adidas bag onto the floor and splayed across the bed.

"Your mother was here," Jez said dully.

"Oh yeah," said Dee, echoing her monotone.

"She had Andy leave a note in my locker," Jez continued, forcing her way through an explanation that obviously wasn't necessary. "I thought it was from you, so I came here for four o'clock, like the note said."

Silent, Dee played a finger across Marilyn's pursed lips.

"Cute little look-alike joke you all played on me," Jez added, anger creeping into her tone. "Is that how your mother dresses everyone she propositions, or just the ones she's sure of?"

"Fuck off," Dee said coolly, as if the words were hardly worth the effort.

"Oh," said Jez. "*Thanks* for the explanation."

"What d'you want explained?" asked Dee. Languorously, she yawned and stretched. "That I get fucked for money? That I'm part of my dad's business? Well, maybe not his *business*. Officially, he's an architect. Officially, I'm just recreation, like his buddies' daughters. They call us the 'Play Pen.'"

"This is what I would like explained, *please*," said Jez, enunciating each word clearly. Officially or unofficially, she too could act as if ice cubes wouldn't melt in her ass. "Did *you* want to make me part of this Play Pen? Was that what this whole goddamn thing was about?"

"No," said Dee, exhaling slowly. "At least, not all of it."

"*Which* part?" demanded Jez.

"The first part," admitted Dee. "Early on. When Andy and my mom were checking you out. They check out all my friends."

"And what were you going to get for me?" asked Jez. "Double your clothing allowance?"

"Hey," said Dee, rolling onto her side and giving Jez her back. "That was before I knew you."

"Oh," Jez said icily. "And now you know me?"

"What the fuck," came Dee's muffled voice, "do I know about anything?"

Everywhere, the air was heavy with shadows coming in

to roost. Fighting off their underbelly of despair, Jez leaned forward and flicked on the lava lamp. "Oh, don't be such a *suck!*" she snapped.

Dee lifted as if pulled by strings. "You're calling me a *suck?*" she asked disbelievingly.

"Yeah," said Jez. "I'm calling you a suck. You lied to me, you set me up twice—once with your brother *and* at that party. And today there was that lovely little pimp scene with your mother. *I'm* the one getting screwed here, in case you haven't noticed."

"Oh, I've noticed!" spat Dee, leaning forward. "I've noticed a lot about you, Jezzie-Jezebel. How you hang around with the rest of us poor fucked-up slobs, pretending to be one of us, but inside your head you're still that snotty Christian goodie-girl playing *judgment.* You think you're some kind of prophet, a messiah for the stoners and the woodies. This whole thing is some kind of experiment, a story out of the Bible that you're playing inside your head because it isn't *real* for you. You aren't *stuck* here like the rest of us. You can always go back, can't you—back to *Mary-Eve.*"

"I don't want to go back," protested Jez, her cheeks stinging. "How can you go back from the Apocalypse? Isn't that the point?"

"Apocalypse?" sniggered Dee, rolling her eyes. "Come on—that's just another game Christians play inside their heads. See? You're still thinking like a goddamn *Christian.* The experiment failed, you didn't make Jezebel, and you'll always be stuck being goodie-goodie Mary-Eve. So go on home now," she sneered with a dismissive wave of her hand. "Run on home to Mommy."

Stunned, all Jez could do was stare.

"Oh," added Dee, her smile a thin, bright wire. "You can take this message to Mommy while you're at it. Here's something else I've noticed. You're a *dyke*, Jez. You hang around with me because you think I'm so easy, I'll fuck anything. Tell me, Miss Goody Two-Shoes—what makes you any different from the guys shadowing my ass?"

Faces ransacked and wasted, they watched each other. "Come *on*, Jez," Dee said finally, sinking back onto the bed. "You *knew*. You can't tell me you saw me working Dinky's party and you didn't *know*."

"I didn't know you were *working*," spluttered Jez.

"Well, I was," Dee said flatly. "For pay. You got jumped for free, and I got jumped for bucks."

"It's not rape if you're *selling* yourself," hissed Jez.

"Sure, it is," said Dee. "Either way, they pour through your asshole like Javex. It's that bad every time."

"So why don't you stop?" asked Jez.

Body convulsing, Dee jerked out a sharp laugh. "You don't *stop!*" she said. "Not with the customers my daddy handles. Big dicks, big bucks. I've been trained; I do special tricks. They'd miss me if I was gone."

"That's *their* problem," said Jez.

"No, Jez, it's mine," Dee said bleakly. "It's all mine."

"So go to the police," said Jez.

"The *cops!*" hooted Dee. "Believe me, you don't want to know what I know about the chief of police."

Jez couldn't help it; her mouth opened into a thin cry.

"That's what it's like on this side of real, baby," mocked Dee, her eyes taking on a satisfied gleam, as if savoring Jez's shock. "Everything's bought and sold. You don't have to go *seeking* to find out—on this side the finding out never stops. So go on home to Mommy, Jez. Go back to Mary-Eve and churchie-church, and wait for your goddamn Apocalypse. I get one every week. The Big A's just another rerun, man."

For the second time in her life, Jez felt it happening—the sensation of hanging on desperately as the pain of something leaving tore through her gut. "No!" she whispered, rising to her feet, one arm clutched to her abdomen. Staggering, she cried out as the coffee table bit into her shin and a copy of *People* magazine slid to the floor. Without warning, then, the world went blind, leaving her shuffling through darkness with no sight to guide her as she fumbled her way toward the door and pulled the jackknife from its position in Farrah Fawcett's former face.

"You knew too," she whispered, gripping it tightly. She and Dee had made blood vows together, she thought, her eyes fixed on the jackknife as her vision faded back in. Together they had cut their tongues on this blade. The words she needed to find now would be as painful—blood-soaked—but if she held on, maybe they would come.

"Knew what?" asked Dee from the bed.

"What we both know," said Jez. Still holding the jack-knife, she turned toward the other girl's careful gaze.

"It was a *game*, Jez," said Dee.

"If it was a game," Jez said heatedly, "you wouldn't have given back my soul that time in the car."

Startled, Dee blinked, then glanced away.

"You weren't supposed to, were you?" said Jez, fingering realization. "That *thing* that has your mother, it wants me too.

I saw it this afternoon—your mother is *possessed*, man. That's what it means to be chosen, y'know—one of the chosen few. You're chosen by something from the other side, and then it possesses you. And if that thing runs your mother..."

Sensing the danger, Jez hesitated. A loaded silence followed as Dee studied her, narrow-eyed, from the bed. "Not quite, Jezzie," she said, grimacing. "Close, but no cigar. That *thing*, as you call it, doesn't run me. Believe me, my mother is not how I want to end up. But she has taught me some useful things. I know how darkness can open you to other worlds. And I can call things—anything I want."

"Yeah," Jez said softly. "Through pain."

"How else do you call something?" asked Dee.

The question hung unanswered between them.

"You called me," said Jez.

"I think that went both ways," said Dee.

"All right," said Jez, taking a shuddery breath. Finally, *finally* things were coming back to themselves, turning away from the abyss. Or perhaps not. Perhaps there was yet one more personal monster to pull up out of that inner chasm. "You're right, this isn't just about your shit. I had...a twin once. She died when I was seven. She was half of me. No— she was everything. And when she died, she took it all away."

"So?" asked Dee, her tone guarded.

"She took it from *inside* me," said Jez, touching the jack-knife's tip to her chest. "I felt her die *inside* myself. Not like a separate person, but part of me. I thought that was the end of the world—my Apocalypse—but I guess it wasn't because I'm still here."

"So?" repeated Dee, her eyes narrowing.

Frustration shot through Jez; she felt her own eyes narrow. "So you're still here too," she said, fighting the quaver in her voice. "You've suffered, you've born a heavy cross, and you know things only someone who's suffered as much as you can know. You've found out about a lot of things I don't know; I don't think I want to know them. And you're right—I could go back…to wearing sperm midis, Inter-Varsity Christian Fellowship, and watching real life through windows.

"But if I did, we wouldn't find out what we're supposed to find out. We wouldn't be seekers, we'd be losers—"

"Oh, for fuck's sake!" cried Dee, her body again convulsing. "What d'you think *I* need to find out about? What the hell are *you* going to teach *me?*"

"Maybe this is a different kind of finding out," Jez said intensely, crawling onto the bed beside her. "A different kind of seeking than what you're used to."

Eyes closed, Dee snorted.

"Come on," said Jez. "You haven't *really* been seeking. Not yet. Everything we did, you already knew it all."

"So?" said Dee, her eyes still closed.

"So," said Jez, "when you know, you're conquered."

Motionless beside her, Dee seemed to stop breathing and Jez opened into the pause. "If I went back to being Mary-Eve now," she said, "it'd be like losing another twin. Maybe not as bad as the first time, but—"

"Shut up," Dee said softly, opening her eyes. "I get it, okay?"

Carefully, *carefully* Jez pressed on. "You're half a person too," she whispered, clutching the jackknife for strength. "Half of you is in your body, and the other half flying around in your demons. Maybe they're not dead, but they're outside you. You're cut in half, like me."

"Would you get that fucking knife out of my face?" exploded Dee, pushing her away. "I thought you were grabbing it to cut my throat!"

"Not *yet*," said Jez, slumping fluid with relief onto the bed. *Thud-thud, thud-thud* went her heart, Louisie's shadow heartbeat matching it, pulse for pulse. Womb-like, the room curved in around her; she was home again, at the beginning of things.

"What the fuck am I going to do about the pill?" she moaned, staring at the ceiling. "For sure your mother will cut me off when I tell her no."

"Jez, you dodo," said Dee. "There's a family planning clinic on Simpson Street."

"They won't tell my parents?" asked Jez.

"Guaranteed they won't tell," said Dee. "It's their *job* not to tell." Quietly, she chortled. "I can't believe you fell for that one. Weren't you listening in health class?"

"Yeah," said Jez, her face hot. "I guess I just believed your mother."

"I stopped believing Mom a long time ago," muttered Dee.

"Does she *know* about the thing that's possessed her?" asked Jez, recalling Mrs. Eccles's vapid expression as she made her flirty toodle-oo wave.

"Yeah," said Dee. "She calls it her astral buddy. She and Dad called it in. I think she's afraid of it, but she won't admit it. She says it tells her things—how to call money toward her, how to have power over men. But she has to feed it."

"With her soul!" Jez burst out.

Dee shrugged. "Mom isn't that hung up about her soul," she said. "She's more into her body. Speaking of which—all you have to do is drop in on the Simpson Street clinic this week and you'll be able to keep on fucking Georgie-Porgie without taking a day off."

"We don't do it every day," mumbled Jez.

Silent, they lay next to each other, parallel heartbeats. Jez took a tentative breath. "When I tell your mother no," she said. "Well…how mad will she get? Will she still let us be friends?"

"Yeah," said Dee, her voice carefully casual. "As long as you keep your mouth shut."

Jez considered. "Who would I tell?" she asked.

"*Exactly*," said Dee. Then, stretching, she drawled, "So, Jezzie-Jezebel. You're not going back to Mary-Eve?"

"Yeah, I'm going back," said Jez, touching the jackknife's tip to Dee's lower lip. "I've got some more finding out to do. But I'm taking you with me. Brace yourself, baby—you're about to meet *my* mother."

TEN

Before the Waiting for the Rapture End Times Tabernacle, before the Divine Sister and the Tongue of Fire, before the house on Quance Crescent, I had a different father, or perhaps simply a different set of circumstances with the same father in waiting. This father carried a noticeable heaviness, moving, it seemed, always close to the earth, as if in giving Lawrence Philip Hamilton his material form, God had left the process of creation incomplete—shaping the man out of clay then leaving him, a human figure with its feet still rooted in mud. Indeed, my father often seemed confused by his body, unsure where he ended and his surroundings began, and could frequently be seen reaching for objects with a tangible intensity, as if through touching them he gained a clearer definition of himself.

His salvation thus anchored itself in the external—that which he could touch and, through touching, remake in his own image. Predictably, this transformed the home that was to have been his castle into the dungeon that held him captive, for the slightest detail could make or unmake him; he was condemned to a perpetual shifting of knickknacks, straightening of wall hangings, and the deft bumping of furniture with knee or hip until everything realigned according to some internal blueprint. Upon sitting down to a meal, his fingers twitched nervously across his place mat, and he tapped each article of cutlery a quarter inch to the left or right and twirled his water glass into a slightly different position. Any dinner table centerpiece called out for his corrective touch, and the ladle in the casserole dish always had to be angled more accurately; certainly no one was allowed to begin eating until all dinner napkins had been placed neatly on laps and every shoulder aligned squarely with its respective chair back. Typically, upon his daily return from work, Louisie and I would be sent to our room to change into clothing he deemed more suitable, and he watched continually to ensure we kept our knees together when we sat, lifted our forks gracefully to our mouths while eating, and chewed the required number of times before swallowing—so much so, it seemed as if he sought out the very rhythm of our breathing, intending to pattern it to his own.

When it came to matters of religion, however, my father appeared content to let others design the landscape. Descended from a long line of Presbyterians, he was a trueblood backbencher, leaving the politics of church and Heaven to those trained for the task. For the most part, his faith restricted itself to the material realm—rules that regulated, for instance, his weekly tithe, manner of dress, vocabulary, and social interactions. If there was a spiritual realm that existed beyond these regulations, he seemed largely to ignore it, regarding it as irrelevant to the daily choices he needed to make, and it was his habit to wade with dense authority through legions of ideas, dismissing entire bodies of philosophy and any hypothesis that did not bend the knee to his opinion.

Even as a very young child, I understood that this granted me enormous freedom. My father took note of the parts of my life he could place his hands upon and relentlessly, inexorably reshape; all other aspects floated like unheard radio waves above his head. Thus I could play leapfrog with Louisie and an invisible horde of rainbow fairies while he laid out the backyard patio bricking, oblivious, and I could babble wildly of the many-splendored possibilities of polka-dot elephants and flying cats at the breakfast table while he disappeared behind *The Globe and Mail*, leaving me to freely birth myself into the wonder of each new idea. My father's world had narrow perimeters and a pedestrian heartbeat; I simply vacated it for others I found vibrating beyond his reach, and he remained entirely unaware that I had left him. All it took was a careful observance of his personal code—dress neatly and comb your hair, don't run in the house, say please and thank you—and my father's ponderous hands moved elsewhere to exact their pound of flesh.

Without question, Louisie was his favorite child. From early on she responded most strongly to him, and he liked to boast that, when she discovered her knees, she crawled to him. His employment required he be frequently on the road; as soon as Louisie was old enough to understand the words "Daddy's coming home today," she could be found with her toys in the front hall, waiting for him to walk through the door. As a toddler, it was always Daddy's lap she wanted to sit on, Daddy for whom she drew all her pictures; she even wrote *To Daddy* on the inside of her first grade Mother's Day card.

But when my father reached for his other daughter, he was met with an extreme case of the squirmies. More often than not, I twisted, slithered, or dropped as a deadweight to the floor, even bit and kicked to escape his embrace. What was obvious to me, though apparently concealed from him, was the overwhelming sense that when my father reached for me, he was actually reaching for a carbon copy of Louisie—*and I was not Louisie.* "Mary-Eve!" he would say, distraught, but all I knew was that his hands were reaching for the Louisie that he wanted to discover inside me—the slow, awed tilt of her spirit, her high, quirky giggle, and the way she dropped everything to run, crying "Daddy!" toward him.

My mother's body remembered. Deep within, she carried the memory of Louisie and me, the way I carried that small nub of pleasure inside the lips between my legs. Sometimes when she gazed at the two of us, I could feel the lostness ringing in her like a dull bell; I could go to her then and be absorbed into its familiar cry resonating through her skin. Once, long ago, Louisie and I had been one—my twin's skin had been my skin, and vibrations had flowed unchecked between us, ethereal as angel song. If our bodies had since separated, still I looked at her and saw myself—evidence that part of me had been stolen, that in some high-crying, long-lost moment, hands had reached into my innermost private place, into that shared heartbeat of the womb, and turned Louisie one hundred and eighty degrees away from me. As evidence, all our father had to do was lift his hands and call "Louisie!" and his word became flesh—*her* flesh, flying toward his.

Our father, it must be understood, comprehended none of this. He was a thief who did not know what he had stolen, a trespasser with no grasp of the territory he was traveling. Still, he came inevitably to represent primarily an intrusion into my life, a situation exacerbated by his road trips, during which Louisie unfailingly reversed the one-hundred-and-eighty-degree shift that normally directed her attention so single-mindedly toward him and realigned herself, albeit reluctantly, to me. As if the greater magnet had gone and the lesser attraction reinstated itself, she would settle with a sigh against my shoulder or flop into my lap, the soft curve of her body as familiar as the taste of my own mouth. Peace opened its inner places then, and mysterious music played through my skin, but the reunion was always temporary, lasting only until heavy footsteps once again claimed the front porch and Louisie tore herself free to rocket enthusiastically toward him.

But if I staggered through my first several years stunned and bereft, I did not trail after my twin, the tail of a comet attempting to rejoin its head. Young as I was, I understood that what had been lost was lost. As our father sat on the living room couch with a chirping Louisie in his arms, I wormed wordlessly behind an armchair in the opposite corner, licked my wound, and called it home. And from this position inside

pain, I noted what Louisie, in her Daddy-worship, did not—
the dark, murky silences that blighted the air between our
parents, unexplained bruises on our mother's arms and legs,
the way she changed when our father returned from a road
trip, and the ways we changed with her.

This alteration took place regularly, silent as fluid poured
from one glass into another of a dissimilar shape; without
acknowledgment, we took on different lives and the keeping
of secrets. As far as I know, our father never realized that our
mother often slept in Sunday mornings when he was absent,
nor did he hear about the skipped sermons, the revamped
Bible stories, or the flannel graph board games. During
those early years, our mother developed a technique of talking around details when she spoke to our father, referring to
the life we led while he was on the road as "the time you
were gone," "the time we spent missing you," or "the time
we waited for you to come home." Louisie was as much an
observer of these scenarios as I, yet if our mother's lips tightened when our father sent us, once again, to our room to
change, I seemed to be the only one who noticed. And if
our mother rubbed her temples as our father launched into
another corrective breakfast monologue, it was a further signal my twin neglected to pick up on. In the end, Louisie,
with her eyes fixed adoringly on Daddy, failed to see the way
our mother lived a divided life—reining herself in tightly
when our father was present and funneling all possibility into
his absence.

It was my discovery of the word *no* that gave me a
creeping understanding of our mother's tactics. This short
life-changing syllable entered Louisie's and my vocabulary

during one of our father's lengthier road trips; had he been present, no doubt our initial fervor would have been abruptly curtailed. As it was, however, our mother delighted in the way we latched on to the word, marching about the house and chanting it at the top of our lungs. The word had me thunderstruck and riding the power of my mouth; everything changed under its auspice; possibilities abounded, and I drew them to me with fierce determination: *No*, I was not going to wear that stupid yellow duckie top. *No*, I was not going to swallow that gucky oatmeal. *No*, I was not going to quit the beautiful sun-singing afternoon to take a nap on my parents' bed with the ugly green-nubbed bedspread that left pock-marks in my skin.

Our mother's response was to dissolve into a fit of giggles, chortling and tickling me in the ribs until I collapsed screech-ing into her arms, then promptly carry me off for the dreaded nap. Instinctively, she sensed the magic the word created for a young child—the way it built an invisible kingdom, boundaries her daughters could strut along in two-year-old magnificence. And she knew well the world coming to us, a world merciless and unceasing in its dictates; as long as she could, she gave us a taste of Heaven and let the consequences be damned.

As a result, our father returned from his road trip to find his daughters mutated into full-blown hellions. Completely unsuspecting, he walked through the front door, scooped the waiting Louisie into one arm, opened the other, and called, "Mary-Eve!" But instead of dragging my feet toward him as usual, I retreated to the opposite end of the hall, stomped one foot, and bellowed, "No!" Finally, I could release it in his presence—the word that had been building inside me for two years—and I trumpeted it with unmitigated triumph. "No-no-no-no-no!" I hollered, flooded with exhilaration and meaning. "No-no-no-no-no-NO!"

Setting Louisie down, our father came at me, grabbed my arm, and slapped me hard across the face. Shattered, I sank sobbing to the floor and curled into a ball. A shouting match erupted between our parents, Louisie watching wide-eyed from the front entrance as I crept whimpering toward our bedroom. Thus ended my twin's protests against the adult world, and our father never realized that the "no" revolution had once claimed both his daughters. But if that was the moment Louisie surrendered permanently to Daddy, my retreat was only temporary. For more than a year I took on our father at every opportunity, yelling "No!" through doorways and across rooms, and bellowing defiance both inside the house and out. In response, he took me on like an obstinate piece of furniture, a bit of the material world gone awry; gradually, inexorably, wearing bruises and my mother's thin-lipped silence, I realigned to the word *yes*. Finally, in a lonely backyard ceremony, I dug a hole among the petunias, spoke that heartbeat syllable deep into the darkness where it would be safe, and covered it with dirt.

For years afterward, the word remained buried—a forgotten memory entombed beneath my father's world while I wandered its surfaces, fighting vague disconnected battles. With Louisie's death, this deficit became more pronounced, for I had lost the yes of my life as well as the no. As for my father, it was obvious that he had also lost his yes, and had thereby been reduced once again to that half-finished figure rooted in mud. Day after day, he returned from work, opened the front door, then stood waiting out the house's long moan of silence before removing his overcoat and hanging it up. Not once did he call out to me; instead, he stared at his coat's dangling emptiness as if something were hidden within it, meaning only his dull eyes could discover. No longer did he go about the house making small corrections to furniture, and I often caught glimpses of him seated in his undershorts on the side of his bed, staring at the tossed heap of his clothing, the window drapes, even a movement of air, as if these things held lost parts of himself—fragments he could sense but no longer touch.

The death of his daughter tore my father's world end to end, leaving him without sanctuary. He was no one; he could have become anyone. When my mother suggested a transfer to a different city, he agreed. When she chose the house on Quance Crescent, he did not protest. When she walked through the door of an innocuous-looking stucco church, he followed, a distraught vacuum looking to be filled. Without remorse, the Waiting for the Rapture End Times Tabernacle descended upon him, then swallowed, digested, and spat him out in its image: Deacon Hamilton—Scripture reader, prayer leader, personalized parking space, and carefully crafted face sinking, ever-bewildered, further into the mud.

● ● ●

"Man, this place has a freaky buzz," said Dee.

They were parked outside the Waiting for the Rapture End Times Tabernacle, Dee frowning through the windshield as she observed the benign-looking stucco building. It was approximately ninety minutes before the Sunday evening service, the mid-December air dense with snow that drifted quiet as the thoughts of God. Across the parking lot sat the only other car—the janitor's ancient Volvo—gently disappearing under an endless fall of white.

"Where'd they get that neon job?" she added disbelievingly, pointing to a large crimson electric cross above the front entrance—a hypnotic glow that flashed three seconds on, three seconds off in the dark.

"They bought it last year," said Jez. "Special order from Louisiana." Butting out her cigarette, she opened the passenger door and stepped out into the crisp evening air.

"What—from the KKK?" demanded Dee as she emerged from the other side, coatless and shivering in Jez's Sunday best—a vermilion midi with a tiny white collar.

"Probably," said Jez, heading for the church door. Right behind her, Dee scurried nervously up the freshly shoveled walk. Having balked at the prospect of borrowing Jez's oxfords, she was wearing a pair of low-heeled black pumps—a bit racy for Waiting for the Rapture, Jez reflected, but they would have to do. It had taken a half hour of intense cajoling to convince Dee to ditch her makeup, and without it her face was surprisingly vulnerable, the startling blue of her eyes less of an attack, the soft flush of her lips a kiss rising direct from the nerves. Even her demon seemed subdued, a vague red shimmer around her head. As Jez pulled open the church door, she shot the demon a nervous glance. What if one of the parishioners tuned into the ferret face's wavelength and saw it? Even worse, the Divine Sister?

With a shrug, she ditched the thought and passed into the entranceway. To her right hung a large banner that displayed Jesus in a white robe and crown of thorns, blood dripping from his forehead as he patted a flock of surrounding sheep. Something about the sheep's stunned-silly expressions—Jez had never been able to pin down exactly what it was—had always conjured up vague memories of long-ago Mouseketeers singing "M-I-C-K-E-Y..."

"Creepy," muttered Dee, glancing at the banner as she passed. "Churches give me the creeps."

"Just imagine the place draped in black," Jez said tersely as she removed her jacket. "A couple of knives stuck in the door. That should make it feel like home sweet home." She was on edge and well aware of it; as she hung up her lime jacket, the coatrack's long row of metal hangers rocked and clanked like the tinny insides of her brain. Dee was right though, she thought, glancing around the lobby. There *was* something in the air tonight—as if the church were alive with static, had blown its wiring and released electricity free-form into its walls.

"Fuck!" hissed Dee, narrow-eyed. "Can't you feel it?"

"You're the one with the Eye," said Jez, ducking the question. The slight deception left her uneasy, but for all she knew, she reasoned defensively, giving Dee a straight answer could result in the other girl's taking off, reneging on her promise to stick out the entire service. After all, she hadn't wanted to come—had whined, grumped, and outright howled about missing *The Six Million Dollar Man*—but both girls knew she owed Jez big time. A heavy dose of guilt, some soft-lipped pleading—Jez had worked anything and everything to

tease the other girl into the vermilion midi, then in behind
Sinbad's wheel. *And for what?* she thought, frowning at the
empty lobby. Jez didn't know what she expected Dee to sniff
out tonight; she didn't have a goddamn clue.

"What's that?" asked Dee, her gaze fixing on what Jez
liked to think of as the "concession stand"—a glassed-in gift
shop that had replaced the original front-lobby sales booth
several years ago. Unfortunately, at least as far as Jez was con-
cerned, it continued to feature photographs of the Divine
Sister and her family, with large blowups facing prominently
outward on the shelves.

"Would you look at that!" exclaimed Dee, pointing to a
recent photo of Jez in which she was holding a white Bible
and gazing sullenly at the camera. "Baby, you sell for $1.95."

"Overpriced," admitted Jez. "I'm not a big seller."
Pointedly, she turned toward the sanctuary, but Dee's nose
remained glued to the glass.

"Weren't you a cute little ducky," she murmured, indi-
cating an early picture of Jez toddling toward the camera in
diapers and a huge grin. Ending abruptly along one side, the
photograph was one of the few survivors of Rachel Hamilton's
scissor rampages, its missing half having disappeared long ago
into obscurity.

"Quack, quack," Jez said dispassionately.

"What gives?" asked Dee, raising an eyebrow at her.
"You're cute, but Jezzie, why are they selling you? What's your
turn-on?"

"There," said Jez, stabbing a finger at a photograph of
the Divine Sister, in which she stood gazing beatifically at
a large wooden cross that dominated one of the sanctuary

walls. "That's my mother, okay? She's a prophetess, famous in Waiting for the Rapture circles. Pilgrims come from all across the country, even the U.S., to hear her. And they like to buy mug shots of her family."

"Your mom's famous?" demanded Dee, her face incredulous. "Like Billy Graham? One million souls saved for Jesus?"

"Close," said Jez, heading into the sanctuary, "but no cigar. Come on." Without waiting for a response, she passed through the archway into the sanctuary. Here too the last few years had brought changes. Oak pews now faced the stage in three sections, and a balcony overlooked the proceedings from the back. Next to the new choir loft stood a baby grand piano, and three scarlet-cushioned armchairs sat ponderously behind the podium. With all the improvements, however, no one had thought to replace the puke-amber glass that partitioned the sanctuary from the lobby or the endlessly whispering ceiling fans, and the baptismal tank still gave off the same creeping odor of chlorine. But the main problem here tonight was something else, thought Jez as she observed the familiar scene—a discordant note that couldn't be heard, something hidden like blood pulsing under skin... an invisible hysteria that could be sensed even without the congregation moaning and calling out from the pews.

"Shiiiit!" hissed Dee, coming up beside her. "What kind of church are you running here, Jez?"

"I dunno," Jez said uncertainly. "It's weird tonight. I've never felt it like this, exactly."

"This ain't new," said Dee, slit-eyed as she gazed around herself. "You're just finding it, baby. Something big's got this place—had it for years."

"You mean God?" asked Jez.

"I mean ugly," said Dee. Slowly, they progressed up the center aisle, Jez watching Dee the way a water diviner watches her rod, trusting it to find what she can't locate on her own. Two steps ahead, the other girl walked carefully, throwing out her mind like radar and scanning realities Jez could barely discern...*as through a veil*, she thought suddenly, realization catching in her throat. Dee, on the other hand, had torn that veil asunder—*she* had been torn, her body the veil. Wary, a hiss constant in her throat, the butterfly girl approached the front of the sanctuary, pausing to stare at the large wooden cross on the wall, the three armchair thrones, and the podium.

"What's this?" she asked. Climbing the stairs to the stage, she walked past the podium and stopped, then passed her hands vaguely through the air. "There's something here," she said, her eyes glazing over. "Right here."

"What d'you mean?" asked Jez, confused. "There's nothing there. Nothing—"

"Right here," insisted Dee, sketching out a large, squarish object with her hands. "Like this. A cage. With wheels."

Jez's mouth dropped open, full of soundlessness.

"A woman's inside," muttered Dee, grimacing. "Some poor screwed-up bitch, her asshole sucked up the back of her head with fear."

Even as she spoke, Jez saw something begin to materialize between Dee's hands—the transparent outline of a life-size wailing woman, her hands scrabbling and clawing at her body as if it were a garment she could tear free. "My...my mother!" Jez whispered, stepping back. "It's my mo—"

But Dee wasn't listening—her face gone blank, her pale

blue stare transfixed. "Not you," she sing-songed, her voice floating aimlessly. "But almost you. A long time ago, almost you—"

"This has nothing to do with me!" yelled Jez, suddenly terrified. "It has to do with my mother. My mother and a guy named Pastor Playle. What you're looking for is a bastard called Pastor Playle."

The wailing woman vanished, leaving Dee blinking rapidly and staring around herself with a confused expression. "Jesus!" she whispered, rubbing her temples. "Where am I? Did I—" She faltered, her voice trailing off. "Did I go... *weird*, Jez?"

Her eyes slid across Jez's, a trapped question, and Jez, staring back, stumbled against the rhythm of her own heartbeat going wrong. Slow realization opened between the two girls—Dee couldn't remember what had just happened, as if for a few seconds she had stepped out of her own awareness. Which left the full truth of the incident only in Jez's hands— hands that were, at that moment, admittedly distraught and devious. The immediate problem facing her, as Jez swiftly assessed it, was that if she told Dee what had occurred, the other girl might justifiably freak and run. And that would leave Jez once again alone in the unbearable labyrinth of her life, unable to discover what she most needed to know.

Because for her the veil hung firmly in place. She hadn't been broken the way Dee had been; for her, those inner gates hadn't been torn open. So she *had* to rely on Dee; there really was no choice. And anyway, Jez told herself, Dee owed her. Seekers on the hunt, they had taken blood vows together, had walked in through tonight's church doors on a mission, and were here—poised, finally, on the front line of the war against God. They were about to *find out*.

So, dropping her gaze, Jez said simply, "Nothing's weird. Shh, baby, nothing's weird." Climbing the stairs to the stage, she grasped Dee's clammy hand and pulled her through a side door into the hallway that ran along the back of the church. "C'mon," she urged. "Let's go check out his office."

"Whose office?" asked Dee, her eyes darting as she scanned the corridor ahead of them. "It's stronger out here, Jez—the buzz."

"That's because we're getting close to *Pastor Playle's* office," said Jez, heading determinedly toward a nearby stairwell. Although their encounter in the sanctuary had been a shock, it hadn't revealed anything new. Upstairs, however, in Pastor Playle's office—now *that*, she reasoned, was where the true mystery took place. Sunday after Sunday, that was the place in which her mother was inexplicably transformed into the Divine Sister.

"It's on the second floor," she told Dee, pulling her up the first few stairs. "C'mon—let's see what you pick up."

But instead of following, Dee jerked backward and out of Jez's grasp, her body gone rigid, her eyes wide and staring. Then she turned and began walking back the way they had come. "Where are you going?" Jez called after her, but the other girl continued along the hall, her shoulders cowed, the usual shimmy of her hips locked into an awkward gait that was somehow *very* familiar. "Dee!" shouted Jez as recognition hit. "Wait, Dee! Wait!"

Oblivious, Dee stumbled onward, now mumbling breathily to herself. "This is the journey," Jez heard her whisper. "The journey of the chosen ones. This is the journey of Abraham, Isaac, and Jacob, the journey of the Israelites in the desert, the serpent lifted up in the wilderness. This is the journey of Joshua fighting for the Promised Land, the Battle of Jericho and the walls tumbling down. Walls come tumbling down, tumbling, tumbling down."

Pausing, Dee felt about blindly, then turned to face a door close to the sanctuary entrance. "Dee?" Jez asked cautiously, coming up beside her.

Breath labored, Dee stood with her forehead touching the door. Sweat beaded her face as tremor after tremor ran her body. "Hush-a, hush-a," she whispered. "We all fall down. Sin and evil and all gone dead. Sins of the mothers visited upon their children. Hush-a, hush-a, they all fall down."

Wordless, Jez fought off a mounting panic. Either by bizarre chance or by instinct, Dee had ended up pressed flat against the door of the storage room in which the Divine Sister's red velvet box was kept. *Thank God*, Jez thought fervently, *that door is always locked*. Open-mouthed, she watched the other girl shudder and whimper, shudder again.

"This is the garden," Dee whispered to the locked door. "The garden where the journey begins. The garden where the body is broken and sin enters in. Hush-a, hush-a, sin enters in and we all fall dead. But the few, the *chosen* few, are lifted out of darkness into a great light. Lifted into the light. Into the light."

Her head snapped up. Then she turned and began a slow, shuffling walk toward the sanctuary, her body taking the same broken posture Jez had so often seen in her own mother. "No!" screamed Jez, launching herself after Dee just as the door to the sanctuary opened and her father came through, followed by her mother and Pastor Playle. Startled, the three adults halted and stared at the girl shuffling toward them, twisted and groping as if half blind.

Reaching Dee, Jez wrapped her arms around the other girl, pulling her out of the high, white scream of the mind and back into the comforting solidity of flesh. "Jez?" mumbled Dee, as the two girls nuzzled and burrowed into each other's necks. "What the jeezus fuckin' shit, Jezzie?"

"It's okay," whispered Jez, hanging on tight. "Everything's okay now, I promise."

A frown on his face, Pastor Playle cleared his throat. "Mary-Eve," he intoned, "explain immediately what has been going on here in the Lord's holy house."

Dazed, Jez stared at him. "Uh…my friend's visiting from school," she stammered. "She has a headache. We—"

To her relief, her father stepped in. "Ralph, we're running short on time," he said. "The Divine Sister needs time to prepare."

"Yes, yes. Of course," replied Pastor Playle, glancing from the two girls to Mrs. Hamilton, who stood beside him in a white pillbox hat, smiling radiantly. No, not just smiling, Jez realized suddenly—her mother was displaying the exact rapturous expression she always gave right before she underwent her transformation into the Divine Sister.

"Come, come," Pastor Playle said to Jez's mother, taking her arm and leading her up the stairs. Without a glance back, Jez's father followed, the sound of his footsteps carrying him out of sight. Heart pounding, Jez stood staring after the disappearing adults. *It's about to happen!* she thought excitedly.

The signs had been with her mother this past week, but not strongly—at least not strongly enough to indicate a visit from the Divine Sister. And so there had been no velvet box session at today's morning service, no divine prophecy, and the congregation had been sent home dissatisfied.

But now, she thought, peering up the stairwell to the second floor, satisfaction looked to be right around the corner. The transformation—or mutation, depending on how one looked at it—was about to take place once again. Only this time, Dee was here. The girl with the Eye. The butterfly girl with the inner gates.

"All right, Jez," came Dee's voice from behind her, and Jez turned to see the other girl slumped against the wall, her closed eyelids paper-thin. "You're not going to fuck with me twice. I went *weird*. I know it, and I know you know it, and this time you're fucking going to tell me what happened."

"I don't know what happened," muttered Jez, edging around the truth. "I think you…Well, all of a sudden you changed. You were trembling a lot, and whispering…things. You talked like someone else."

"Yeah!" exploded Dee. "That was some bitch! What was she talking about—sins of mothers, children dying, and a great light? I must've run into some kind of memory of her."

"Memory?" asked Jez.

"Things she's done and said, left behind in the air," said Dee. "People leave them everywhere all the time. Usually they just fade, but this one was so strong it took me over. And then, when I was in the middle of it, something tried to come after me…the way it goes after her, I guess. It was something that feeds on souls. It's not human, whatever it is."

Jez swallowed around the fist in her throat. "What does it do to…that woman when it gets her?" she whispered.

"*Uses* her," snapped Dee. "To connect with the other losers in this church. All it needs is one torn-open soul and it's got a gate straight into everyone else. The thing that has this church is really big." Dull-eyed, she stared down the hallway. "You have to be pretty far gone for it to plug into you. I got blasted so bad, I barely remember anything."

Jez swallowed again. Even with everything she had just witnessed, everything she *knew*, she felt herself pulling back, not wanting to take this in. "How come it went after you and not me?" she asked.

With an effort, Dee pushed away from the wall. "*Fear*, baby!" she hissed. "You ain't got enough fear. When you came after me now, it took off. Which way is Sin? I'm outta here."

"No!" cried Jez, grabbing her arm. "Please, there's one more thing. It's up in Pastor Playle's office, where they went—Pastor Playle, my father, *and* my mother…the bitch you found in the sanctuary. At least, that's what she turns into *after* she goes into Pastor Playle's office. But not before— you just saw her, right? She's not like that now. Something happens to her, every week, in that office. I've been trying to figure it out for years, but I can't on my own. I *can't*."

Desperately, Jez stood watching as Dee rose and fell on one shuddering breath. "It's Pastor Playle," she pleaded. "He's fucking my mother; he's got her under some kind of spell. He's the one who must've called in that *thing*—whatever it is."

Eyes lowered, Dee continued to hesitate somewhere deep within herself. "Okay, Jesus-girl," she said finally, her voice cobweb-soft. "But don't think I don't know you lied when I needed the truth. Don't think I don't know you'll play me the way I play you."

Their eyes met, and in a fierce, singing rush Jez felt the invisible barrier that had always resonated between them tear wide open; then, in some naked virgin place, they were flushed and rooted against each other.

"No one—not you, not *anyone*—is fucking better than me," whispered Dee. Exultation, almost beauty, crept across her face. "We all turn into the same inside-out asshole crawling across the floor and begging in the end, don't we?"

"I'm sorry," whispered Jez.

"Don't be," hissed Dee. "It's *freedom*." Gingerly, she straightened, the cat returning to her body. "Okay," she said, "I'll stay. But remember—that thing comes after me, not you. So what I say goes. If I say we're outta here, we're gone. Got it?"

"Got it," mumbled Jez, wiping tears from her face.

"That was a shitload to carry, Jezzie," Dee added quietly, watching her. "Always having to be better than everyone else."

"Not as bad as having to be worse," said Jez.

"Maybe," said Dee. Without speaking, they climbed the stairs to the second floor and walked along the upstairs hallway until Jez paused opposite a closed door.

"Here," she mouthed, and Dee nodded, studying it. "It's locked," added Jez, "and you can't hear anything through it. Believe me, I've tried."

With another nod, Dee leaned one shoulder against the wall and closed her eyes. "C'mere," she whispered. "Put your forehead to mine and close your eyes. Then wait. Just wait."

Hesitantly, Jez touched her forehead to Dee's and closed her eyes. Immediate darkness enveloped her; she became aware of her heartbeat and the sound of her breathing.

"Usually you need blood," murmured Dee, her breath a gentle pulse against Jez's mouth. "But with the freak-out I just had..." As if in response to something, her voice trailed off, and gradually Jez also began to sense it—a growing heaviness, a density of mind. Then she seemed to be turning ninety degrees and passing through the wall, but so unhurriedly she could see the grain within the plaster and wood. Next, this vanished, and she found herself gazing directly into Pastor Playle's office with its familiar curtained windows, framed theology degrees, and family photographs. In an armchair opposite sat her mother, face serene and beatific. Perched beside her on the edge of a large desk was an intent-looking Pastor Playle; across the room, Jez's father leaned against the outside wall. Motionless, both men were watching Rachel Hamilton the way a heron scans the water's surface for the prey that swims underneath.

"I dreamt of angels," she was saying in a high breathy voice. "Amber and rose-pink angels that were weaving songs of light through my body."

"Ah," murmured Pastor Playle. "Truly a vision sent by the Lord, sister."

Catching Jez's father's eye, he gave a quick nod. Instantly, Deacon Hamilton straightened and began to pace, his breath growing labored and a flush darkening his face. Between his hands, a softcover Bible twisted in and out of an angry curl.

"*You* slept!" he hissed in a tight voice, pointing the Bible at his wife. "*You*, with your sins covering you like maggots!

Yes, the Devil paints *your* sleep with false visions of angels and light."

Dismay pleaded Rachel Hamilton's face. Mouth open, she stared at her husband.

"But the rest of us?" he continued, striding to his wife and gripping her shoulder. "The rest of us who sleep with the blood of Jesus dripping in our faces? The rest of us who suffer endlessly, knowing the price the good Lord paid to save us from evil? Do I sleep, Rachel? Have I slept for the last ten years?"

As if waking to the intentions of the room, Rachel Hamilton cringed back in her chair. "No!" she whispered, clutching her small white purse. "Please, no!"

The eyes of the men met, and again Pastor Playle nodded. Lips tightening, Jez's father turned back to his wife, and the room contracted around them like a throat.

"You killed Louisie," he said. The words were quiet, almost conversational. Like a favorite Bible verse, they left Deacon Hamilton's mouth, flowed toward his wife, and blew her wide open.

"Arrogant," he added steadily. "Willful. Slothful. Your sins mounted around you like the stones of a sepulcher, and you *knew*."

Wordless, Rachel Hamilton stared back at him.

"You knew the wages of sin was death," accused her husband. "You knew someone would have to pay the price. You knew and you chose the one who would pay—*Louisie*. You chose *my* Louisie to atone for *your* sins. Ten years ago, you took a helpless, God-fearing child and placed your sins upon her, knowing God would have to claim *her*. Your sin killed Louisie. *You killed my little Louisie.*"

Eyes closed, Jez's father vibrated through his last words as if suspended along a high, singing note of pain. Then, something released, he grunted, opened his eyes, and stepped back. Slowly the flush left his face, his breathing quieted, and the Bible untwisted in his hands. Glancing at Pastor Playle, he nodded, and both men focused on the woman quivering in the armchair before them.

For Jez's mother had begun to shake. Neck and spine now rigid, she sat plucking at the front of her dress. "No," she whimpered, her eyes darting side to side. "I could have been more faithful. I was lax, I know that as God's truth. I mocked the Lord's holy name and disobeyed His commandments, but I always loved my little girl. I always loved Louisie."

"Love isn't enough," Pastor Playle said gently, getting down on his knees and taking her distraught hands in his. "Human love is selfish and blind. Was it human love you offered Louisie, mere hu—"

"It was the love of a mother!" cried Rachel Hamilton.

"Was it *self*-love?" Pastor Playle continued inexorably. "*Self*-love—the greatest sin of them all?"

"No!" cried Jez's mother. "I *never* loved myself. *Never*. You could *never* fault me with the sin of self-love. It was always my little girls; everything was always—"

From across the room, her husband erupted. "Why did you choose Louisie instead of Mary-Eve?" he thundered, again pointing the Bible at her. "I'll tell you why—because Louisie loved me, and Mary-Eve loved you. Mary-Eve was inferior, the insignificant one. Any fool could have seen how pure Louisie was standing next to her, how much closer to God. Even you could see it, and it filled you with envy.

You coveted the love Louisie had for me. You had to steal it somehow."

"No!" whimpered Rachel Hamilton, her hands scrabbling furiously at her bodice. Long and relentless, a shudder convulsed her body.

"You killed her," repeated her husband in a thick, empty voice.

"Confess everything to the Lord," said Pastor Playle, still on his knees and stroking Rachel Hamilton's hands. "God forgives everything, even the secret sins of the heart."

And then, for a second time, Jez saw it—the white wail of a woman rising within her mother's body, its twisted hands clawing open a hole deep inside her spirit. A hole, Jez realized, stunned, that was brilliant with light—a gate to the other side.

"Yes," whispered Rachel Hamilton, her head sagging. "Yes," she sighed, and the transformation was complete— the radiance vanished and tremors once again haunting her limbs. *This*, thought Jez, staring at her, *is the way she's always led out of the office.* How many times had she seen her mother exactly like this—her head down, shoulders slumped, shuffling toward...

At that moment, Rachel Hamilton started to jerk, her purse swinging wildly from her wrist. As a look of dismay crossed Pastor Playle's face, she spewed several hoarse grunts and raised both hands toward the ceiling.

Looking equally dismayed, her husband stepped toward her. "No, Rachel!" he said sternly. "Not here! Not yet!"

Undeterred, Rachel Hamilton continued to grunt and jerk, sprays of saliva flying from her lips. *Something's wrong,* thought Jez, watching in consternation. *She's not supposed to do this until after she's been strapped inside the box.*

"Holy shit!" whispered Dee beside her. "She's calling."

"Calling what?" asked Jez, then fell silent as the air above her mother's head began to shimmer and spin, creating a tunnel of light that extended upward. At its tip a distant Tongue of Fire could be seen, unfolding delicate wings and preparing to make its descent.

"Why the fuck didn't you tell me about this?" demanded Dee.

Fervor mounting, Rachel Hamilton rocked and jerked in the armchair, sending out her voice in a series of low circling cries that rose and fell like a landscape. Wrapped in her own arms, the swaying woman set out along the journey of her voice, a collage of sound that captured every tortured stumble, every blunder, trial, and betrayal of the human soul. As Jez listened, the landscape of her mother's pain opened like an ethereal travel map, and she saw how her mother's heart had been torn from the flesh to live in the shimmering lies of the mind, those illusions that protected her from the truth of her life: an early-morning sun rising in a garden lush with fruit and promise, two stumbling figures being chased through a gate by fiery angels, a man and his son leading a mule laden with firewood up the side of a mountain.

All this pain on the road to no pain, thought Jez as her mother's wail slid through itself, knife-edged and empowering falsehood after falsehood—the high holy figures of archangels, the four horsemen of the Apocalypse, and the small white stone that held her secret name. Like an ecstatic mountain climber, Rachel Hamilton's voice rose and rose, ascending its scale of wonder, and as it shredded on the very peak of sound, Jez saw vibrating within her mother's body a figure of such light, her eyes burned to look upon it. Wings, she was sure it had wings…and horns—many horns growing from its head. Its eyes glowed like sapphires, its tongue forked like a snake's, and it had the breasts of a woman and the groin of a man. But for all this, it was the face that brought the terror of recognition, a face that had not changed since that long-ago day when she had been forced to her knees in front of the congregation to receive forgiveness for trying to break the code of her mother's babbling and had looked up and seen it—remote, Sphinxlike, and as far from pain and suffering as the human mind could travel: *the face of the Divine Sister.*

Without warning, Jez felt herself yanked back through the wall and into the heaviness of flesh. Disoriented, it was a moment before she was able to tune into the nearby sound of high-pitched screaming. Whirling around, she saw Dee, her eyes wide and staring as she backed away from the office.

"Jezzie, babe," the butterfly girl hissed, terrified. "Your mom's calling *death.*"

Turning, she took off down the hallway, heels skittering as she made a mad dash toward her car.

ELEVEN

When we were five, Louisie and I invented a secret game we called Mirror See. Having stumbled upon it by chance, we played it in front of our bedroom full-length mirror, where we would stand hand in hand and stare directly into each other's mirrored gaze, letting ourselves go quiet until we rested on an inner emptiness the way a house without inhabitants stretches into silence, and knowing, and doorways the living like to keep closed. If we were able to reach this inner calm, and often we were not, we would find ourselves shifting gradually into a shared pattern of breathing and heartbeat, our eyes closing and opening in synchronous slowed-down blinks until everything settled into the same rhythm and our separateness dissolved.

At this point, a shimmering landscape opened around

us, a realm of vibrations, pulse, and motion—that fabric of absolute possibility from which the material world evolves. All known structure disappeared, along with the slightest memory of it, and Louisie and I would stand awed and watching multiple levels of reality interweave like the many individual melodies in an intuitive symphony. Completely at rest together, we then merged into a single vibration within that greater symphony and, as one, explored other vibrations—mingling with the celestial, the merely disembodied, elementals, and all that could not, or was not allowed to, manifest on the material plane.

Within this vibratory realm, thought was simultaneously as singular and as collective as a wave releasing itself onto a shore then plunging back into the deep. Voices spoke to us; angels appeared and disappeared within mundane molecules of air; the singing of a lone siren could call up entire worlds or end them. As long as Louisie and I were able to remain merged, this womb of utter imagination continued to weave us through its fabric of possibility, but the material world presented so many interruptions—a car door slam, footsteps in the hall, the voice of an urgent parent. Without being told, we knew enough not to be caught in such togetherness, and so reserved the mirror game only for those days on which our parents' attention looked to be otherwise engaged for some length of time.

Sometimes we used mirrors in separate rooms. In this version of the game, Louisie took up position before our bedroom mirror while I climbed onto a chair in front of the guest room's mirror-backed dresser. Alone and intent, I would sink into the rhythm of my breathing, all the while watching my disembodied face in the glass and waiting for the moment Louisie's breathing surfaced out of nowhere into my own; without a sound, my body and the surrounding room then vanished from my perception and, together with my twin, I passed through the mirror into another realm.

This realm was of a lower order than the one we had discovered standing hand in hand before our bedroom mirror, and it seemed to exist only between the household mirrors. Once Louisie and I had merged minds and exited our bodies, we could together look back and see my head and chest leaned over the guest room's dresser, my nose plastered to the mirror glass, and, in the other direction, Louisie standing serious and prim against a backdrop of pink rose wallpaper, both hands pressed to her chest. Then, leaving this behind, we moved onward into a shadowy, muffled world. Poking and prodding about its obscure nooks, we gradually mapped out a murky landscape that appeared to represent our physical home in reverse—a dimension packed with the thoughts and vibrations that were not normally allowed to surface on the other side of the mirror. These thoughts, by and large, had a shape—hunched, for instance, or scuttling along nervously— and belonged for the most part to previous inhabitants of the house. As such, their outlines were vague and their speech indistinct, close to dissolution. Thought forms that belonged to my parents, on the other hand, were clearly identifiable but generally full of such anger that Louisie and I steered well clear of them.

We also came across thoughts that belonged to her and me. My thoughts, not surprisingly, tended to stomp and yell a great deal. Many of Louisie's, however, dragged an intense sadness, so much so that both she and I kept our distance. As a result, I did not discover the reason for this grief, the secret burden that weighed them down—one so enormous, even Louisie seemed to have banished it from her awareness. I did not learn it, that is, until one afternoon late into our sixth summer. On that day, as I took up position before the guest room mirror, I heard a distinct giggle coming from Louisie's and my bedroom across the hall. To my astonishment, before I had a chance to begin quieting myself, an intense pulling sensation rose up from *within*, sucking me out of my body and through a quick whir of darkness, then out through the mirror and back into my body. Disoriented, I stood letting my confusion dissipate, and when it had cleared, looked around to find myself standing not in the guest room but before the mirror in the bedroom I shared with Louisie, sur-rounded by pink rose wallpaper.

Immediately, I noticed small things were wrong—my mouth tasted unfamiliar, the air came too thin and quick into my nose, and my toes pointed inward as I stood. Bit by bit, I became aware of a high-pitched noise in my head and a fish-hook of pain in my chest. Try as I might, I could not figure out how I had gotten from the guest room to the bedroom, and the room itself seemed confused, fading in and out of its outlines. Sweaty and shivering, I climbed onto the bed I shared with Louisie and gave myself over to the dizziness that sang through my brain in a high, white voice.

When my twin entered the room several minutes later, I barely noticed until she clambered onto the bed and strad-dled my hips. Squinting through blurred eyes, I noted her unkempt hair and sagging socks, the carefree movements of her body, and on her elbow a large scab where I had scraped myself falling off a neighbor's tire swing several days earlier.

"You're me!" I whispered, horrified.

"Don't tell," she said with a preposterous grin. "It's a secret."

"But you can't be me!" I protested, fighting the blur in my head. "I didn't say you could!"

"Oh yes, I can!" she said, breathing triumph. "I've been thinking lots about how to do it, and now it's done."

"Give me back!" I whined, pushing at her.

"I don't want to," she replied, bouncing slightly on my hips. "Not yet."

"Louisie," I whimpered. "I don't like being you. You're tired and sick."

"Not now I'm not!" she sang. Scrambling off the bed, she headed for the door.

"I'll tell Mom!" I howled as she ran out of the room, but we both knew I could not—who but Louisie knew enough to believe me? Sprawled limp on the bed, I stared at the empty doorway and listened to the oversized thump of my heart. *No, not my heart,* I thought, terrified. *Louisie's.* While I had heard it often enough lying beside her at night and during the mirror game, this close its rhythm seemed full of odd angles—sharp pieces of glass or nails. Every few beats, I felt a pain like a bright, ripping sensation. It was as if I had been naughty and was about to be punished, but the punishment was hidden and lurking *inside* me, and I did not know how or when it would come, just that when it did, it would be part of me—an inner apocalypse, some part of my body going horribly, finally wrong.

Fighting nausea, I slid off the bed and stumbled through the house to the backyard, where Louisie crouched next to my mother, chattering happily as they painted the rock garden stones a startling unblemished white. Splayed in the shade of a nearby poplar, I watched their bright, blurred forms, determined not to degrade myself completely by sinking into one of Louisie's frequent naps. About me the air sang with heat, and the ground felt as if it was rippling beneath my back. Every now and then, huge flames of color rose from the earth and danced through the trees. Bright, jagged moments came and went with each heartbeat; the air flashed crystalline edges as unseen spirits sang wild, lonely notes.

It was the world of Mirror See, I realized, horrified, as I stared around myself, or some distorted version thereof— either way, a realm I had assumed Louisie and I could access only together, through the mirror game. Now, however, it was becoming rapidly obvious this had been her constant reality for years, forced on her by a weak heart that kept her continually on some sort of threshold, one foot in the material plane and the other God knew where, and constraining her to live a drippy watercolor kind of existence—an existence, I thought, as fear crawled up my throat, to which she was not likely *ever* to want to return. And, having experienced it directly myself, how could I blame her? This was not the paradise of the womb, but a vague headachy place that could not keep its sounds and colors straight. No wonder she had been scheming to switch bodies, and now that she had succeeded, her obvious goal would be to keep as far away from me as possible.

Trapped within incommunicable panic, I lay fighting

the heart that clenched within me like a fist. Cicadas called back and forth, their harsh cries drilling through the afternoon; gradually, my best intentions dulling, I drifted off to sleep and woke sometime later to find my father leaning over me. In that surrounding sea of shifting color and sound, he reached down to me, solid and steadfast, an underlying, ever-abiding reference point for all that changed; gathering me in, he lifted me toward the fortress of his body, where his sturdy heartbeat caught and carried mine. Cradled in the strength of his arms, I knew that as long as he held me I was safe.

"There, there, Louisie," he comforted. "Daddy's home now. Tell me what's wrong."

I wasted no time considering what it must have meant for my twin to have lived this way. For her part, she expended no sympathy on me, refusing to sit in her usual place beside me at the dinner table and plastering herself against the opposite car door whenever we had to share the Valiant's backseat. Desperate and silent, I waited three days for her to relent and return my birthright. Interminable, indescribable, those three days were a Persephone between-world existence, waiting for mercy; when it did not come, I started attacking the body that imprisoned me—slamming the head against walls, clawing the skin, and gouging at the eyes.

There is no telling how much damage I caused Louisie's body during this period. As my assaults continued, my parents grew frenzied, my twin merely more distant. Finally, one night when the sky roiled with clouds and the wind howled and pulled at corners of the house, I climbed on top of a sleeping Louisie, placed my mouth to hers, and began to suck. Deeply asleep, she did not fight. For one brief moment, I felt her rising out of my body toward me—next, that fleeting second when, in transit, our souls met and merged. Then, leaving her behind, I reentered my body and pushed hers emphatically away, reducing us both once again to permanent isolation.

Without remorse, I reclaimed my singular identity. The world returned to its proper alignments; colors and sounds behaved themselves, and I was no longer forced to endure thresholds to other dimensions. Rooted again firmly in the physical plane, I began to observe my twin from a careful distance, watching for evidence of her precarious existence. The frequent naps were obvious, but I also noted the delicate blue smudges that lived beneath her eyes and the way she often paused in the middle of an activity and stared about helplessly, as if having forgotten where or who she was. It was not much, I decided, considering what she had to live with. Over the years, Louisie had learned to chart her course between the worlds with the consummate skill that grows out of extreme loneliness. Unfortunately, no means was ever given her to communicate her situation, and other than our Mirror See explorations and her brief respite within my body, she was condemned to live as trapped and alone as an Old Testament prophet amid the bewildering mysteries of God.

After the mirror-game switch, Louisie made no further attempts to steal my body. Instead, she turned to Billy Graham and the ethereal night visitors that were visible only to her. In the year before she died, we never again played Mirror See, and for months after her death I struggled with the certainty that it had been God's will that we switch bodies, His divine plan that my twin go on living in my skin while the Devil bore my soul to Hell on a pitchfork. Guilt grew in me, a series of stacked coffins; within them, I placed the memories of Mirror See and Louisie's and my explorations of other realms. As time went on, these coffins sank deeper and deeper into an internal graveyard; in the end, I was left with only an odd pull toward mirrors and the sense that something awaited me on the other side of the glass.

• • •

The stairwell rose, a now familiar habit, muffling the sound of Jez's footsteps in new-fallen snow. At the landing she paused, suspended in a quiet so weighted, the evening carried it like a sleeping child. Pensive, she stood letting the winter silence sink down through her and gazing over a sepia snow-covered landscape that stretched before her like a prayer cupped in the hands of God. A god, she thought wistfully, that could still confuse by unfolding in her sometimes like blurred doorways of light, like breathing.

It was midway through the week, four days before Christmas. Normally, Jez would have been about to head out the door with her parents for the Wednesday evening prayer meeting, but she had begged off, claiming the need for last-minute library research on a history paper. Trudging along the alley a minute ago, she had looked up to see such a faint light coming from the garage window ahead of her that she had panicked, certain Dee had been called out on her father's "business," or worse—had decided she preferred the company of someone else. Dee did that sometimes—her whims seemingly deliberately erratic—and it always caught Jez unawares, the flick of a knife through bliss; she always bled.

But tonight's knock brought an immediate call of "Come in," and Jez oozed relief. Opening the door, she stepped into a room once again draped in black and lit by a single candle. From one corner came the glow of an electric heater.

"Close the door," said Dee. On her knees before a black candle on the coffee table, she was wearing the skull T-shirt and a pair of black jeans. About her head shimmered the usual red haze.

"Does this have to be so dramatic?" asked Jez. Shutting the door, she noted the large bump in the black sheet tacked over its inner side—the red-handled jackknife, still stored in Farrah Fawcett's face. *Old jokes die hard*, she thought.

"Close your eyes," said Dee.

"Can I sit down first?" asked Jez, on edge. "Can I take off my jacket?"

"Just close them," snapped Dee.

Sighing, Jez complied.

"What d'you see?" asked Dee.

"Darkness," said Jez, irritated.

"The mind sees in the dark, got it?" said Dee, equally annoyed.

"Got it," said Jez. Shrugging out of her jacket, she kicked off her boots. Then she unzipped her green and red plaid midi, dropped it carelessly to the floor, and donned the black T-shirt and jeans Dee had laid out for her on the bed. "Okay," she said, turning toward the coffee table. "Am I dark enough yet?"

"We'll see," said Dee. "C'mere."

Slowly, her body awkward with unease, Jez knelt opposite the other girl. Though she had asked for this—begged for it, even—now that they were about to begin, she found herself overcome by quick, miniscule shudders. Caution whispered through her, lace-curtain warnings in a window breeze.

"Did you bring it?" asked Dee.

"Yes," said Jez. Reaching for her jacket, she drew a flannel-backed paper doll out of a pocket. "Here," she added, giving it to Dee. "This was hers—her favorite thing. It was like a real person to her. She talked to it, carried it everywhere with her."

Eyebrows raised, Dee took the faded Billy Graham cut-out from her hand. "A million souls saved for Jesus," she murmured, studying it.

"Louisie was only seven when she died," said Jez. "She didn't know about that kind of stuff. Billy Graham was like, y'know—Elmer the Safety Elephant or something. A guardian angel, one step down from God."

Face expressionless, Dee continued to study the flannel-backed figure.

"I remember," Jez continued hesitantly. "Well…we used to play this game we called Bible Guys. She would pick a Bible character and I would pick a different one, and we would make up a game pretending that was who we were. Lots of times we picked Cain and Abel."

Obviously not getting it, Dee just looked at her.

"You know," said Jez, "the twins. They were Adam and Eve's kids. Cain was a farmer and Abel was a shepherd. One day they both made sacrifices to God and He rejected Cain's by sending the smoke back down to the ground, because it was fruit and vegetables. But Abel's sacrifice was accepted because it was an animal, and the smoke went up to Heaven."

Dee frowned.

"Well *then*," Jez stumbled on, a flush rising in her face, "Cain got angry and killed Abel. Something like that had never happened before—someone killing someone else— because this was near the beginning of the world, and it was the first murder. So a mark was put on Cain's forehead to set him apart, and he was banished from his family and sent out to wander the wilderness. And..."

She paused, considering how to put her next thoughts into words. "Well," she added reluctantly, "when Louisie and I pretended we were Cain and Abel, she was always Abel and I was always Cain. So every time, the game would end with me murdering her...as part of the story line, see?"

Dee's eyes honed in, intent. "How?" she asked slowly.

"Just a butter knife," said Jez. "Nothing sharp-edged; don't get excited. The last time we played Bible Guys, we were at a birthday party for a girl from our church. The rest of the kids were out in the backyard running an egg-and-spoon race, and I was stalking Louisie with some red Freshie and the knife that had been used to cut the cake. And she was running all over the house and the yard, trying to keep away from me, with this Billy Graham in her hand, whispering to it the way she always did." Jez gave a small hysterical laugh, remembering. "God, when I think about it, we were so *weird*."

"No kidding," said Dee, grinning slightly.

"I finally jumped her," said Jez, grinning back. "By the rose bushes. Poured the Freshie all over her dress for blood, and held the knife to her throat. And the whole time, she was waving Billy in my face and shouting, 'You have to sacrifice a sheep, stupid! Carrots aren't no good. Kill a sheep and then maybe Billy'll let you into Heaven.'"

"Huh," said Dee, a thoughtful look on her face. "Not so weird, actually. Everything I've met on the other side wants blood."

"Not everything," said Jez. "There were times…" She faltered, her voice trailing off. Because when she thought about it further, she realized Dee was partly right, even when it came to the long-ago game of Mirror See. While that hadn't involved blood per se, there had been pain—Louisie's pain, that bright, ripping sensation that had accompanied her every heartbeat. And as for the solstice figures of light that had appeared among the congregation the year Jez was ten—well, Jez thought, they had entered and exited this level of reality through the hole in her own soul that Louisie had torn open at the moment of her death.

But why? she wondered suddenly, fighting back a sharp rise of tears. Especially when there was so much beauty on the other side. Why did the body have to be wounded in order to create a gate for the mind? Why did it take so much pain to *see*?

"Y'know what is absolutely the worst thing about all this?" she blurted, her gaze skittering past Dee's. "Before Louisie died, it was like my father said in Pastor Playle's office—he loved Louisie best, and my mother loved me. Because I was most like my mother—at least the way she was *then*. But after Louisie died, well…I could see it in both their eyes. They *both* wished it had been me. They *both* wished I had died instead. And I can see them still thinking that now, every time they look at me. Every day my mother and father look at me and think, *I wish you were Louisie.*

"And they're right," she whispered, the words shuddering

cold and deep through her body. "It should have been me. *I* should have been the one to die. Because if I had died, my mother and father would have been left with Louisie, the good daughter. The three of them would have made the perfect Christian family, with no one suffering or going mad, and God would have stopped punishing everyone else for my sins.

"Because…" Here Jez paused, both arms wrapped tightly around herself and hovering on the edge of the abyss, that inner depth she had never dared look into alone. "Well," she wavered, then pushed mercilessly onward. "It was really *me* who destroyed everything. Because *I* was the one who couldn't let anyone else love Louisie. I had to have her all to myself. That's what it's like being a twin—you're cut in half, part of you always missing, running around inside someone else. And so I wanted her always to be with me, and no one else. So I could have more of myself with me, okay?"

Jez paused again, her lips, her arms, her entire body trembling. "And I think," she said haltingly, avoiding the gaze that watched steadily from beyond the candle flame. "I think I slowly sucked the life out of her. Bit by bit, to pull her back into myself. So we could be one again, y'see? So everything could be back together again. That's why her heart got weak; that's why she was always tired and sick the way she was. And then when she died…well, I thought all I had to do was hold onto her real tight. Dying is like going backward, back to how you were when you were conceived. Louisie and I used to be one person, and I figured…well, that she would come back into me when she died. But she didn't. At least not the way I thought she would. I held onto her while she died, like

I said—I didn't let go—and when she died she came into me, then went *right through me*. I felt it, man. I know it happened.

"But I think, somehow, she didn't quite make it to where she was supposed to go—Heaven, I guess. She got stuck somewhere deep inside me that really isn't inside me at all. I don't know where she is now, but sometimes I can feel Louisie out there and I don't think she's happy—like I'm not happy. Do you think, maybe, if we find her tonight, I could pull her back into my body and trade places with her? Our bodies were made from the same blueprint; I'm sure we could do it. No one would have to know about it except Louisie and you, and she would make the perfect daughter for my mother and father—finally they would be one happy family."

A long silence stretched out on the other side of the coffee table. Jez couldn't look, couldn't look. "Oh, maybe not," she mumbled, looking down. "Maybe this is a dumb idea. Maybe we shouldn't try to contact Louisie at all. Because, y'know, I probably wouldn't be able to do it. I'm too selfish. I…"

She swallowed hard, swallowed again. "Well," she blurted, the words awkward, reluctant, dragging themselves inexorably free. "More than anything—more than helping Louisie or helping my mother—I want to live. I *should* want to give my life to Louisie—I'm the bad girl, full of hate, and I don't deserve to live. I deserve to die, I know that, I've always known that…but I want to *live*."

Raising both hands to her eyes, Jez wept, a voice shoved out of itself and wandering through grief. Empty, she felt oddly empty, as if something jagged and gargantuan that had lived submerged within her for years had just departed. Hugging herself, she rocked and wept, rocked and wept, oblivious to the soft shifting sounds coming from across the coffee table. Then, gently, as if from a great distance, arms crept around her and pulled her close.

"Shhh," whispered Dee, nuzzling her hair. "Shhh, bad girl, shhh. Shhh."

Exhausted, Jez rested within those arms and floated on the inner emptiness like a sleeping child; the evening carried her, without resistance, toward some primal knowing of herself.

"Shhh," soothed Dee. "Shhh."

Out in the alley, a car idled past the garage, reversed, and braked to a halt. Headlights shattered across the frosted window and dimmed. A car door opened.

"If that's Andy..." muttered Dee. Rising, she blew out the candle, crossed to the window, and peered out. "What d'you know," she muttered. "It's snowing cats and dogs." Quietly, she slid up the single pane of glass and leaned out to get a better view, then quickly pulled back in. "Shiiit!" she hissed, holding herself like an indrawn breath. "Jezzie, you're not going to believe this. It's your dad."

"My dad?" gasped Jez. Getting to her feet, she joined Dee at the window. There below her, almost blotted out by falling snow, she saw the parked Valiant and the dark shape of her father, casting about the alley like a hunting dog.

"Shiiit!" she echoed, retreating from the window. "How did he know I was here? He'll absolutely kill me if he finds me."

As if in response, her father veered around the side of the garage and footsteps started up the staircase. Panicking, Jez scooted across the room, pausing only to grab her jacket, dress, and boots before ducking down into the narrow space between the wardrobe and the bed. Seconds later, there came a loud knocking and the squeak of hinges as the door swung open. Pressed flat to the floor, Jez could see nothing except the small shadowy opening between the legs at the foot of the bed. In the silence that followed, she heard her father breathing heavily and then the slow closing of the door. Cautiously, she inched herself up until she was peering over the top of the mattress.

Dee was crouched between the couch and the coffee table, relighting the candle; Deacon Hamilton stood just inside the door. "You!" he said heavily, eyeing her. "You streetwalker, bitch, *slut*! Where is she, my daughter? I've come to take her home."

"I don't know what you're talking about," said Dee. Her voice was calm, almost bored, but Jez saw her hand shake as she tossed a pack of matches onto the coffee table.

"I've seen the two of you!" snapped Deacon Hamilton, his voice rising as he pointed an accusing finger. "Seen you driving in a blue car, both painted and dressed like whores. Consorting with boys at the 7-Eleven and…" His mouth twisted. "God knows what else."

Eyebrows raised, Dee just looked at him. "Oh yes," he hissed, stepping forward. "She thought she had me fooled, Mary-Eve. Dressing you like herself and bringing you into the church. But I saw you for what you are. Whore demon. *Jezebel!* Out to steal my daughter and lead her into Satan's ways."

Slowly, Dee got to her feet. "Your daughter…Mary-Eve," she said carefully, "is trying to save me. She goes around school handing out Jesus pamphlets. I thought I'd give it a try."

"The hell you did!" roared Jez's father. "I've been watching the two of you, keeping track since I saw you at the church. She's not changing you—you're changing *her*. My daughter has become a liar, a deceiver, a whore slut...like *you*." Mouth trembling, he drew a shuddery breath, then added, "She came here tonight. I was following in my car and lost her a few blocks back, but I picked up her footprints in the alley. She's here and you're hiding her. I know you are."

"You're crazy," said Dee, her face deadpan. "Get the fuck out of here."

Instead of responding, Jez's father went into a moment of absolute stillness, rooted to the spot and staring bug-eyed at the coffee table. Then he darted forward. "This here!" he shouted, snatching up the Billy Graham paper doll and shoving it into Dee's startled face. "This was my daughter's. My *only* daughter's. You must have gotten it from her. She's here—I know you have her here somewhere. Give her to me, you goddamn whore *slut*!"

His face was contorted, his eyes strangely bright. Watching him, Jez felt such a wash of fear that she was left boneless, her mouth collapsed and sucking on itself. Abruptly, her father lunged at Dee, overturning the coffee table and toppling the candle. The next few seconds were crazed, impossible—two figures grappling beside the couch, Deacon Hamilton's hands around Dee's throat, her hands begging against his as gurgling, grunting sounds issued from their mouths. Then, with a sigh, the toppled candle gutted completely and the room was reduced to shadows, outlined faintly by the heater's red glow.

And in that moment, the gray-robed Chosen Ones came stepping into the womb of that room as if they had always been walking toward it and Jez had always been waiting. Enveloped by their low-throated hum, they slid a robe over her head and placed a curved ceremonial knife in her left hand. As she grasped it, Jez sensed vibrations keening from the spirit knife, and felt herself tilt and turn as if her very molecules were realigning to some new axis. Then, without thinking, she was rising to her feet and stepping out from behind the bed, tearing the black sheet from the door and drawing the red-handled jackknife free of Farrah Fawcett's face.

Her father was wearing his camel-hair overcoat, a damp weight too thick for the jackknife to penetrate. The collar was upturned, every part of his upper body covered. Thinking she would have to come at him from underneath, Jez dropped to her knees and began struggling with her father's lower buttons, his left elbow all the while knocking the side of her head but he didn't seem to notice, his gurgling, glaring focus entirely on Dee. And Dee was weakening—Jez could feel that as certainly as she felt her own stopped breath. The last button undone, she wormed in between the two pairs of staggering legs and positioned herself so she faced her father's waist.

Still he had not noticed her, so intent was he on choking the life out of the Jezebel. Already Dee's gurgles were fading, her knees sagging against Jez's back. A quick jerk of a hand brought Deacon Hamilton's coat open, exposing an unbuttoned suit jacket and a cotton shirt stretched tight across his belly. With a cry, Jez brought her hands together, merging the spirit knife with the jackknife, and thrust forward, shoving repeatedly, her mouth grunting as her father's grunted, her arms gaining strength as his lost their rigidity and blood burped from his gut out onto her hands. Abruptly, the weight against her back slid free, and Dee, released, sank to the floor. Jez's father staggered backward, his eyes darting wildly, then fixing on her dimly lit face above the upheld knife.

"Louisie?" he croaked.

Later, she would relive endlessly the way he lurched toward her, his arms circling and pulling her close, straight into the open wound. Then his hands slipped free of her, past any meaning of her, and she realized they reached merely for the wound, working its edges frantically, trying to draw it closed. Shoulders slumped, her father reeled and tottered. Sounds dribbled from his mouth, dying sounds, but he hung on, working the hole in his gut shut; Jez could see the life in him, fierce and determined, not yet ready to lose its grip on flesh.

His face sagged, red-lit by the heater's glow, the anger deserting it, the bitterness. In that moment, Jez wanted to reach out and stroke its final vapid emptiness. She so understood its creed of loneliness, hymn of pain, its beautiful complex code of martyrdom—she was the daughter who knew him best; he had been wrong about that.

At the very end, she saw something like wings rise from his back—a clear, blue-white flickering that carried every possibility of the father she had never experienced. But Jez had learned; ducking, she let the hope of it pass her by, allowed no part of her father's soul to touch and hang onto the living of her life. Then, as she stood open-mouthed and trembling, his body slowly caved in around her, embracing her in death the way she had never allowed him to hold her in life.

Behind her, Dee moaned and shifted. "Dee," Jez cried, her knees buckling under her father's weight. "Help me. Please. I don't know what to do with him."

Whimpering and unsteady, Dee rose to her knees. For a moment she simply gaped at the dead man, collapsed and bleeding in Jez's arms. Then, without speaking, she took hold of his feet and began to angle his body toward the door.

"Too far," gasped Jez, thinking of the long haul down the stairs. "The window."

In the room's red-lit darkness, their eyes locked as they remembered. Then they were grunting and heaving, pleading with a corpse that flowed like the Manawaka River, torso slumping one way and legs another as the head jammed itself stubbornly against the bottom of the raised window.

"Fuck, he's staring right at us!" hissed Dee.

Twisting the right arm up and out, they forced the head through, and for one last moment the body rested, balanced on the small of its back. Then, scraping loudly, the butt slid over the ledge and Jez's father began his fall through the snow-white air, down onto the hood of the car parked below.

TWELVE

The night of my father's death marked the beginning of a two-day near-record snowfall that descended on central Ontario like the end of the world, closing schools and bringing much of the pre-Christmas commerce to a halt. As Dee and I sat, however, trembling at her kitchen table, the future was yet unknown—the coming snowdrift that would enshroud the Valiant, magnified by a ten-foot-high snowbank piled soon after onto the snowed-over car by an oblivious snow-removal crew, and, finally, the seemingly never-ending wait for the discovery of Deacon Hamilton's body, well into the spring thaw.

For Dee and I that night, the man about to become the subject of a province-wide search was not a church deacon or a father, not even a splayed hapless corpse, but an unspeakable horror that continued to clutch at our throats, fingers locked tight and refusing to let go. This psychic nightmare was made even worse by the surrealistic normalcy that surrounded us—the well-decorated Christmas tree visible through the Eccles' living room doorway; the naked-woman sugar bowl next to my elbow, cradling its concealed cock; the erratic thumping that could be heard from the basement rec room as Dee's father and some friends played out a game of darts. Mrs. Eccles was at work, Andy out with his buddies. Since the death in the room over the garage forty minutes earlier, Dee and I had showered and changed, our movements slow-motion, dense with shock. The bloodstained clothing that we had been wearing now lay at our feet, shoved into a garbage bag. Slightly more distant behind the garage, but equally bloodstained, my father's corpse slumped facedown in the Valiant's backseat.

"Over by Joe's Tavern," rasped Dee, her voice quavery with the effort of speech. Reddish-purple fingermarks circled the base of her throat. "We'll dump him behind the pub— him and his car. Cops'll think it was a drinking thing."

"My father doesn't drink," I said automatically, then caught myself, shuddering long and deep. "Didn't, I mean," I corrected myself. "He *didn't* drink."

"So he had a secret life," croaked Dee. "Something you didn't know about. Lots of dads do—d'you think I know everything *my* dad does? Come on, Jez—get your brain in gear. The last thing that can happen is the cops nosing around *this* house, got it?"

Dully, I nodded. "Got it," I said.

"All right, let's get moving," she said. Picking up the

garbage bag, she got to her feet, then stood for a moment, leaned heavily on the table. "Believe me," she whispered, her face pale, her eyes gripping mine. "My dad can't *ever* know about this, okay?"

"Okay," I whispered in reply.

It was a tense, to-the-point funeral procession, consisting of Dee in the powder-blue Bug followed by myself driving the Valiant with its backseat corpse. That night, Eleusis was eerily still, the falling snow muffling the sound of the occasional passing car, the only other sign of life the odd caroling group trudging between houses brilliantly outlined in Christmas lights. Even so, it was all I could do to remain focused, the tears pouring steadily down my face as my brain staggered around the inside of my head. *My father is dead*, I kept thinking as we drove across town. *My father is dead and I killed him. I* killed *him*. Finally, Dee flashed her signal lights then turned into an alley that ran behind several pubs and pawnshops. Coming to a halt beside a Dumpster, she got out of the Bug and came over to the Valiant.

"Pull in there," she rasped, pointing to an empty area between the Dumpster and a scraggly copse of trees. "Then get in with me. We're outta here."

As she returned to the Bug, I edged the Valiant into the mounting snowdrift behind the Dumpster and shut off the engine. But instead of getting out and following Dee to her car, I continued to sit, my mind also shut off as I stared out at the whirling snow. In that densely falling world, then, I felt silence open about me in slow folds—silence so deep, it went on unfolding into the next universe. And in that moment, it came to me, an understanding that rested deeper than heartbeat, quiet within quiet, absolute stillness: The essential quality of all survival is its impassivity, its ability to move inexorably onward. No matter how I longed for it, there would be no forgiveness coming to me from beyond the grave; what had happened tonight had been born out of terrible necessity, and I had now to release those events and allow the dead to pass on, without judgment, to whatever realities beckoned.

But how was this to be accomplished? All my life I had spent hanging on—to Louisie, to my mother's approval, my father's disapproval. To Dee. How did I now reverse a lifelong habit of obsessive clutching, and open to absolute emptiness?

Without warning, the driver's door was yanked open. "Jez!" croaked Dee, leaning into my face. "What the hell are you doing? Get your ass moving!"

All I did, however, all I could seem to do, was sit clinging to the steering wheel and staring straight ahead. "He was all right, y'know," I whispered to no one in particular. "Before I was born, that is. He was okay before *me*."

"Don't give me that shit!" yelped Dee, shoving my shoulder so hard she sent me sprawling across the front seat. "Don't you go crybaby over *that* bastard!"

Pushing up onto an elbow, I stared at her.

"You seek and you find, Jez," spat Dee, leaning into the words, shaping them with her body. "So you found out what a bastard your daddy was. That doesn't make him special. A lot of guys are bastards. As long as you keep your eyes open, you're going to find that out."

"Well, I didn't want to find that out!" I yelled, sudden rage jerking me upright. "Not that, *specifically*."

"Boo hoo for you!" Dee hissed back, her voice giving out on her completely. "Too bad if you didn't get what you wanted, *specifically*." Then, turning on her heel, she headed for the Bug. As I watched, she got in and slammed the driver's door. Sinbad's headlights flared in the darkness; AC/DC screamed briefly from the dash and bit the dust.

Two minutes, I thought dully, *before she takes off and leaves me for good.*

Turning, I looked into the backseat. A shapeless mass, my father's body lay splayed, head tilted off the seat, upside-down in darkness. "I'm sorry," I whispered to the silence that resonated back at me. "I'm sorry I wasn't Louisie. I'm sorry I never loved you."

Then I got out, shut the driver's door, and trudged through the falling snow to the Bug. As I got in, Dee held out a joint. I shook my head.

"Come on," she snapped. "Who's sane here and who ain't?"

She had been crying; her eyes were swollen and rubbed raw. Taking the joint, I dragged deep as she put the Bug into gear and headed down the alley. Outside the car, the sky continued to fall toward earth, covering the good and the gone.

"Sweetie," Dee said quietly as she drove, "you've got guts. You did what you said you'd do. I owe you."

"But he was killing you!" I burst out. "And he was *my* father. If it hadn't been for me...if we hadn't been friends, none of this would've hap—"

"So you owe me too," croaked Dee, and I felt the crevices of fatigue that ran through her—deeper than moral bargains, agonized debates, any of the codes.

"Okay," I mumbled, half-sobbing with relief. "But we're not done yet. Now I have to go get my mother. She's at the church with that *thing*. We have to get her out of there."

Dragging on the joint, Dee drove through a long pause. "Y'know, Jez," she said, hinting at sanity. "I'm tired; you're tired. It's been a big night. For her, it's just one more fling with the supernatural."

"My mother needs me," I said, my voice rising. "I feel it. She needs me *right now*."

Dee breathed deep, then let out a shuddery sigh. "Promise me one thing before we go into that nuthouse," she said, glancing at me. "You're not going to kill her too?"

Wordless, I stared at her.

"Okay," she said. "Just checking. It's on Fern Street, right?"

I nodded, then sat slumped and silent as she turned the Bug in the direction of the church. What I was going to do upon arrival was unknown to me; all that mattered was that I was headed toward my mother. Or rather, *our* mother. Because somewhere within, seemingly at the very core of my being, I could feel something beginning to stir. It was the gate, the place Louisie had torn into existence as she passed to the other side, and it appeared to be singing. There was no other way to describe it—at the center of my being, I felt the long calling wave of a song. As I slouched in Sinbad's front seat, that calling wave grew and grew, filling me with its urgency. And, gradually, it came to me that the gate was going to open tonight, that it was calling out that the way be made ready between the worlds—the world of Louisie and the world of Mary-Eve.

The Waiting for the Rapture End Times Tabernacle looked like it always did on a Wednesday evening—the crimson cross flashing on-off over the front door, the parking lot full of vehicles. Pulling up at the curb, Dee gave the building a hostile glare. "That place is a bad trip," she muttered, taking one last drag from the joint before butting out. "And I'm not up to it tonight. Sorry, Jez, but this is your baby. You go in and get your mom, and I'll wait for you out here in Sin."

In the cross's flashing light, she looked haggard. Gently, I reached over and traced the darkening outline of my father's fingermarks on her throat. "Okay," I said. "But keep it down on the AC/DC, would ya?"

"Yeah, okay," she rasped, then leaned back her head and closed her eyes. Getting out alone, I pushed open the church's front door and entered the lobby. To my left, coats filled the coatrack and boots were lined neatly on plastic floor mats. But to my surprise, the sanctuary's amber barrier glass displayed the blurred outlines of members of the congregation on their feet, hands uplifted as wild trilling sounds came from their mouths. This was unusual for the normally sedate Wednesday evening prayer meetings, and experience told me it could mean only one thing—that even without my father's guiding presence, the Divine Sister had once again taken hold of my mother's body and was riding her like a surfer seeking the biggest wave.

Hit by my own wave of adrenaline, I grabbed a nearby stacking chair and heaved it at the despised glassed-in gift shop. "Louisie!" I screamed as it plowed through neatly arranged photographs of a scowling, lonely Mary-Eve. Glass exploded, flying everywhere, and as if in reply I felt the gate

in my gut blow wide open. Turning, I headed into the sanctuary, where the congregation's cries were so loud, the sound
of shattering glass had gone unnoticed. As I started down
the central aisle, people to either side swayed in the packed
pews, letting loose long ululating cries. My attention, however, was drawn upward to what hovered above their heads,
for with the reopening of my inner gate I seemed to have
gained enhanced perception, and what had previously been
veiled was now visible. Everywhere I looked, the sanctuary throbbed with light, a light that shape-shifted through
splendid image after image—glowing castles, radiant domed
cathedrals, marble mansions, and other common fantasies
of Heaven. Beneath the congregation's feet burned a lake of
fire, the four horsemen of the Apocalypse galloped sternly
past, and angels clasping swords of fire circled the room. On
the stage stood the Divine Sister's red velvet box, with its
ascending tunnel of light, but for the first time I was able
to discern how the tunnel's spinning motion threw off fine,
lit threads that floated toward members of the congregation
and slid into their brains, trapping them like insects within
a gigantic web.

And that web, I realized as I watched in stunned amazement, functioned as a conduit to suck energy from individuals
within the congregation and transfer it to the Divine Sister.
The more frenzied the members of the congregation became,
the more energy they produced, and the brighter and stronger grew the web that held them all entrapped. This included
my mother, who was, as expected, rocking and slamming in
her box, but this time with a gaping hole clearly visible inside
her chest, or that area of her spirit that resided inside her

chest—an inner gate like my own, except hers was spewing a heated, vicious, acrid light.

Oblivious, Pastor Playle knelt at her feet, spouting the usual verbiage about sacrifice, suffering, and the Apocalypse—an apocalypse, I thought, glancing at the congregation's feverish faces, that was being artificially produced and maintained. At the core of my being then, my inner gate roared its call; I raced forward, shoved aside a startled Pastor Playle, and reached into the velvet box. "Mommy!" I cried, my voice abruptly plaintive and seven years old. "Mommy, Mommy, look at me!"

About us whirled the tunnel of light, its spin fierce and unabated. I grabbed my mother's hands and held on. "Mommy!" I cried again, my voice Louisie's and at the same time Mary-Eve's. "Look at me! Look at *me*!"

Slowly, almost imperceptibly, the Divine Sister's rigid upward stare began to falter.

"Not up!" I half-shouted. "Down! Mommy, I'm down. I'm down *here*."

Hesitantly, my mother's face turned toward me, her pale eyes meeting mine. "Mary-Eve?" she whispered. "Mary-Louisie-Eve?"

Yanking open the velvet box's half-gate, I reached toward the scream of light bleeding from her chest—the heart wound my father had created with his accusations, the gate she herself had torn into existence through repeated self-attacks. And it was also the gate, I now realized with horrifying clarity, that had called in the entity of light that controlled her—an entity that might otherwise have sniffed out the portal that Lousie's dying had torn open within *me*. Fervently, I pressed my hands against my mother's chest, trying to staunch its brilliant flow, but the gate continued to bleed light, the tunnel to spin madly about us. Then, as if on another level of knowing, I saw two transparent child's hands rise from deep within me and pass like a dream directly into our mother's flesh, where they cupped themselves around the wound of light. Delicately, they fluttered back and forth as if weaving, and gradually the gate to the realm of the Divine Sister began to close, the flow of light to diminish. Finally, the wound healed over and light ceased to stream from our mother's chest. For a moment, the child's hands remained cupped around the scarred mother-heart, fluttering like butterfly wings; then they withdrew back into my body.

A long shudder ran through my mother. Raising her head, she whispered, "Where am I?"

"With me," I whispered back, and began undoing the bonds that held her in place. Immediately, Pastor Playle stepped forward, protesting, but I turned on him in such fury that his eyes widened and he stepped back. Carefully, I helped my mother to her feet. As we started down the platform stairs, her knees buckled, but then she seemed to gain strength and we continued along the sanctuary's central aisle amid a dense silence. With the healing of my mother's inner gate, both the tunnel of light and the multiple visions of Heaven had vanished; all about us, the congregation now sagged in the pews, drained empty husks. Step by step, my mother and I pressed forward against the enormous disapproval that clung to us, trying to impede our progress; inch by inch, I fought the weight of Pastor Playle's eyes, glued to our backs and desperately hanging on. Ahead loomed the doorway to the lobby;

like a weary but successful Orpheus, we gained its threshold and passed through. Sliding my mother's coat from its hanger, I placed it around her shoulders.

Perhaps it was exhaustion, perhaps an understanding that this was an ending of sorts, a cutting of all ties, but not once did my mother glance in the direction of the shattered gift shop, nor did her eyes flick back toward the sanctuary and the Divine Sister's velvet box. Past the mural with the bleeding Jesus and His docile flock we plodded, through the outer door and into the crimson cross's sullen heartbeat flashing across the mounting snow. As I opened the Bug's passenger door, Dee came abruptly awake and began shoving packages of cigarettes and marijuana into the glove compartment while I settled my mother into the backseat. Reluctantly, Sinbad's engine wheezed and coughed, then eased into its familiar idle.

Alone, I stood a moment outside the car. The air about me was quiet, resting without wind, no hint of apocalypse or portals to other worlds. As I watched, countless snowflakes drifted downward in utter peace, each kissing the earth, a love intricate beyond comprehension.

"Louisie?" I whispered, not expecting an answer, my mind simply adrift with the snow. "What's it *really* like up there? Y'know—Heaven, Billy Graham, God?"

For one last time then, the gate within me opened wide, and I saw a vast array of angels singing so intensely, they roared with joy. And it came to me suddenly that what I was seeing was the fundamental underlying essence of all matter, the molecules of the universe, and that all of it together, this radiant *roaring* consciousness, was God.

And then the gate at my core began to close. Briefly I saw them again, the two shimmering child's hands, fluttering within me in a delicate weaving motion. Lifting my own, I pressed them firmly to the outside of my belly and watched the inner hands complete their healing work. Gradually, gently, the long-ago wound closed over, folding into a double-winged scar. One gateway between the worlds, and all the pain that had created it, was gone.

I stood alone in the dark and the snow fell toward me, kissing my face.

• • •

Pressed against the long song of Dee's body, I rose and fell on the sleepy cadence of her breathing. Outside, the wind blustered through ice-silvered trees and the snow continued its tortured pilgrimage down the alley, but here in the room over the garage the mind rested—a sanctuary set apart from the rest of the world. In one corner, the electric heater hummed its blood-red light; on the opposite wall, Mick Jagger's lips defied all natural laws; across the bed stretched the eternal gleaming smile of Marilyn Monroe. Things, I thought musingly, were much as they had always been; at the same time, so much had changed. Still tacked to the inside of the door, Farrah Fawcett's mutilated face gave out its familiar warning, but the red-handled jackknife was gone, probably tossed months ago into a randomly selected Dumpster, along with a certain garbage bag of bloodstained clothing. The bloodstained floor had since been scrubbed and bleached and painted over black.

"Always wanted to do that, anyway," Dee had said tersely when she showed me the finished job. "Walls and ceiling are next, when it gets warm enough to ventilate. When I get the guts."

Which left only the frozen pool of blood waiting under the snow at the back of the garage, and my father's body, yet to be discovered. With the calendar currently standing at mid-March, that was bound to happen soon. Although Lawrence Philip Hamilton's disappearance was at this point considered officially suspicious, the missing-person investigation had been put on hold. There was simply nothing to prove he hadn't deserted Eleusis, along with his wife and daughter, for something he found more appealing. Faced with more pressing concerns, the police had let the matter drop, and neither I nor my mother had taken it upon ourselves to encourage them.

In fact, I thought with more than a trace of envy, rather than preoccupying herself with her husband's disappearance as might have been expected, Rachel Hamilton seemed to be shedding his memory like an old skin. While I still woke regularly thrashing about my bed, heart in an ugly thud as I tried to shake off a blood-soaked, clinging dream-father, it had been weeks since my mother had mentioned his name. Ever so gradually, the deacon's widow was beginning to move more freely about our house, to look me in the eye when she spoke, even to laugh on occasion. Several days ago, to my astonishment, she had broached the possibility of applying for a job.

Beside me Dee continued her sleepy breathing, quietly conducting my thoughts. And as ever, come hell or high water, those thoughts pressed on. Since the night of my mother's rescue, I reflected, neither she nor I had returned to the Waiting for the Rapture End Times Tabernacle. Pastor Playle still called the odd time, but by now I had learned to let go of my panic attacks, having seen my mother repeatedly hang up on him. With the healing of her inner gate, Rachel Hamilton seemed to be returning to a firm-boundaried sense of herself; her night prowls had ended, she habitually slept until daybreak, and the house walls were slowly losing their high-frequency field. The change this brought to the home on Quance Crescent was so tangible, I could feel it in the air—something unclenching and opening, by degrees, to easier breathing.

If only, I thought as I lay listening to the heater's quiet drone, my father *had* simply taken off. If only I hadn't brought that Billy Graham paper doll to the proposed *séance*. If only…if only…Ultimately there were countless if onlys, and one dead body under a ten-foot snowbank, awaiting the inexorable approach of spring. Things had happened the way they had happened, and if I was completely honest with myself, my father's death was an apocalypse that had been in the making for years. It could have occurred so many times earlier—like the instance in the kitchen when I held the bread knife to his throat. So many times, I thought heavily, but it had waited for my grad year, a particular room over a garage, and Dee.

Briefly, then, I wondered if the entity that had transformed my mother into the Divine Sister had somehow also entrapped my father, but I ditched the thought. That *thing* fed on pain big-time, and Deacon Hamilton had never exhibited the slightest inclination toward self-abuse. As far as I could tell, neither he nor Pastor Playle ever figured out what was really driving Rachel Hamilton, never glimpsed the true visage of the Divine Sister.

What had been evident to both men, however, was that Mrs. Hamilton was the conduit for a mystery called the Tongue of Fire, and if they set themselves up as her keeper and translator, they would thereby gain enormous power. It probably hadn't taken Pastor Playle any longer than it had his right-hand deacon to connect Rachel Hamilton's access to the Tongue of Fire to her personal suffering, and further, to realize that his own power depended upon maintaining that agony. Only men without internal sanctuary—men who were no one—could have done what my father and the good pastor did…to my mother, to myself, to Dee. In the end it was that simple, that clear, and a relief to see it without judgment or apology—how the wreck of my mother's life had been created out of the wreck of my father's. The only thing left now was to climb out of the debris and carry on.

Nuzzling my face into Dee's damp hair, I snuggled a hand around her naked breast. What had surprised me most about our loving, when it came to us, was the uninhibited wetness of it and the startling inconsolable cries that erupted from us sometimes, as if our souls were soaked with grief. Sex was another kind of twinning, really—a reaching through short-lived ecstasy toward oneness. Afterward, all one could do was lie on the bed, returning to the exile of one's body as if it were a place from which one had been gone a long time—these arms, legs, hips the prison guards of division, separation, all the questions and loneliness of flesh.

And that flesh was still lonely. Not for the loving that could be created body with body, but for those worlds beyond the body, those other realms that could be called open by pain and need. For with the closure of Louisie's death gate and her final departure, I, Mary-Eve Hamilton, had been left healed and at one within myself in a way I had not previously experienced. In tandem, the external physical world had also mended, presenting now solidly to me within boundaries, no longer continually bleeding color, energy, *soul,* as had been its wont. While the gains this had brought were undeniable, in the process something had been lost—something ephemeral, beyond, the quintessential mystery of all things.

The question was: *How to regain it?* How could I once again seek and call out to other realms and *their* questers without creating wounds so profound that they caused irreparable damage? How much blood was required to see; how did one learn where and when, how deep to cut? Restless, my mind on the prowl, I lay pushing mentally against the physical plane and its restrictions, that curse of the mundane with its oversized thumb pressed down, as ever, upon the world; then, as if some psychic fault line had given way, I felt a gentle rippling and a buckling, and a cave-like darkness opened up around me and flowed outward to envelop the room. Off to one side flickered candlelight, accompanied by the rustling of robes. Raising myself onto an elbow, I watched a line of gray-hooded figures approach and encircle the bed. It had been a while since The Chosen Ones had dropped in, more than ten weeks—the winter solstice, to be exact, the night of my father's death.

Mumbling their endless indecipherable chants, the robed

figures surrounded and held me within the vibratory plane of their circle. *Who are they?* I wondered as I floated on the gray hymn of their voices—guardian angels, the dead, a gathering of personal phantoms? Whatever their identity, it was entirely disconnected from the mind-searing brilliance of the Divine Sister and the miasmic black sludge that had entrapped Dee's mother. Those two entities inhabited extremes, whereas this particular set of Chosen Ones seemed to resonate *between* dimensions, close to the human but not quite of it. Deep in a gut-world of tunnels and caves, lost parts and loneliness, they had traveled from some place of collective knowing and bequeathed themselves to me.

But that bequeathing, I recalled as I watched them, had been for the purpose of the Apocalypse—to guide me toward and through it, to give me the necessary strength. And the Apocalypse, at least that particular apocalypse, was now over. What could they possibly have to communicate to me tonight?

As if in response to my thoughts, the robed figures standing about the bed lifted their arms. Then, as I watched wide-eyed, The Chosen Ones turned their hands, open-palmed, toward me. *Empty!* I realized, staring at their circle of raised hands. Every one of the curved spirit knives they usually carried was gone.

Quietly, then, a voice began to speak inside my mind. *Pain is not the only way*, it said. *There are others. Thought. Memory. The inward gaze. Look inward, but do not force the veil. Force creates wounds, and wounds call out in the vibrations of anguish and despair that created them. Whatever conscious-ness enters this world enters through you, your mind a delicate sounding board that vibrates between realms, receiving the stories of other universes and reenacting them in your flesh. But you can choose what you receive. Hear this—hear it as a song: You were conceived not as a chosen, but as a choosing one.*

With this, the empty hands began to lower and the chanting to trail off. And it came to me then that The Chosen Ones were fading out on me, probably for the last time. Dismayed, I pushed aside the quilt, rose to my knees, and reached toward the nearest figure; it did not flinch, did not pull back. Swiftly, my heart thudding, I slid back the hood, then cried out as the entire robe collapsed formless to the floor.

Empty! I realized again. Each robed figure currently standing around the bed was, and possibly always had been, uninhabited. As I stared in amazement, the rest of the robed figures collapsed in like manner, leaving me surrounded by a circle of empty cloth.

There were no chosen ones. They had never existed beyond the empty forms I had given them. And the message those cherished thought-forms had come to bring to me tonight was the same one I had been sending myself for years: *There is no code, no law—only possibility and the desire of the seeker.*

And it was flesh that contained all the stories and the mirrors, all the names necessary to each seeker's finding out. *Jezebel*, I thought, smiling down at the girl sleeping next to me. Maybe the nickname hadn't come written on a small white stone, and it certainly hadn't been secret, but it *was*, arguably, divinely inspired. What an incomparable gift Dee had given me through the alias Jez—truly an identity ready-made for seeking, for finding out. Could I return the favor?

Was there a name I could bestow upon Dee that she could use to dream herself toward truer selfhood?

Beside me, Dee shivered as she often did in her sleep, clutching herself and whimpering. "Can you find me?" she whispered in a high broken voice. "Can you find me?"

Leaning toward the beloved, I murmured, "Yes."

ABOUT *the* AUTHOR

Beth Goobie grew up in Guelph, Ontario, where the appearance of a normal childhood hid many secrets. Beth moved to Winnipeg to attend university, became a youth residential treatment worker, and also studied creative writing at the University of Alberta. She is the award-winning author of 23 books, written mainly for young adults, including *The Lottery* and the CLA award-winning *Before Wings*. Also a published poet, Beth makes her home in Saskatoon.